THE SINS OF SHADOWMERE

ROTTEN SCOUNDRELS - BOOK 1

ADELE CLEE

The Sins of Shadowmere
Copyright © 2026 Adele Clee
All rights reserved.
ISBN-13: 978-1-915354-69-3

Cover by Dar Albert at Wicked Smart Designs

CHAPTER ONE

By definition, Dominic Hawke was a scoundrel.

He was not a wastrel—he had amassed a fortune to rival Midas. Nor was he a rogue; rogues charmed their way into ladies' hearts before ruining them, and he lacked the stomach for seduction.

With a commotion erupting in Lord Templeton's marble-clad hall and pallor spreading through the ballroom, he might be a villain. Yet a man avenging a murdered mother was a hero. So why did matrons eye him like a bloodstain on brocade?

Amused, he adjusted his cuffs, offered a wolfish grin, and descended the stairs with the swagger of a man who held a trump card.

Lord Templeton was at his side before Dominic's foot touched the polished parquet. "Good God, Hawke. What the blazes are you doing here? If this is about the misunderstanding last week, we'll discuss it in my study." Templeton offered a tight smile, the sort worn by men trying not to soil their breeches. "Curse the devil. My wife will expect me to throw you out. What am I to tell her?"

"Anything but the truth, unless you want to break her heart." Best he didn't mention warming a widow's bed instead of tending the tenant accounts.

Men like Templeton thought rules were for lesser mortals, the sanctity of marriage for peasants. He should have thought of his wife before tangling himself in Shadowmere's web of secrets.

Dominic turned from the gaping horde and tapped the lord's chest, as one might silence an anxious servant. Templeton, still in his thirties and desperate to preserve his reputation, flinched.

"Step aside. It's not your neck in the noose tonight. Though I do bring a letter from Monique. Perhaps your wife would care to learn you spent the weekend at my estate in Kingston upon Thames."

A violent flush crawled up Templeton's neck. He grasped Dominic's arm and drew him closer. "What about the contract? What happens at Shadowmere is never spoken of beyond its doors. You gave your word."

Dominic looked at the hand as if it were a beetle on silk, with faint disgust and the urge to flick it off. "I suggest you retire to your study and read it in depth. Buried in the small print is a clause. I'm permitted one favour. Refuse me and the contract's void. If you want to attend the next gathering, you'll remove your manicured hand from my arm and placate your wife."

Templeton stepped back, doing a passable impression of someone in charge. "Just be aware, not everyone will welcome you tonight."

Let them call him Lucifer. He hadn't spent nine years amassing the ton's sins to be turned away by cowards. They would have to kill him to silence him—though most were too weak to resist their base appetites, let alone act on conscience.

"They don't have to welcome me. They only need to get out of my way." He smirked at the panicked lord and gave his cheek a playful tap. "Monique sends her regards."

Head high and shoulders squared, he cut through the crowd with ease. Whispered speculations trailed in his wake. Was he here to claim a debt? To expose a scandal? To inform a lord of his wife's infidelity?

Men quaked as he passed.

Women shrank behind their painted fans as though he were a harbinger of doom. A daring few brushed his hand with theirs, a fleeting caress, as obvious as a beckoning finger. To bed him was considered the epitome of conquests.

But he had only one woman on his mind.

Miss Daphne Harland.

Daughter of the bastard who had driven his mother to an early grave. Daughter of the lord who had preyed on a widow's poverty and blackmailed her into handing out favours. The villain's identity had remained a mystery until a few weeks ago. But the best enquiry agent in London had succeeded where Dominic had failed.

The thought grated.

He'd be in no one's debt. Least of all the illegitimate son of a duke who liked playing detective.

He snatched a flute of champagne from a passing tray, downed it in one swallow, and tossed the empty glass into a potted fern.

Everyone watched *him*, not the demure debutantes scrambling to secure a suitor now the end of the Season was nigh. The orchestra struck up a lively reel, but the room held its breath, waiting to glimpse the poor fool bold enough to coax the devil from Kingston.

For his own wicked amusement, he paused beside a

gentleman long enough to watch the blood drain from his face. Others exhaled, relieved they'd been spared his attention for now.

He hadn't come to talk.

He'd come for vengeance.

To storm through the heart of the ton, take the serpent's spawn in his arms, and kiss her so thoroughly that no one in the room, not even a scandal-hardened dowager, would doubt they were lovers.

The plan was simple: cast aspersions on her character and force her father to call him out.

Let the gossips sharpen their knives. It would be worth it if it forced Harland's hand. If the whispers were true—if she was to be wed against her will—then scandal might prove her salvation.

Would that not make him a hero in her eyes?

Yet some part of him knew it was wrong. Miss Harland hadn't been forced to barter her body or bury her pride for coin. She would pay the price for another man's sin. Just as his mother had.

Firming his jaw, he reminded himself why he'd come. For justice. For retribution. For the woman who'd given up everything to protect him. For the need—

That's when he saw her.

Miss Daphne Harland.

A dove trapped in a gilded cage.

The music faded.

Conversation died.

All eyes shifted to him, then to her.

It wasn't her silky dark hair that caught his attention, nor the braided Apollo knot fastened high at the crown. Not her skin, pale as candlelit alabaster, untouched by vice. Not even her mouth, composed with the restraint of a woman who guarded her thoughts.

It was her eyes.

Sad as a mourning song.

By God, he'd be damned if his step didn't falter.

He considered turning back and abandoning the plan he'd nurtured for weeks. He would find another way to destroy the man he despised to the marrow.

But then came the whisper of his mother's voice, brittle with shame.

Forgive me, Dominic. I had no choice.

He bit back a curse, gathered himself, and strode up to the lady he intended to ruin. "Miss Harland." He took her hand, dainty in her pristine white glove, while her female companions stood bleating like lambs in a wolf's shadow. "I know what we agreed. But I couldn't stay away."

Everything else faded to the ragged catch of her breath and the swift rise of her breasts. A frisson of awareness chased up his arm and settled somewhere far more dangerous.

Damnation.

"Release her, Mr Hawke." The sharp voice to his right belonged to Miss Harland's aunt, Lady Sanders, a commanding figure with hair as pale as steel and a will to match. "I don't know who you're searching for, but I'm confident it is not my niece." She turned to her companion. "Don't stand there gaping, Loretta. Fetch Templeton. Better still, drag my brother from his precious game of piquet."

Dominic should have moved quickly. He should have hauled this sheltered little innocent to his chest and scorched her lips with the fire of vengeance.

But one damning truth held him still.

The angel he'd dragged to Hades did not pull away.

Curse it all, that only made her more intriguing.

"I hear the strains of a waltz, Miss Harland." He cupped

her elbow, eager to prove his heart was blacker than a Whitechapel alley at midnight. "Will you honour me with this dance? Indulge me, or make a scene. Either suits me fine."

Miss Harland looked at him, her gaze unreadable. "The damage is done, sir. I may as well enjoy a turn about the floor. I expect it will be my last."

He felt a twinge of regret and dismissed it. "Then I shall endeavour to make it memorable." What the blazes was wrong with him? He shouldn't care if she wept through every turn.

Lady Sanders caught hold of her niece's sash, gloved fingers bunching the fabric in a vice-like grip, and gave him a glare that could crack stone. "Cease this nonsense. Or you may find yourself summoned to a dawn appointment."

"Then I hope Lord Harland has made peace with his maker."

A duel would give him exactly what he came for.

Lady Sanders swept a hand towards the gentlemen nearby. "Well? Do you mean to stand there and permit this heathen to ride roughshod over us? Does no one here possess a backbone?"

But the whispers had begun to circle like vultures scenting ruin. Protecting their sordid acts and salacious affairs mattered more than defending a woman with a tainted reputation.

Miss Harland was the only one with the strength to argue her corner. "If I'm to salvage anything, you'll let me dance with Mr Hawke. I'm sure he'll leave once the ton have had their fill." She turned to him. "Well, sir? Is there a shred of honour beneath that armour? Will you leave after one dance? Villains rarely linger past the last chime of the bell."

That she saw him as such struck a nerve, one buried deep. But revenge came with consequences. Ones he'd need to swallow. "One waltz with you, Miss Harland, and you'll never have to lay those sorrowful eyes on me again."

She sighed, then whispered a remark that made her aunt's fingers go slack. "Some things are more important than reputation. Neither of us can afford for my father to die tonight."

With clear reluctance, Lady Sanders let go.

Trying not to look too smug, Dominic guided Miss Harland onto the floor, weaving past gilded gowns and the cloying scent of perfume and pomade. He paused beside the musicians. "Play the same waltz twice without pause."

Revenge was sweeter when savoured.

He meant to relish every second.

"I suppose you plan to scandalise me further." She shivered beneath his palm as he laid a hand on her back. "I'm surprised you know how to waltz with your clothes on. I hear the only dances at Shadowmere amount to naked romps with strangers."

Her tone was calm. Her aim precise.

So, she knew how to spar.

He wrapped his fingers around hers, ignoring the jolt that followed—one he suspected had less to do with the woman and everything to do with a well-executed plan.

"Who told you about Shadowmere?" He doubted she'd heard her father boast of bedding a desperate widow so she might keep her house. "I'm surprised you can say *naked romps* without blushing."

He drew her into the first sweep, holding her so close he could feel the warmth of her, soft, delicate, unmistakably feminine. It had been years since he'd held a woman. Years since he'd let himself feel anything at all.

"Your name tops the list of men to avoid. Shepherds are warned to guard against savage dogs; innocent maidens, against hawks hunting field mice."

He might have laughed, were this about pleasure. "You call yourself a mouse, Miss Harland, yet you wield injustice like a Roman gladiator."

The flicker of satisfaction in her blue eyes was brief but unmistakable. "Perhaps you should have chosen your prey more wisely, sir." She lifted her chin, her mouth softening as if this were a triumph, not the worst moment of her life. "I happen to be rather skilled with a trident."

Clever.

Who knew the mouse had wit?

"I'll give you this," he said, pulling her close enough to make every chaperone reach for her smelling salts. "Whatever guilt I had left, you've stripped it clean. If I didn't know better, I'd think you lured me here just to parade your resilience."

"You disappoint me, Mr Hawke. Only a fool would invite someone to trample over her reputation before the beau monde." She studied him. A lesser man might have faltered. "Am I permitted to know what my father has done to warrant such disgraceful behaviour?"

The memory of his mother's frail body had him firming his jaw, but he'd be damned before sullying her name in the same breath as that degenerate. "His cruelty knows no bounds. The rest isn't fit for your ears, angel."

She eyed him curiously. "I might accuse you of the same. You call me angel and claim my ears are delicate, yet you mark me a sinner before all the world."

"Take solace, Miss Harland. You may find yourself elevated in the eyes of some," he said, desperate to banish the damned twinge in his chest. The last thing he'd expected was for her to prick his conscience or be mildly entertaining. "Before tonight, you were invisible. See how women look at you now. As though you possess something they can never obtain."

She didn't glance around the ballroom, keen to test the theory. She seemed unfazed by her newfound infamy. "You're in danger of sounding like an optimist, Mr Hawke, not a man who dwells in shadows. I may not know what my father did, but I know it cost you dearly."

The comment found a chink in his armour. He'd expected to dance with a fawn, all weak-legged and body aquiver. Instead, she met him step for step, spine straight, chin lifted, a challenge in silk and lace.

"You know nothing about me, Miss Harland."

"I know you expected me to whimper, to cling to my aunt's skirts like a frightened child. Yet here we are, waltzing before the beau monde as though you'd written your name on my dance card."

His instincts had failed him, it seemed.

This maiden had mettle.

His hand slipped lower, settling with deliberate pressure at the base of her spine, a bold touch masked by the rhythm of the dance and the sweep of her skirts. He waited for a gasp, a flinch, for the telltale flush that never came.

"Careful, Miss Harland. Hold your nerve like that, and I might forget which one of us came here to play the villain."

She looked him in the eye, a task few men achieved. "I expect, once you're home with your brandy, you'll still be debating it."

He laughed, much to the delight of those engrossed in the show. But suspicion flared. She spoke with the confidence of a lover. Perhaps Miss Harland was a perfectionist. Even her ruination must be flawless.

"Perhaps you've done me a great service, Mr Hawke."

She cast a glance at the men who hadn't taken their eyes off her since he'd marked her as his target.

The sight soured his stomach. That they pictured her in their bed brought bile to his throat. He wasn't jealous. He wouldn't bed Harland's daughter if she were the last woman on earth. He just prayed she never arrived at Shadowmere on a degenerate's arm.

"Not that I'm one to offer guidance," he said, slipping on sheep's clothing despite the poor fit. "But find a quiet village, where word of your downfall won't reach the young pastor. Though I doubt you'd make him a biddable wife."

She considered it. "Yes, the country air might suit me better than the choking fog in town. Thank you, Mr Hawke, for sparing a moment to consider my welfare."

"Think of it as a parting gift."

"Like a rose left on a lover's pillow?"

"More a diamond parure before I give you your congé."

She sighed, though her hand slid a little higher on his shoulder. "I suppose I must grow accustomed to rejection. After such a display of gentlemanly prowess, it's only right you should be my first."

First. The word lodged like a splinter.

It summoned an unwelcome vision, her body beneath his, innocence yielding to vengeance. He tamped it down like a flame that had no business being lit.

"I pray you take rejection as well as you do ruin."

It was time to end this farce.

His gaze swept the crowd, hunting for his nemesis, but the bastard was nowhere in sight. The news would have reached the card room by now.

"My father may be struggling to get through the crush," she said, her perception as sharp as her wit. "Or perhaps he's on a winning streak and cannot bear to leave the table. Money is everything, after all."

Not everything. Some days he longed to be a simple farm-hand, concerned with nothing but the weather.

"I confess, I wanted to see the horror on his face."

"The damage is done," she said with calm resolve. "Will you escort me back to my aunt, or would you prefer I collapse into a heap on the dance floor? I could swagger back alone, play the true scarlet woman. You could tear the neckline of my gown, though it's one of the few I possess."

An unwelcome flicker of regret passed through him, one easily buried beneath his determination. Harland hadn't spared his mother a second thought. This was for her. He needed to remember that.

"It's your choice, angel."

"How magnanimous of you."

"I aim to please."

"Yet you've fallen dreadfully short tonight, Mr Hawke."

He shook his head, amused. Few had the confidence to imply he was lacking. "You were no one. Now you're notorious. I think that qualifies as memorable."

"Not quite memorable enough."

He should have mocked her, reminded her she was just a mark. Instead, he found himself noticing the slope of her neck, the defiant set of her mouth, the maddening softness of her curves. He could have any woman. Yet this one made revenge feel complicated and an affair almost tempting.

The music faded, the final strains of the violins marking the end of the dance and a plan brought to fruition.

Yet his competent partner took a sudden misstep on the final turn, causing him to catch her about the waist. She reached for him to steady herself, one hand gripping his lapel, the other clasping the back of his neck.

Miss Harland should have graced the stage. If titles were given for theatrics, she'd be royalty. Yet it wasn't the sudden press of her body against his that sent his world spinning, nor the feel of her sumptuous breasts crushed to his chest.

It was the sweet mouth that settled on his.

Warm. Soft. Deliberate.

And for one impossible moment, he forgot who was ruining whom.

CHAPTER TWO

To most, Mr Hawke was a rotten scoundrel, a dangerous degenerate who preyed on the weak, a cunning master of manipulation. To Daphne, he was a light in the darkness. Her saint. Her saviour.

She'd heard the gasps when he entered the ballroom with the confidence of Lucifer come to collect his due. Men clutched their hearts. Some shrank into the crowd, hoping they were invisible. Others tossed back their champagne as if it might be their last.

"God help us all," Aunt Augusta had muttered.

"Hawke takes no prisoners," someone added.

Daphne had just stared.

What must it be like to wield such power? To watch the ton cower? To stride through a room with your head held high while people cursed your name? What kind of life bred that sort of pride?

She'd spent sleepless nights praying for a solution to her dreadful predicament. She'd wept in silence, weighed hopeless options, and come within a breath of surrendering to her fate. Never had she imagined salvation would arrive in such a dangerously handsome package.

Yet it wasn't Mr Hawke's brooding good looks that made her throw herself at him. It wasn't why she kissed him now, or clung to him, knowing he couldn't push her away without ruining his own savage scheme.

She didn't want to feel the heat of his mouth or hear the hitch in his breath. She didn't want to taste brandy on his lips or breathe in the maddening spice of his cologne.

She needed but one thing from him.

Ruination.

He played his hand as she'd known he would, with devilish intent, as if this had always been the plan. He clutched her hair roughly, scattering pins across the floor. The hand at her waist slid lower, bunching the silk in his fist, sparking a strange heat in her belly.

Her breasts felt heavy. Her head too light. She forgot there were people in the room, forgot that he was a means to an end. That this mattered.

Then Mr Hawke dragged his mouth to her cheek, her jaw, and the sensitive spot below her ear. "I hope you've got thick skin, angel." His breath sent a shiver skipping down her spine. "Own this moment, and you'll be the toast of the demimonde."

She pulled back and met his gaze.

His green eyes softened, perhaps part of his act.

"Never let them see you cry," he said, releasing her and smoothing her gown. "Play the role. Carry a weapon. When it comes to conquests, you'll top every man's list. You could ask for the world, and they'd give it."

A hundred pairs of eyes watched them, so she smiled. "Thank you, Mr Hawke, for an enlightening experience, and for making this the most memorable dance of my life."

A muscle in his cheek twitched. Something passed between them: a flicker, a beat, a breath. Then he took her gloved hand, his mouth warm through the fabric as it brushed her fingers.

"Goodbye, angel."

"Goodbye, Mr Hawke."

He hesitated, then bowed and led her from the floor.

Her father appeared, his face flushed, half his waistcoat buttons undone, his grey eyes as cold as a winter's frost.

Mrs Foster scurried after him, lip rouge smudged, her hair wild, as though she'd been caught in a gale.

The sight angered Mr Hawke, and for the first time that evening, she noticed a flaw in his composure. "Evidently, you weren't playing piquet."

"What the devil is this about, Hawke?" her father demanded, but didn't wait for an answer. He shouted to the musicians, who sat frozen in their chairs, instruments braced. "Play something, you imbeciles!"

Daphne had never seen him so at odds.

He turned to Lord Templeton, whose next event would be a crush. "For Pete's sake, man, insist they dance. Ring the damn supper gong. Do something other than stand there like a preened hen."

The orchestra launched into a reel, all sharp strings and stomping rhythm. Daphne had the absurd urge to join in.

"You know what this is about," Mr Hawke said coldly.

She watched her father, waiting for a reaction. He glanced away briefly, but it was enough. He had done something to warrant her degradation.

She bit back a smile, a delicious surge of triumph bubbling in her chest. Who could he blame but himself? What excuse would he offer Mr Irving now?

She resisted the urge to clap her hands in glee.

Unbeknown to Mr Hawke, he had saved her from a fate worse than death. A life of abject misery, where the plan was to see her swollen with child by St Stephen's Day.

"He insisted they dance," Aunt Augusta said quickly, eager to excuse the fact that she was the world's worst chaperone. "Then he kissed her shamelessly in the middle of the floor. We were powerless to stop him."

Daphne held her breath, waiting for Mr Hawke to correct the mistake. She'd likely feel the crack of a birch for the part she'd played. Still, better that than marry a man thrice her age who smelled of stewed cabbage.

Mr Hawke stared at her father like a wolf on the prowl. "Ruining your daughter was only the beginning."

That should have been her cue to weep. To collapse into despair. To feel the hopelessness of her situation, the utter hatred for the masterful man beside her.

Perhaps she should reach for her handkerchief and pretend to dab a tear, or appear a little unsteady on her feet.

"What is this about, Father?" That seemed like the appropriate thing to say. She sniffed and coughed lightly. A touch of meekness would do no harm. "Why would a man like Mr Hawke seek me out?"

Her father leaned closer, so close she caught a whiff of Mrs Foster's sickly lavender scent on his coat. "You tell me, Daphne. I've a mind to think this is your attempt to sabotage our plans. If you think playing the harlot will free—"

"Don't call her that," Mr Hawke snapped, much to everyone's shock, for he ran a house of ill repute. "I'm the villain here. Nothing she could have said or done would have deterred me."

"Mr Hawke seemed intent on taking pleasure in my misfortune," she agreed, the sudden memory of his mouth on hers warming her cheeks.

Excellent. They'd mistake it for shame.

"This isn't about pleasure, angel. It's retribution."

Her aunt lifted a limp hand to her brow. "Good heavens. He has a moniker for her. Are we to hear of a new apartment in Mayfair? Accounts opened at every famed modiste? A new barouche delivered to the door?"

"I may have no option but to retire to the country. Perhaps even move as far afield as Flanders."

She might have winked at Mr Hawke, but that would be beyond the pale. Besides, how was he to know she welcomed his attention? The scoundrel had intended to ruin her life.

A sinister shadow passed over her father's patrician features. "You'll go where I tell you." He bared his teeth. Froth gathered at the corners of his mouth. "This charade ends now. We'll discuss the matter of your exile at home. Irving has a house in Bengal."

A cold chill swept through her. Bengal.

A place so distant she was unlikely to see home again.

She felt the blood drain from her face.

Surely he didn't expect Mr Irving to marry her. The man might have overlooked her lack of a dowry, but not the possibility she was no longer chaste.

Mr Hawke didn't seem to care either way. He tugged his cuffs and brushed imaginary dust from his coat sleeves. "I shall await a dawn summons. You'll find me at Mivart's Hotel."

With that, he strode away, the crowd parting in his wake.

All eyes in the house turned to her, crows keen to feast on the bones of her anonymity. Every distasteful glare was another vicious peck. Whispers rose behind gloved hands and raised fans. They noticed everything.

The small stain on her hem where it had caught the step.

That her breasts were a touch too full for her slight frame.

Yet her first thought was for Mr Hawke. How did one ignore their spite? How did one walk through ruin with confidence carved into their spine?

"I hope you're pleased with yourself," her aunt complained. "Judging by the cool reception, I'll be your companion in Bengal." She turned to the man who wielded patriarchal dominance like a sabre. "I don't know what you did to rouse his ire, but we'll all pay the price."

"What Hawke thinks I did, and what transpired, are different things entirely. I'm not the only man to pay court to his mother, nor the only villain here." Her father muttered a curse, a scourge on wicked men. "It was years ago. Had I known the blackguard bore a grudge, I'd have dealt with it then."

Aunt Augusta scanned the onlookers and swallowed. "We should leave before they descend like a pack of jackals." She turned to her companion, Loretta, but the woman had already made herself scarce.

Her father gave a wry snort. "Let them look. I'm not leaving until I'm good and ready."

"What about the dawn appointment?" Daphne asked. "Who will you name as your second?"

She didn't want him to meet Mr Hawke on the common, but the event seemed inevitable now. No doubt the scoundrel shot with expert precision. And who in their right mind would stop him?

Her father straightened to his full height. "I have no intention of feeding Hawke's need for vengeance. It's not as if your honour hangs in the balance. Irving will have you regardless."

The thought froze her blood.

Had she humiliated herself for nothing?

She wasn't thinking of the dance, but of the kiss. A stolen

moment with a man she should have feared. Yet it had confirmed one thing with painful clarity: she could not marry Mr Irving.

The truth slotted into place with sickening ease.

"So that's it, then. This is all about money," she bit back.

What was she but a mere commodity?

At least with Mr Hawke, she'd seized a sliver of power. She'd twisted the scandal to her advantage. There was no advantage in marrying a man who made her skin crawl.

Her father stared at her from beneath his heavy brow. "If I don't pay the Moseley brothers by month's end, they'll have my head on a spike. Then you'll wish you lived in Bengal."

She'd rather take her chances with the crooks from Drury Lane. How her father had landed in such a predicament, heaven only knew.

"I'll call on Irving tonight and make sure he'll take you, though there will be some negotiation on the price."

He spoke as if she were a brood mare, and he meant to pair her with a flea-bitten nag.

"Perhaps I could find work." It was a last-ditch attempt to stop this madness. Though who would employ her now?

"Even if I'd permit a daughter of mine to sully her hands, there's only one profession open to you." His mouth twisted into a sardonic grin. "If your mother were alive, she'd cast you out in shame."

The words struck like a blade to her heart. Her mother's soft smile rose in her mind, along with her final warning.

Trust no man, for they all betray you in the end.

Tears welled, but she fought them back.

Never let them see you cry.

Strange that her mother and Mr Hawke should share the same sentiment. Perhaps it was a sign from the gods.

"Excuse me. I need to visit the retiring room."

"Don't let me find you in an alcove with your skirts hiked," came her father's coarse warning.

"Jacob," Aunt Augusta muttered sharply. "As I understand it, it wasn't Daphne's mistake. If we're to salvage anything from this debacle, we must show a united front."

A united front.

Somehow, she needed to sever ties with these wicked schemers and put more than an ocean between herself and Mr Irving. For a lady without funds or reputation, it was an impossible feat.

"I'll accompany you to the retiring room," her aunt said.

"She can do the walk of shame alone," her father cut in. "Perhaps it'll convince her that a comfortable home with Irving is the best option all round."

It *was* a walk of shame.

Ladies stepped aside as if scandal were a disease they might catch. Had they carried stones in their reticules, they might have used them.

But the prospect of Mr Irving's damp, grasping mouth caused her to stiffen her spine and walk with the deliberate sway of a courtesan. It took strength to look ahead and not at the carpet.

If only Mr Hawke were her tutor.

If only she possessed a measure of his charisma.

As she made her way down the corridor to the retiring room, someone whispered her name, low and unmistakably male. Her heart gave a traitorous jolt. The thought of seeing Mr Hawke again set her nerves alight, and not in any respectable fashion.

But it wasn't the indomitable Mr Hawke.

Lord Templeton beckoned her towards an alcove, waving a slip of paper as if it might entice her. "I have a note from Hawke."

Her dratted pulse rose a notch.

Perhaps Mr Hawke had offered her a financial reward for being a pawn in his game. Wishful thinking. By the time she reached the lord, it was clear he had read the missive.

"Hawke suggests if it all goes to hell, and it will, you should seek out Lady Soanes. You'll find no safer place this side of disgrace."

She took the note from the lord's hand and thanked him for his trouble. But he caught her wrist in a serpent's grip and drew her closer.

"I have a better alternative, Miss Harland. A house out of town, away from prying eyes. Use of a carriage. Any fripperies you desire."

Her instinct was to stamp on his toe and bloody his nose, but she offered a sweet smile, the kind that warned of arsenic in the tea. "How generous of you, my lord. But I'm already quite ruined. It would be greedy to take more than my share."

Lord Templeton's thumb stroked her wrist. "It's a practical offer, Miss Harland. A promise you'll be well housed and well kept." He moved nearer than courtesy allowed. "No lady has ever found my terms lacking." He tapped the note in her hand. "Hawke no longer assumes responsibility for your upkeep or your virtue."

How naive she had been.

Was this how her life would be now?

Not one leering gentleman to endure, but a horde of them.

"I shall give it some thought." She tugged her wrist free. It was the only way to be rid of him.

"I'm extremely wealthy, Miss Harland. I'll more than match any offer you receive. Your father won't object. I doubt he'll live to see sunrise."

Too afraid to visit the retiring room in case the lecherous lord followed, she tucked the note into her bodice and promised to give him an answer by week's end. Though she would sooner burn in Hades than waste another moment on this Lothario.

Damn Mr Hawke.

She was of a mind to challenge him herself.

A duel would be another foolish notion. She didn't know the first thing about loading a pistol, let alone firing one with any accuracy.

But there were other ways to make a man bleed.

Not with a blade.

Knowledge was the only weapon she needed. The kind that could ruin a man's name with a whisper, turn a rumour into a scandal, a secret into currency. If Mr Hawke thought he'd seen the last of her, he'd underestimated her badly.

She drew a breath, plucked the note from her bodice, and read Mr Hawke's parting gift.

> *Angel,*
>
> *The secret's out. Let them whisper. You always did look good in a storm. Smile like you know something they don't. You will soon enough.*
>
> *Find Lady Soanes. She knows how to win at this game and finish it. She'll see that you're armed.*
>
> *Hawke*
>
> *P.S. I'll miss those sweet lips and that clever tongue.*

She studied his confident penmanship. What sort of man ruined a woman and then wrote her a note? Perhaps one with a conscience. Or one who knew Lord Templeton would read the missive and wished to convince the ton they were lovers.

Well. If he wanted her to seek out Lady Soanes, that's what she'd do. A woman like that didn't survive without influence. Daphne didn't want sanctuary. She wanted training and help to overcome the obstacles. Who better to provide it than a woman who'd turned scandal to her advantage?

As soon as her father left the house to visit Mr Irving, and Aunt Augusta fell asleep in a fireside chair, Daphne dragged her packed valise from the blanket box and slipped out through the servants' door, taking a hunk of bread and a square of cheese with her.

The walk to Wimpole Street took five minutes, though her heart thumped in time with every step. Would Lady Soanes receive her or turn her away like a common beggar?

As legend had it, the diamond of her Season was once found locked in an orangery with a wicked cad. The scandal should have ruined her. Instead, it forged her into something far more dangerous. Judging by the grandeur of Soanes House, infamy suited her well.

Daphne lifted the lion-head knocker, polished to a mirror sheen, and made her presence known. The young butler answered promptly, a frown flickering beneath his reserve as his gaze dropped to her valise.

"If you've come from the Registry, miss, Sir Gascon Phillips lives next door. He holds interviews between ten and noon."

That he'd mistaken her for a servant did not bode well.

She pressed the note into his hand. "Please give this to Lady Soanes. I shall await her reply."

"Lady Soanes is indisposed." His tone was polite but noncommittal as he returned the note. "You may try again tomorrow. After her afternoon calls at three."

She might be halfway to Bengal by then.

Daphne stepped closer. She was not averse to barging past him. "I must leave London tonight. I'm sure Lady Soanes will appreciate the urgency of a woman down on her luck." She offered the note again. "Mr Hawke advised I call, and gave me this missive two hours ago."

Before the butler could respond, a feminine voice floated down the stairwell. "Did he now? It's just like him to catch a lady unawares."

A truer word had never been spoken.

A figure appeared on the landing, wrapped in a robe of midnight blue trimmed with white fur, her auburn hair coiled loosely, as if she'd only just risen from bed.

Lady Soanes descended with the confidence of a woman who'd fought the patriarchy and won. "Allow her in, Braisby. One never ignores a summons from Hawke."

Braisby took her coat without comment, though his brows lifted at the worn hem and the heavy valise.

The drawing room was all pale blue silk and gold damask, with marble-topped tables and gilt-framed portraits. Every polished surface spoke of wealth and security, things she could only hope to possess.

Lady Soanes poured two glasses of sherry, then crossed the room and handed one to Daphne, but not before giving her figure a brief appraisal.

"I've had many requests from Hawke over the years. Never one involving a woman. May I ask how you're acquainted?"

Daphne took a fortifying sip of sherry. "He came to Lord Templeton's ball to ruin me, so my father would have cause to call him out."

The evening had not gone entirely to plan.

Lady Soanes' gaze dipped to her lips. "Did he succeed?"

She told the story from the beginning. Soon, all of London would be able to recite it verbatim. "A dance was all he intended."

"Dance with a devil and you'll burn on a pyre."

"I confess, I did more than stir the embers."

"You did? How intriguing."

She explained her father's devious plan to see her wed. "I let myself stumble into Mr Hawke's arms as the waltz ended, then kissed him."

The lady tightened her grip on her glass. "You kissed Dominic Hawke? Before a room full of people? Without his permission?"

"What else could I do? I need Mr Irving to withdraw his suit."

Lady Soanes shook her head. "It will take a little more than a kiss in a ballroom. My dear, your father needs money. Desperately so, from what I hear. Mr Irving needs heirs to prevent his brother from taking control of the family business. He won't care about gossip. He means to emigrate to India."

Yes, and he intended to secure an heir before the ink on the register dried.

"Could I not pretend to carry Mr Hawke's child?" Desperate times called for desperate measures. And things were already spiralling out of control. "After tonight, no one would doubt it."

Lady Soanes's eyes widened in alarm. "Good God, no.

Have the ton believe he left you with child and turned his back on it? Hawke would never allow it."

"But everyone believes he's a rotten scoundrel."

"And he is. Ruthless to the core. But he has principles."

"Forgive me if I fail to see them."

Lady Soanes glanced at the scrap of paper in Daphne's hand. "You have the proof of it there. May I see the note Hawke left?"

"Of course. That's why I came." She handed Lady Soanes the letter, written in the intimate tone of a lover.

The lady read it, glanced up and arched a brow. "Angel?"

"That's what Mr Hawke called me when we danced. And *mouse*. Though I imagine he thinks me a tiger after the way I pounced."

Lady Soanes laughed, her green eyes bright with wicked delight. "What an interesting creature you are, Miss Harland."

"I'm glad you think so, my lady."

Interesting was better than useless or ungrateful.

"Yes, you're wasted on the men of the ton."

It was said Lady Soanes had once ruled the ton without a title or a husband. If anyone could teach her how to wield ruin as a weapon, it was her.

Scandal or no, she had no intention of marrying.

"My options are rather limited." She hated how calmly she could say it now. "The wax had scarcely cooled on the note when Lord Templeton made me a scandalous offer."

Lady Soanes muttered something decidedly unladylike under her breath. "I trust you refused him. The man hasn't a shred of decency. Does Hawke know?"

Why would he care?

"No, I doubt he'd be surprised. He's at Mivart's tonight, expecting a visit from my father's second." Another mistake. Her father was the king of cowards. "But he's averse to violence when the odds aren't favourable. He decided to visit Mr Irving instead."

"And now you're in a dreadful predicament."

The statement hung in the air like the threat of checkmate.

Lady Soanes refilled their glasses, her brow knitting as though she were contemplating which move on the board might save the queen.

"*Angel,*" the lady muttered. "Who'd have thought it?"

"Maybe he meant to soften the blow."

Lady Soanes smiled. "Yet I've never known him let his guard slip. I can understand why he wrote the endearment, a clever ploy to cement his position. But not why he'd bother to flatter you."

Was it flattery, or merely mockery?

"Who can say what he intended?" Other than to make a spectacle of her to satisfy his own devious ends.

"Who indeed?" Lady Soanes studied her as one might an odd curiosity. "Of course, he expects me to take you under my wing. Teach you the art of making men fall over themselves despite never knowing the pleasure of having you."

Daphne imagined all eyes on her as she entered the ballroom. Fake smiles, empty compliments, and men waiting for the chance to catch her alone in a dark corner.

She shivered as though someone had walked over her grave. "My father may be a coward when it comes to his peers, but not so with his kin. Mr Hawke is wrong if he believes I can avoid capture. I expect my father is already sourcing a ticket to India."

"You possess the qualities to succeed, Miss Harland."

"Yet I'd prefer a simple life in the country."

"Without funds, how would you survive?"

"I'd have to work, my lady." Twelve hours of toil was

preferable to twenty-four with Mr Irving. "And pray my father never finds me."

The lady's gaze roamed over Daphne's figure. "There is somewhere you might put your talents to good use. Somewhere your father would never reach you."

Daphne's heart skipped a beat. "The Americas?"

"No," the lady said, grinning. "Shadowmere."

Shadowmere.

An image of Mr Hawke crashed into her mind, sending her heart pounding. He was formidable when calling her *angel*. How would he react when she invaded his territory? "He'd never permit me over the threshold."

"He's not there. He's at Mivart's. I could write you a note. My coachman will take you directly."

A pang of trepidation hit her squarely in the chest. "It's a house of ill repute. Tales of the wicked—"

"It's Hawke's home. He merely hires out part of the house on weekends. Don't believe all the gossip. Judge for yourself. Stay for a month. If you decide to leave after that, I shall find you a safe place to live."

She fell silent, a little dumbfounded.

"Use what you have: your poise, your perception, your unfailing ability to see through a man. You're not as powerless as they'd have you believe."

She shook her head, doubting she'd survive a night.

"Mr Hawke is not a man open to charm."

"Yet you've done something right."

"I've packed nothing but a few serviceable dresses."

Lady Soanes' eyes brightened. "Perfect. You must endeavour to be yourself, Miss Harland. No masks. No clever tricks. Refuse any other role he gives you. He's accountable for his actions, and you shall remind him of that."

She couldn't deny the thought of confronting Mr Hawke

had appeal. A few days away from London would keep her out of harm's way and give her time to think. And she wouldn't have to waste precious funds on a stage ticket.

"Very well, my lady."

"Excellent. And you must call me Charlotte." The lady couldn't hide her elation. She captured Daphne's hand and squeezed it tightly. "Come. Let me write a letter, and we'll devise a plan. The first being how you get past the guard at the gate."

CHAPTER THREE

Of all the craven bastards in Christendom, Lord Harland topped the list. Did the man have no shame? He could debauch a widow, blackmail her into silence, permit his daughter to face humiliation, and still sleep soundly in his feathered bed.

Dominic had paced through his suite at Mivart's hotel for the better part of eight hours, the carpet near threadbare beneath his boots. He would have downed an entire decanter of brandy had he not needed to keep his wits. Hell, he'd opened the gold case on his full hunter so many times he'd nearly worn out the clasp.

Was Harland arrogant enough to believe himself untouchable? Did he not have a shred of honour to his name?

Dominic had considered seeking the blackguard out, dragging him from whatever vice-ridden corner of London he currently infested. But what greater insult was there than silence? Harland hadn't sent a second. Hadn't issued a reply. He'd ignored the challenge entirely, as though Dominic and the disgrace he'd orchestrated were beneath his notice.

Now, on the road to Kingston in the cold light of day,

Dominic thought of the woman he'd tried his damnedest to forget.

Miss Daphne Harland had been a surprise. A pleasant one.

Few people left a lasting impression. Perhaps that's why he'd done the unthinkable and offered her a way to escape her predicament.

But that wasn't what bothered him now.

He should have been plotting to destroy Harland. Or, at the very least, sleeping against the squab so he didn't feel half-dead. So why did every thought circle back to the woman he'd ruined?

Had her father locked her in her chamber?

Was she already warming some profligate's bed?

The last thought landed like a punch to the gut, ridiculous, given she owed him nothing. So why the hell did he care?

Had she taken his advice and sought out Lady Soanes? Was she at the modiste's, seeking ways to display her sumptuous body to perfection? Which licentious lord would earn the privilege of that clever mouth?

They were all undeserving.

A darker thought took root.

Someone else would have the gift of her virginity.

For some baffling reason, he kicked the seat.

The carriage slowed, his coachman mistaking the sound for a summons. "Drive on, Jones," he barked.

He never raised his voice.

He never assaulted the furniture.

Woe betide anyone who crossed him today.

Keen to put his thoughts in order, he had Jones stop at All Saints Church. He took the posy from the seat, the one he'd bought before leaving London, and walked the gravel path to his mother's grave.

He knelt—she was the only woman to bring him to his

knees—and picked the few weeds, brushing dust from the new Carrara marble he'd had imported from Italy.

He laid the posy for his mother, her beloved white roses, and refused to glance at the lichen-covered stone marking his father's plot.

"I'd hoped to bring good news. To say you could finally rest in peace, that the debt was paid." His throat tightened at the memory of her final breath. He had failed her again. "But my mission is far from over."

A bitter vow pulsed beneath his ribs.

God help him, he would avenge her.

He took the single rosebud and said a prayer for his sister. He'd never met her. Never would. But his mother had been certain the child growing inside her was a girl, and he'd never doubted her word.

He left the churchyard, the chill of loneliness seeping into his bones.

It was the reminder he needed.

The coldness that gave him the will to fight on.

If only he'd known the truth years ago. But his mother had been secretive; Harland, cunning. Which begged the question: where had London's finest enquiry agent found the information?

With a new sense of resolve, he returned to Shadowmere.

Some called his castle-like home *Lucifer's Palace*. It certainly rose from the earth like a curse on the landscape. Its old stone walls had surely witnessed many sacrifices, none more so than his mother's.

Had she not sold her soul to keep it, he would burn it to the ground.

He approached the great studded doors and tugged the iron bell crank, its peal echoing through the vast entrance hall, the belly of the underworld, some said. Shadowmere was barred to visitors. Few came or went unless he was hosting an event. Even then, the doors were locked after the guests were patted down like common thieves, their fine leather luggage rifled through.

Ramsey opened the door hatch, suspicion giving way to relief when he eyed Dominic. "I was beginning to fear the fool had shot you." He slid the heavy bolts with the ease of a man who enjoyed keeping enemies out. "Or you'd been tossed into Newgate to rot."

Broad-shouldered and sharp-eyed, with hair that held the amber depth of good cognac, Ramsey served as Dominic's bodyguard, butler, and occasional second. In short, he was damned indispensable.

Dominic marched into the entrance hall, where the crimson walls drank what little light the day offered. One look at the gilt paintings of naked nymphs, and he thought of Miss Harland.

Bloody hell.

"Harland didn't give a damn that I danced with his daughter." Anger sparked at the memory. Perhaps insulting the lord's paramour would have drawn a reaction. "I could have stripped the girl bare and he wouldn't have batted an eye."

Miss Harland was no mere girl.

She was every bit a woman. A devious one at that.

"He left me waiting at Mivart's like a buck with a measly grudge."

"Can't say I'm sorry." Ramsey closed the door and drew the locks, plunging the hall into shadow. "I'd rather not see you hanged for murder. Happen you must have been three sheets cut when you cooked up that plan."

Humiliation had been the primary goal. Then isolation. Most would distance themselves from Harland now. He'd wanted him to feel the indignity of having doors slammed in his face. Yes, he might have shot him, but only to maim, not kill.

"And it's not like you to cause an innocent woman distress, even if she *is* the spawn of Satan. Did you tell her you'd see her right? Give her that windfall we discussed?"

"Not in so many words."

If he'd had a cat-o'-nine-tails, he'd have whipped his own back. But the moment he'd entered the ballroom and seen arrogance worn like a buttonhole bloom, something inside him had snapped.

"I believe she wanted me to ruin her." He should have phrased it differently, because all the ways he might deflower Miss Harland filled his head. "We danced, albeit too close for propriety, but she kissed me as the musicians struck the final notes."

It was brief, closed mouths, so why could he still feel the hot press of her virtuous lips, seared like a brand?

Ramsey stepped back, his frown giving way to a mocking grin. "She kissed you? An innocent threw herself at the Prince of Darkness, in full view of the ton? Were you drinking?"

"A glass of champagne foul enough to sober a corpse."

Ramsey laughed so hard he had to clutch his ribs and gasp for breath. "That's the funniest thing I've heard since you told Lord Burrows his wig needed a valet. I mean the kiss, not the drink."

"The lady has a titan's courage," Dominic admitted.

Ramsey wiped his eyes, still grinning. "Did she know who you were? That she was besting the devil?"

"Apparently, I top the list of men to avoid." Doubtless the next three places belonged to his friends. A quartet of ruin, as one scandal sheet had called them.

"By a mile, I'd say."

Dominic managed a smile. He'd rather be feared than feel that crippling vulnerability again. "Might I remind you I paint, play piano, and read Virgil. There is an elegant man beneath this villainous charm."

"Aye, you could compose a concerto with one hand while torturing a man with the other."

"Nothing would please me more than strapping Harland to the rack and stretching that lily-liver inch by inch." Keen to wash road dust off his skin—and the elusive trace of Miss Harland's perfume, something floral and far too memorable —he strode towards the dark oak staircase. "Have William bring warm water for the shower-bath. Then meet me in the study. I want to run through the preparations for the Autumn Masque."

Ramsey called after him. "Beattie has compiled a list. It's exact down to the number of berries on the wreaths."

"I'd expect nothing less," Dominic said, mounting the steps. Beattie ran the house like a field marshal and did nothing by halves. If he ever plotted murder, it would be timed to the second, not a drop of blood left behind.

"I'll have him join us once he's finished with the new maid." Ramsey chuckled. "He's putting her through the usual paces, though there are more crosses than ticks on his list."

Dominic froze mid-step. Slowly, he turned. "New maid?"

"The one you had Lady Soanes hire while in town."

"I didn't ask Lady Soanes to hire a maid. You know my views on employing female staff. I keep them to a minimum." The last thing he needed was virtue in a house that catered for vice. Monsters needed little encouragement once free of their cages.

Ramsey's smile died. He approached the stairs, eager to explain. "She came with references. Carried a note from you.

I know your mark like I know my own name. She arrived in Lady Soanes' carriage."

Dominic did not move, but his mind raced.

What the devil had Charlotte done?

Ramsey gripped the newel post. "She knew the code word."

"Of course she bloody did," Dominic snapped. "Lady Soanes told her." Give him strength. "Where is she now?"

"Lady Soanes?"

"No. The maid."

Ramsey rubbed the back of his neck and grimaced. "With Beattie. He had her lay the fire in the servants' hall three times this morning. Now she's polishing silver. Said he doubts she's buffed anything in her life."

He didn't know whether to laugh or groan, to applaud Miss Harland's gall or chastise her for it. Assuming, of course, it was the lady who'd disgraced him on the dance floor. Who else would be so bold?

"Let me guess," he said, though he hardly needed to conjure a vision of his despoiler. She had lived behind his eyes since last night. "Ebony hair. Skin smooth enough to be marble. Blue eyes, as I recall." Like a faraway ocean. Distant. Untouchable.

Ramsey shrugged. "Can't say I noticed."

He felt like marching down the stairs, propping Ramsey's eyes open with sticks and checking he wasn't blind.

He should be relieved.

How could a man *not* notice Miss Harland?

Perhaps he was jumping to conclusions. Perhaps there was a rational explanation. Even so, he knew it was her. He could feel it in his bones. Who else would invade his house disguised as a maid, armed with forged references and that clever mouth wielded like a weapon?

"Shall I give her a month's wages and turn her out?"

Dominic hesitated, the urge to say yes dancing on his tongue, though he'd left his better judgement in Templeton's ballroom.

"No. I'll assess her abilities myself. Have her bring up the water for my shower-bath. She's to carry two buckets up the servants' stairs."

He allowed himself a thin smile. He would see how long that composure lasted. See whether she truly understood the game she had chosen to play.

The image forming in his mind was wicked enough to make a priest sweat.

They didn't call him the Prince of Darkness for nothing.

If Mr Beattie asked her to polish the silver again, she'd tell him exactly what to do with his chamois cloth. No doubt Mr Hawke liked staring at his own reflection while he dined. One glint of a knife at the window was enough to summon an infantry from a mile away.

Wasn't it the job of the footman? Or the under-butler?

Trust him to break with convention.

Her shoulders ached. Her hands smelled of vinegar and soot. She could lay a fire with military precision, and still Mr Beattie was dissatisfied.

He loomed over her like an ageing bloodhound as she sat at the crude oak table in the butler's pantry, his long, mournful face sagging under the weight of Mr Hawke's expectations.

"Miss Smith, I can't comment on your previous employer's standards. But at Shadowmere, everything must be first rate."

Anyone would think Mr Hawke entertained the King, not a pack of lecherous libertines. Since when did debauchers and opium-eaters care about polished tableware? Most probably ate with their fingers.

Just when she thought Mr Beattie might pull out the boot polish and ten pairs of muddy Hessians, Mr Ramsey appeared at the door.

He stared at her from beneath hooded lids, as if the word *liar* were carved on her forehead. Then he turned to Mr Beattie.

"Hawke is home. And he's not in the best of moods."

Her heart shot to her throat, though it had nothing to do with the man and everything to do with his cold manner.

Well … that might be a small lie.

It had a little to do with the man, the one whose eyes were the shade of moss at dawn, and whose arrogance was utterly unmatched.

"He wants two buckets of water for his shower-bath."

Shower-bath?

So, he might live in a fortress, but he wasn't a heathen. He liked to indulge in modern comforts.

Perhaps the wicked ladies of the ton sat in velvet chairs, drinking ratafia, watching him tend to his ablutions.

"I'll have Cook heat the water at once, Mr Ramsey."

The sly curl of Mr Ramsey's lips warned he had something shocking to say. "Hawke wants the new maid to carry the buckets upstairs. I'll follow behind. Make sure she can find his chamber."

Her stomach dropped. She'd been hoping to spend a few days moving about the house unnoticed, to delay the inevitable confrontation. Lady Soanes expected her to stay a month. At this rate, she would be lucky to last the hour.

Mr Beattie eyed her as a major would the worst cadet in the barracks. "I'm not sure Miss Smith is up to the task."

Daphne straightened her spine. She'd carried burdens heavier than buckets and insults sharper than Mr Beattie's stiff little moustache.

She smiled through gritted teeth. "I can manage the buckets, sir."

"It isn't a question of managing, Miss Smith. Hawke was quite specific."

Of course he was. He'd make her climb the stairs, sweat dripping down her spine, just to gloat.

The buckets were heavy. Heavy enough that Mr Ramsey took pity and carried one to the top of the stone staircase. She adjusted her grip, ignoring the splash against her skirt.

"There's more on the floor than in the bucket."

"Alas, I lack your brawn, Mr Ramsey."

"What you lack in brawn, you make up for in courage. Pity the same can't be said for your father. Hawke won't rest until he makes him pay."

So there had been no duel at dawn. No blood spilled in her name. Mr Hawke hadn't hunted him down and fired regardless.

He had chosen restraint.

He was not a complete scoundrel.

Her father had done more to disgrace her than Mr Hawke with his scandalous waltz. At least *he* fought for a cause, one she had yet to understand. Her father fought only for himself.

Mr Ramsey led her down a narrow corridor, stone yielding to wood so polished it shone like old wine. Mr Hawke might be short on scruples, but he didn't cut corners.

They stopped outside a door with two keyholes and a

plaque that read: *Enter upon pain of death*. One had to admire a man who didn't mince words.

Mr Ramsey knocked twice.

"Enter."

The rich sound of Mr Hawke's voice stirred the hair at her nape. Her belly fluttered, which she put down to nerves. This would be their second round. She had to win this bout.

Mr Ramsey handed her the bucket and opened the door. He didn't set foot over the threshold, merely closed it behind her.

Daphne took a moment to scan the room, not him.

The deep reds and plush velvets that dominated the house were absent here. The walls were painted hunter green, the wainscoting and heavy oak poster bed evoking the quiet hush of a forest. The furnishings were spare but elegant: an escritoire scattered with papers and numerous quills, a book he was midway through reading.

She knew the traits of the man who owned Shadowmere.

Not those of the person who slept here.

She noticed the monstrous shower contraption raised on a tiled dais in the far corner, and reluctantly drew a breath. The room smelled of him, as she feared it would, that tantalising mix of dark spice and danger.

"Put the buckets beside the shower-bath, Miss Harland."

She caught him in the corner of her eye: grey trousers, a loose white shirt, and—lord help her—bare feet.

"It's Miss Smith while I'm working here, sir. A lady on the run should remain incognito."

He closed the gap between them, his fingers warm as they slid over hers to take the bucket. "I'm sorry to say you've been misinformed. There is no vacancy."

She turned to face him, ready to fight, but he was too close for comfort, her eyes level with the open neck of his shirt. Her hand trembled. Water slipped over the rim of the remaining bucket, splashing onto her feet.

"You've made a puddle on the rug, Miss Harland, and I've not touched you yet."

"Hell will freeze over before you touch me again, Mr Hawke." She met his gaze and wished she hadn't. Mischief lived in those compelling green eyes.

"Then I'd better buy a fur coat."

She set the bucket down with a thud. "I used you last night. I've no plans to do so again."

The slight jerk of his head said he'd felt her bite.

"We used each other. And now it seems the advantage is mine. I don't want a maid, and you need employment."

"Is this where you make me a different offer?"

"I don't want a mistress, either."

He probably burned through them at a rate of one a week.

"I was referring to your guests for the Autumn Masque. You said I'd top most men's list. Why not use me to your advantage? I could be the entertainment."

He clasped her elbow. "Over my dead body."

Satisfied she'd achieved the desired effect, she tugged her arm free. Somehow, she had to persuade him to let her stay.

"You hurt me. And now you must make amends. I'm your responsibility, whether you like it or not. I deserve a home. An income. You stole my airs and graces, and so I'm more than happy to work as a maid."

He stepped back, dragged his shirt over his head and threw it on the leather chair. "It's not safe for you here."

Her gaze dropped of its own volition.

Cook had always said she was a greedy minx, and she couldn't help but sneak one look at Mr Hawke's muscular chest.

Well. Maybe two. Three, if one counted the slow glide to where that trail of dark hair vanished beneath his waistband.

"Pour the water into the basin. If you want to work as a maid, let's see if you can follow orders."

He began unbuttoning the fall of his trousers.

Good heavens above.

"I can be obedient. You'll scarcely know I'm here."

"A man would need to be deaf and blind to miss you, Miss Harland. Now hurry. Before the water goes cold. Consider this a test. You'll need to grow accustomed to nakedness if you want to keep your position."

There was no danger of the water chilling. She was warming it with the heat from her cheeks. She lifted the bucket with as much grace as she could muster and poured, determined not to spill a single drop.

She saw him fling his trousers onto the bed.

"Once I step in, take a firm grip and pump hard."

"I beg your pardon?"

"The mechanism, Miss Harland. How else shall I bathe?"

She might have shot him an irate glare, but daren't look above his firm calves. Dark hair lay against skin drawn taut over corded muscle. And she cursed her own curiosity.

She gripped the handle with both hands and began siphoning water from the basin into the tank above.

"Faster, Miss Harland. A man might freeze to death."

"I'm going as fast as I can. It's extremely stiff."

Thank heavens Mr Beattie wasn't listening at the door. Doubtless he'd insist she empty the water and start again.

"How long should I pump?"

"Until I'm satisfied you're up to the task." She could hear the laughter in his voice. "Look at me, Miss Harland, so I know you're listening."

She knew what he wanted. To embarrass her. To remind

her this was a house of sin. To suggest his weekend guests might expect more than a steady hand at the pump. And to see where her greedy eyes would settle.

She didn't look at him. Didn't take the bait.

Lady Soanes' warning echoed like a bell.

Be yourself. Refuse any other role he gives you.

She stepped back from the contraption, wiping her hands on her pink muslin dress. Mr Beattie had refused to issue a uniform until she proved herself capable.

"Pull the chain, Mr Hawke. I'm confident the tank is full. Do try not to drown." She crossed the room and gripped the doorknob. "How would you avenge your mother then?"

CHAPTER FOUR

It wasn't the lukewarm water raining over his head and chest that chilled him, nor Miss Harland's refusal to play his scandalous game. It was her comment about his mother. How would he avenge her if Harland refused to step onto the battlefield? How could he beat a man who didn't mind being called a coward?

Miss Harland had a way of slipping past his defences, striking the old wound with little more than a well-aimed word. Did she know he felt it like the jab of a blade to the—

"Hawke." Ramsey snapped his fingers, more amused than impatient. "I'm starting to think you left your wits in Mayfair because your head sure as hell isn't here."

Dominic blinked, realising he was seated in the leather chair behind his desk, not standing naked in the wretched basin while his angel ogled his calves.

What the devil had possessed him to strip off his clothes? Yes, he'd planned to have Miss Harland pump the water, but not while he was in it.

"Shall I repeat the question?" Ramsey flipped through five pages of notes and sighed like a man faced with a monumental task. "Who will you refuse? Lord Stapleton or Sir Graham? They brawled in the paddock over Mrs Langford when they came for the Bacchanal."

He didn't care if they throttled each other in the pantry. The ton was overrun with deviants. Two less would be a blessing. "Accept both. But charge a reparation fee for the trouble they caused."

Ramsey took up the quill and made a note on the first page. "Mr Hearst listed his valet among his party. I'm told he likes to wander the house in the dead of night."

A vision of the valet creeping into Miss Harland's room tightened Dominic's gut. Not that it mattered. She'd be gone before sunrise. "Hearst dresses himself or he doesn't come."

"He was hoping for a little privacy with his servant."

"Then he should keep his lover on a leash. Put Hearst next to Smithers. He had a taste for the man and his wife at the Crimson Carnival."

Talk of guests' habits might shock some, but nothing was as obscene as the sounds of them feasting like the citizens of Sodom and Gomorrah.

And so it went on—lists of sickening requests, a house tailored for those addicted to pleasure. But there was nothing pleasurable about inviting another man into the marriage bed.

He was about to consider the next depraved demand when a sound drifted in through the half-open door.

"What the blazes is that?"

Ramsey tilted his head. "Singing, I'd say."

"I *know* it's singing. I'm not a fool."

"That's open to debate, considering the new maid is your enemy's daughter. You should have had Jones drive her back to London. But I suspect you enjoy having her at your beck and call."

Dominic scoffed. As if Miss Harland would ever bend to

anyone. She hadn't come to grovel. She'd come to hold him to account, chin high and claws bared, a walking reminder of his failings.

"Only days ago, you suggested I offer her a handsome reward. Now you'd have her bundled out before morning. Make up your mind."

"You're the one walking around as if you don't know your arse from your elbow." Ramsey leaned back in his chair, arms folded, watching him with a knowing smirk. "Since when did a woman leave you rattled? Maybe we should arrange a wager. There's men who'd pay a king's ransom to see you come undone."

"They'd be wasting their coin."

The singing drifted down the hallway, an old folk song about love, red roses and sweet summer meadows, one that had no place in this iniquitous den.

"My confusion stems from not knowing what to do about Harland." *Or his distracting daughter.* No man wanted to look weak within his own walls.

A light rap sounded at the door, followed by the clatter of a tea tray. She appeared, bright as a button, not a tear in sight. But he knew sadness lingered behind the bravado. He wouldn't put it past her to hide a dagger beneath the short-bread biscuits.

"I bring the coffee pot, Mr Hawke. I believe you ordered enough to quench a desert army."

Miss Harland strode into his study in the plain pink dress that made her look biddable, wearing a smile where he'd expected a scowl.

Her eyes skimmed the papers on his desk. "Should I make space, or will you?" She tilted her head towards the door, voice dropping. "Mr Beattie would insist on a tray table. One more cross on his list, and I'll be demoted to the stables."

"Yet a home for the depraved suits you better."

She set down the tray. "Careful, Mr Hawke. That almost sounded like an invitation to stay."

"You'll not sleep a night in this house," he said flatly. But even as he spoke, he imagined passing her door in the dark. Wondering if she'slept. If she dreamed of revenge or of him. "We'll discuss your removal once I've finished here."

"Then I shall retreat and prepare my terms." Like a general in training, she swept from the room, humming her little tune as she closed the door.

"Terms?" he grumbled. As if he'd agree to her demands. "We're not pirates haggling on the high seas. Perhaps it's time I bared my teeth."

Ramsey chuckled. "You look like a man in sore need of a bite."

What he wanted was to hate Miss Harland as he did her father, but the minx had charm and courage in abundance. He could not name another soul bold enough to knock on his door, let alone stage a coup.

"One has to admire her tenacity," he said.

"When you left for London, you said she was as docile as a dove."

"Chalk it up to the only time I've been wrong." A mistake he would rectify once he'd finished preparing for the Masque.

Charlotte was meant to guide her. To teach her how to hold the world in her palm without ever taking a man to her bed.

Independence was the reward for playing her part in his charade. So what the hell was she doing at Shadowmere?

"What does she want from me?" he muttered, then cursed, realising he'd said it aloud. "What possessed her to think this was a safe option?"

"Happen she likes the taste of danger on her lips."

He wished he'd never mentioned the kiss.

"It was barely a peck." Yet he had threaded his fingers through her hair, bunched her skirts in his fist like he needed her bare beneath him. "Forgettable."

Ramsey rubbed his jaw, as he always did when weighing lies on the scales of justice. "So forgettable you can't even think straight."

"That's what happens when plans go awry." He should be celebrating, raising a glass to his mother, reminding the world that those who crossed him paid the price. "Let's go over the list, so I can finish what I started, and see Harland ruined."

Ramsey shifted in his chair. "You're sure there's been no mistake?"

Mistake? The word had no place in his vocabulary.

"Trust me. I never gave the chit a second thought after I left the ballroom. Her being here is nothing but a temporary inconvenience."

Ramsey's lips twitched. "I meant Harland being the enemy. You're certain this old neighbour can be trusted?"

His mind turned to the letter, to the tremble in his hand as he accepted the folded parchment, hatred rising. The villain finally had a name. One he would grind into the dirt.

"The men who work for the Order don't make mistakes."

And they knew better than to test his resolve.

"Besides, when I questioned Mrs Seagrove, she described my mother down to the mole on her cheek and the white streak in her hair."

He'd looked the woman in the eye. She'd not wavered.

"She might have been persuaded to lie," Ramsey said.

What was this, the Spanish Inquisition?

He slammed his palm on the desk, rattling the inkstand. "I deal with adulterers for a living. I know guilt when I see it. Harland knew exactly why I danced with his daughter."

"Ruined his daughter," Ramsey corrected. "Don't dress revenge up with ribbons and pearls. No decent man would offer for her now."

"There are no decent men in the *ton*," he snapped, refusing to include himself among them. "Perhaps she should pay me. I've saved her from a life of misery."

Ramsey shrugged. "You are the injured party. It's not every day the infallible Dominic Hawke is ravished at a ball."

Would he ever live it down?

The most feared man in London, outwitted by a woman.

"Be thankful I can think on my feet. From every angle, I looked the heartless rake." Yet his reaction to the way she felt in his arms had been anything but staged.

The sooner Miss Harland was on the road back to town, the better. He'd send her to Charlotte with a list of instructions. And a terse reminder that he did not run a boarding house for wayward girls and fallen angels.

Steeling himself, he rang for Beattie.

"The new maid. Limit her duties to the servants' quarters. I've no wish to see her in the house until I'm certain she's staying."

Beattie surprised him by speaking in her favour. "I doubt she's used to hard work, but she's light on her feet and pays attention. I'm confident she'll come right, given the chance."

Bloody hell. Was there no end to Miss Harland's talents? She'd worked with Beattie half the morning and would probably make sergeant within the week.

"Remind her there's no place in this house for singing."

Beattie nodded and was halfway out the door when a footman intercepted him and muttered something in his ear. The housekeeper gave the younger man a reassuring tap on the shoulder, then turned back to Dominic.

"The local magistrate is here, sir, with a sergeant from Bow Street. They're asking for you. Said it can't wait."

Dominic inwardly groaned. *Sir Lionel Deane.* Obnoxious prig. His wife occasionally attended Shadowmere's gatherings, always when the man was out of town.

What crime did Sir Lionel wish to accuse him of now?

Luckily, he had an alibi.

Still, Ramsey looked a shade uneasy.

"Show them in." He answered to no one, and he'd make damn sure they didn't forget it. "No need to draw two chairs. They won't be here long enough to catch their breath."

As soon as Beattie left the room, Ramsey leaned forward. "A man doesn't travel from London to Kingston over some rumour about a duel. They have something on you."

Dominic eased back in the chair. "They have nothing."

The footman returned, opening the door. Sir Lionel entered, puffed up and as self-important as ever, trailing a waft of expensive cologne that failed to mask his stale breath.

The younger man behind him smelled of damp wool and horse sweat.

One spent his days sipping port behind a desk; the other walked the streets come rain or shine. A wise man would trust the one with mud on his boots.

Dominic remained seated. He wouldn't stand even if someone lit a fuse beneath him. "Sir Lionel. To what do I owe the pleasure, and with Bow Street in tow, no less? If you've come begging for tickets to the Autumn Masque, I'm afraid you're too late."

Sir Lionel's imperial moustache twitched. "We come on a serious matter, not to discuss your lewd parties. You ought to be arrested for the disgraceful things that go on here."

"Private orgies aren't a crime." Dominic rather enjoyed

the blush that rose to Sir Lionel's red-veined cheeks. "I count members of the bench among my regular patrons."

It was his way of saying they'd better have a bloody good reason for disturbing his meeting.

"Sergeant Carter rode from London this morning." Sir Lionel gestured to the man in the ill-fitting coat. "He wishes to question you regarding a scandalous incident that occurred last night."

Dominic made a quick mental calculation. Whatever crime they meant to accuse him of must have happened before dawn.

Had Miss Harland left a note naming him her abductor?

Was this punishment? A warning not to cross her again?

"Scandalous incident?" Dominic echoed, noting that Carter watched him from beneath hooded lids. "If something shocking happened, I'm hardly the one to ask. Such things are common occurrences here."

"What about murder, Mr Hawke?" Sergeant Carter spoke as if he had no patience for jests. "Is that shocking enough?"

The threat of the noose forced him to straighten.

"Not in London, no. Do I need an alibi? I have one. I checked into Mivart's yesterday afternoon, attended Templeton's ball, and left around ten. I returned to the hotel and remained there all night. The man at reception will confirm I left this morning, sometime around eight."

Carter took a notebook from his pocket and scribbled with a stubby pencil. "May I ask what business you had in town?"

"Thursday's scandal sheet will tell you everything you need to know." No doubt it would show him with horns and hooves, standing over Harland as he burned. "I went to dance with Lord Harland's daughter. My reasons are my own."

Sir Lionel snorted. "After one dance with you, what's left for the poor girl but a life of penance in a nunnery?"

Clearly, the magistrate had never met Miss Harland, not *his* Miss Harland, at any rate. "I don't know. She seemed like a resourceful creature to me."

"There's a suggestion she may have visited your hotel room." Carter flipped through his worn leather book. "Her aunt found her missing from bed in the middle of the night."

The implication that Miss Harland was his mistress pricked his temper. "No one visited me in my room. I paid a porter to guard my door until dawn."

"Guard *your* door?" Sir Lionel scoffed.

"You'd be surprised how many married ladies long to seduce a dangerous rogue." He had even written a clause into the contracts for those attending his raucous events. He was strictly off-limits. "As for Miss Harland, she's too proud to be anyone's mistress."

No. She'd rather scrub floors than warm a man's bed.

She was a conundrum in a world of predictability.

"Do you know where she is?" Carter asked.

Dominic met his gaze without flinching. He could give a masterclass on deception. "Not since I left Templeton's ball last night. I have no plans to see her again. I imagine if I did, she'd likely shoot me."

"So you had a grievance with her father?"

"A long-standing one." He could feel Carter circling towards the point. "Why is that your concern? Are you suggesting Lord Harland is the victim?"

The blackguard was anything but.

"He was found floating in the Thames just before dawn." Carter spoke with the cool reserve of a man who'd seen too many corpses. "Someone struck him with a blunt instrument and tossed him off Blackfriars Bridge. A witness reported the incident."

It took Dominic a moment to absorb the news. If the

witness had seen the perpetrator, Carter wouldn't be standing here asking questions.

"You're confident it's Harland?"

"Certain, sir."

He ought to have felt elated. Someone had saved him the trouble. But it stank of a trap. A neat way for some sly bastard to see him hanged for murder.

And yet it wasn't anger or fear he was battling.

It was guilt. And a strange wave of sadness as he anticipated breaking the news to his new housemaid.

"It wasn't me. I only wish he'd spent years drowning in debt and rotting in misery."

Carter paused, letting the silence settle. "His sister confirmed he owed money to the Moseley brothers. That he planned to force his daughter to marry a wealthy merchant, and was out visiting her suitor when he met a tragic end."

None of this surprised Dominic. "Perhaps the men you mentioned have taken Miss Harland hostage."

"Or the lady did away with her father and is presently on the run," the sergeant countered. "Of course, there's always the possibility she had an admirer, and he committed the dastardly deed for her."

Dominic gave a disinterested huff, yet his mind ran through endless possibilities. Had she got rid of the problem and sought refuge at Shadowmere? Did she have a beau and—

No. He would not entertain it.

"It's not natural," Sir Lionel said, "to sit there and show not the smallest flicker of concern. A man is dead. Have you no—"

"I've seen a naked judge don furry ears and bray like a donkey. Few things rouse a reaction." Except, perhaps, an unexpected kiss from a chaste maiden. One who would never forgive him.

He stood, so abruptly Sir Lionel flinched. "Is that all, gentlemen? If you wish to continue this conversation, you'll need to drag me away in shackles. If you have proof I'm involved, fetch the prison cart. Ramsey will show you out."

He had more pressing concerns.

Somehow, he would have to find an ounce of compassion when he informed Miss Harland that her father was dead.

"The corner of the sheet must be mitred, Miss Smith. Folded at precisely the right angle to prevent the material from slipping." Mr Beattie gave the footman's mattress a sharp tap with his gunner's stick. "Try again. Mr Hawke won't tolerate wrinkled bed sheets."

Daphne forced a smile and dismissed all thoughts of Mr Hawke lying sprawled on his feather-stuffed mattress. How strange that a man who lived to break rules should be so exact.

Clearly, Lady Soanes had never worked under a housekeeper with a military background. It had been less than a day, yet Daphne felt as though she'd marched across a dozen battlefields. How was she meant to survive a whole month?

As Mr Beattie continued issuing orders, she pictured an idyllic cottage on the banks of Loch Tay, the reward Lady Soanes had promised if she completed the task. Somewhere remote. A place her father would never think to look. A place Mr Irving would never find her.

Yet there was a complication.

"Will I be expected to tend to guests during the Masque?"

What if one recognised her and told her father? Worse, what if Lord Templeton cornered her in some dark corridor, no chaperones, no witnesses, and no chance to refuse him?

Perhaps she should warn Mr Hawke?

But convincing him to let her stay would be no small feat.

"Mr Hawke won't permit you to work during the Masque. He'll send you to stay with Mrs Buckley for the weekend. She was the housekeeper here some years ago."

So, the master was happy to disgrace an innocent before the *ton*, but would protect his maid like an honourable knight on a moral crusade.

"And in the meantime, I'm to have a room in the servants' quarters?" Preferably one farthest from the devil who tested her mettle with naked bathing.

"No," came the commanding voice behind her. "You'll be given alternative accommodation."

She turned to find Mr Hawke leaning languidly against the doorjamb, dressed in black. He looked infuriatingly at ease, the very picture of masculine arrogance. The glint of mischief in his eyes seemed a permanent affliction. And by *alternative accommodation*, he clearly meant anywhere but Shadowmere.

"May I have a private word, Beattie, while Miss *Smith* finishes making the bed?"

The request did little to soften the curious frown on the housekeeper's brow, but he followed Mr Hawke into the corridor and closed the door behind him.

She couldn't hear what was said, but when Mr Beattie returned, he looked at her as one might a war widow receiving sad news.

Mr Hawke motioned to the corridor. "Shall we?"

She looked at his outstretched hand. Last night, he'd led her onto the dance floor, and her world hadn't stopped spinning since. Why did she sense something similar was about to unfold?

Reluctantly, she followed.

He said nothing as he led her through the basement corridors and out into the garden. The afternoon sun warmed her cheeks but did little to ease the tension.

"Are you leaving me at the gate?" It wasn't the main gate. They were heading in a different direction, along a narrow path and past a walled garden.

"Few people surprise me, Miss Harland." He kept his gaze fixed on a point ahead. "Fewer leave a lasting impression. Fewer still stir a flicker of admiration."

"You didn't expect me to come here."

His mouth curled, almost into a smile. "No."

Was that it? No?

Not *How remarkable you are, Miss Harland?*

Not *I've never known a woman with as much gall as you?*

"You left me with little option, sir."

"I made a mistake," he said.

"Oh." And yet she was not sorry he had stormed into her life, a tempest bent on ruin. "I suppose I should commend your honesty. You forced me to confront the problem."

"I assumed Charlotte would take you in."

"Then you're less astute than I thought. Charlotte fought her way through the prejudice and lies. That's what gave her the strength to prevail."

Lady Soanes had made it perfectly clear: rewards were earned in battle, through hardship, through pain. What she hadn't mentioned was how terrifying it felt to be set adrift.

"I'm happy to work for my keep. You must take account of your actions, sir. I'm not saying you weren't right to seek vengeance, though I doubt your mother would have approved."

She heard his sharp intake of breath, but his mask remained firmly in place. "Says the woman who tripped just so she could kiss me. It's a damned good job I turned the situation to my advantage."

How was it that one brief kiss had caused such mental torment? It had been a means to an end. In that, they were alike. And yet, for some baffling reason, it felt like the only honest moment of her life.

"I was desperate."

He cast her a sidelong glance. "As was I."

"But you're not responsible for me, is that it?"

"You could have said no."

"No?"

"You could have looked horrified. Slapped my face in indignation. You could have clutched your aunt's arm and hidden behind her silk skirts. But the truth of it is—you needed me as much as I needed you."

The fact that he wasn't wrong needled.

Yet their lives were worlds apart.

Never more so than in this moment.

He stopped outside the rickety gate of a cottage. The garden was overgrown, but the structure itself stood firm beneath its sagging thatch. From his coat pocket, he withdrew an iron key, took her hand, and placed it in her palm.

"The key to your new home, Miss Harland. You may do as you see fit with the grounds and the decor. Though I should warn you, it's been empty for years."

Daphne glanced at the key, then at him.

Gratitude rose, a sudden wave that brought tears to her eyes. It took three swallows before she found her voice.

"I can work at Shadowmere? Live here?"

"You can live here, but you'll not work in the house.

Cook will deliver fresh produce twice a week. For anything else, you'll speak to Ramsey."

Every syllable was devoid of emotion, or else he hid it exceptionally well.

"And I thought you were a rotten scoundrel."

"I am." He hesitated, the slight shift of his feet telling. "You may add kidnapper to my list of transgressions. I'll not permit you to leave."

The wave of gratitude she'd felt receded with the tide.

"I don't understand."

He clasped her elbow, his fingers firm, the sudden contact stirring that wicked heat in her belly.

"Brace yourself for bad news." The bob of his throat belied an inner struggle. "Your father is dead. Murdered last night. I swear on my mother's grave, I never saw him after our confrontation in Templeton's ballroom."

She blinked, wondering if she'd misheard.

He was dead. How could that be?

She'd hoped never to see him again.

But murdered?

By whom?

"I expect you hate me," Mr Hawke said as if he didn't care either way. "But I won't lie. It's less than he deserved. Still, I need you to answer one question."

He paused.

A second. A minute. She wasn't sure.

Her mind was awash with confusion. She tried to recall the last words she'd spoken to her father, but nothing came.

Her heart pounded so fast it might burst from her chest.

The rest of her, except for that place where he held her, was cold and so dreadfully numb.

"Did you get into a fight? Kill him in a fit of temper? I can help you, but you must tell me the truth."

She jerked her head. "Kill my own father? I despised him, but kissing a rogue on the dance floor is the worst of my sins."

"The magistrate came with a man from Bow Street. They were looking for you. They seem to think you may be involved. They don't know you're here, but …"

He kept talking, but she barely heard a word.

His voice faded to a distant hum as horrible images flooded her mind, her father slumped in a back alley, his pale hand clutched to a bloodied chest, eyes glassy and accusing. Cold on the common, a lead ball lodged between his brows. Poisoned, perhaps.

She had defied him. This was all her fault.

Guilt twisted through her, coiling tight around her chest.

It hurt to breathe. Her vision swam.

The key slipped from her fingers and hit the ground with a dull thud.

Her knees gave out. And before she could hit the dirt, Mr Hawke's strong arms were around her.

CHAPTER FIVE

Dominic had heard many women cry.

Usually because they'd forgotten a vital piece of their costume. Drunk too much wine. Realised their lewd antics weren't nearly as thrilling in the light of day. Or their husband hadn't returned to their bed.

Only once had he heard a woman sob from the depths of her soul. A wracking sound that didn't rise from her throat, but from some hollow place grief had carved inside her.

He'd been eighteen. His mother too thin, too frail to support her own weight. Her skin as cold as winter marble.

Miss Harland was soft and warm, every curve a delicious temptation, but her cry reminded him why he filled his corridors with music and laughter. Why he'd rather hear beds banging and pants of pleasure than the sound of someone breaking.

He wished he were standing in the midst of an orgy, just to drown out her heartfelt whimpers. Wished he wasn't holding her in his arms, something he'd sworn never to do again. Wished he didn't feel every inch the devil.

"If you want to leave Shadowmere, I can make the

arrangements." His tone was as blunt as ever, the offer more than he'd give to another living soul.

Miss Harland straightened, blinking tears from her dark lashes onto her cheeks, though she didn't step out of his hold.

"You said I couldn't leave."

"Whoever killed your father may come looking for you." He didn't add that he was afraid she might meet the same grisly end. Or be made a scapegoat by a Bow Street sergeant desperate to make inspector. "Trust me. There's nowhere safer than here."

He glanced at the rundown cottage, half convinced she might perish from the cold within the week. But he couldn't have her in the house.

She gathered herself and stepped back to a respectable distance. "Can you prove you didn't murder my father?"

He gave a mirthless snort. "Would I waste my time creating a scene if I'd planned to kill him? Half the staff at Mivart's can confirm my whereabouts. I never left the hotel room."

Her gaze dipped to his mouth. "You had company?"

Did she think he used pleasure the way other men used opium? "No. I didn't invite a woman to my bed."

"I wouldn't care if you had." She dashed a tear from her cheek and lifted her chin. "I'm merely trying to decide if you killed my father."

He'd wanted to—every day since receiving the letter.

"As a logical woman, you know I'd have done it without leaving a trace. I have no reason to spare you the truth." He met her gaze, unflinching. "I've dreamt of driving a dagger through his heart more times than I can count."

She searched his face. "Why?"

"Does it matter?"

"Of course it matters. If I'm to stay here, I need to understand your motives. How else are we to find the real culprit?"

That should have been his cue to step back.

To deliver a line that cut to the bone.

He didn't care who had done his dirty work for him.

He should get rid of this woman. Hand her a thousand pounds, send her away, and put the past behind him.

"You said it was retribution. That his cruelty knew no bounds." She laid a hand on his upper arm. "He did something to your mother. Mine hated the ground he walked on."

He stilled, every muscle rigid, his face a mask of stone.

He could have shaken her off. He didn't.

Seconds passed. His mouth thinned.

He couldn't bear to say the words.

"Fine." She shook her head, loose strands tumbling from the comb. She bent and picked up the key to the cottage. "Can you ask Mr Ramsey to meet me here in an hour, so I might give him a list of what I need? When you're ready to discuss it, you know where to find me."

She turned away from him and marched through the open gate, noting the weeds on the path as she made for the door.

He waited until she was inside before walking away. Yet he knew she watched him from the window. That she would cry again. Curse the day he forced her to dance. Seek her own form of vengeance.

For some reason, he welcomed the battle. The thought of tussling with her roused something primitive in him.

He found Ramsey in the morning room, standing beside the long table where Beattie had spread out a linen cloth and several neatly folded menus.

"Miss Harland needs supplies delivered to the cottage. Give her whatever she requires. Whatever it takes to prevent her from leaving until I discover who bludgeoned her father and threw him in the Thames."

He told himself it was about answers. His guilt. Her safety. But he wasn't quite sure why he insisted she stay.

Both men nodded.

"I suspect you'll want the coroner's report, sir."

Beattie was more than his housekeeper. He'd fought at Waterloo and had comrades in town—men whose lives he'd saved and who were eager to repay the debt.

"Yes, but I can't risk leaving Shadowmere until I know more."

"I'll have what you need delivered within two days."

Ramsey was quick to offer a word of caution. "Sir Lionel wants an end to your wild parties. He won't care if it means the end of you. And that sergeant from Bow Street looks as if he'd frame his own mother to get ahead. Do you want me to call a meeting with the Brethren?"

Let his friends think he couldn't handle a measly magistrate? Hell, no. Besides, they were all preparing for their own wars.

"No. We'll meet next week as planned."

"What about Daventry?" Ramsey said, naming the master of an elite group of enquiry agents. "He's the one who found Mrs Seagrove. Happen he'll have a list of men who wanted Harland dead."

"Daventry may be a fountain of knowledge, but no man holds me by the ballocks. I won't pay his price. We'll manage without him."

Beattie stood firm. "Sir," he said, in that parade-ground tone of his. "We all remember Papelotte. Looked like a weak point. Turned out to be bait."

"What are you saying?" He knew damn well what Beattie

implied. That he'd been fooled into blaming the wrong man. "That we find out who really put Harland in the river?"

"It won't hurt to make our own enquiries, sir."

"The coffers are full of favours," Ramsey added. "About time we called some in. Want me to use one to get the name of the witness?" He paused. "And you could ask Miss Harland for the name of her suitor."

The first was an excellent idea.

The second … less so.

"If the witness exists, I want to know everything about him." He was curious about the man who'd offered for Miss Harland, but he'd rather be damned than ask her himself. Ramsey could do it. "You speak to our guest in the cottage when you collect the list. I've a task of my own to deal with."

He had one job, truth be told.

Avoid Miss Harland like the plague.

For four days, he'd succeeded.

Four days without asking Ramsey what the devil he was doing with Miss Harland after dark. Four long nights wondering if she was cold or hungry. Yet he'd spent most of his time at the upstairs window of the coach house. It was the only place with a decent view of the cottage.

His men were beginning to ask questions.

He'd been called many things over the years.

Wicked. Arrogant. Ambitious.

Never obsessed.

He'd never stalked a woman's movements.

Never dreamed of one in his bed.

All this talk of vengeance and murder had left him

unhinged. Any man would feel unsettled after being named a suspect in a crime. His preoccupation with her likely amounted to nothing more than guilt.

But guilt didn't usually make a man hard.

This was need, plain and punishing.

He wanted to strip her out of those dusty clothes, silence her clever mouth with his own, and bury himself between her soft thighs.

He'd punch his own face, but his men already thought him half mad. Gouging his eyes wouldn't help. She lived in his head now, haunting its dark chambers at night, humming that sweet little song.

He had no defence against her, not even in his own mind.

And what in blazes was she doing now?

He pressed closer to the window.

Miss Harland was outside, dressed in old breeches and a gentleman's shirt. He'd shoot Ramsey if they belonged to him, but the garments hadn't been stylish since before the dawn of Waterloo.

She disappeared behind the cottage and returned with a wheelbarrow. He watched her slide her hands into leather gloves as if they were fine silk, then kneel and sift pebbles from the soil.

Was this what he'd driven her to?

Manual labour?

He'd pictured her naked on his bed, draped in diamonds.

Now she was elbow-deep in dirt.

She took up a spade and dug.

Where the hell was Ramsey?

Unable to watch, he marched out of the coach house— nearly broke into a sprint—then slowed to a languid stroll the moment she looked up.

"I didn't realise you had a fondness for gardening, Miss Harland."

She stood, brushing dirt from her cheek with the back of her hand. "I'm not sure *fond* is the right word, Mr Hawke. But there is something immensely satisfying about tackling a project."

He felt another flicker of admiration.

"I assumed Ramsey was helping you."

She tugged off her gloves. Her knuckles were red. "He was beginning to fall behind with his own work. And I'd asked too much of him already."

He hated Ramsey, he decided.

"Have you come to survey my work?" She met his gaze. "Mr Ramsey thought you'd be satisfied with everything I've done so far. That you'd have no complaints."

His traitorous gaze slid over her. No corset. Breasts that would spill over his palm. More than enough curve to her hips for his hands to grip.

Yes, he'd be more than satisfied.

And that was the bloody problem.

"Ramsey mentioned you'd helped yourself to furniture and linens from the house."

She gave a nervous smile. "He said you agreed."

"I did."

She paused as if expecting more, but he needed to tread carefully. Discovering what she knew about her father *should* be the only reason he was speaking to her now.

"Would you like to come in?" She spoke with the polite distance of a hostess receiving an afternoon caller. "The tea is steeping. You're welcome to join me. I'll just move the barrow."

He should have refused, but his feet betrayed him.

"I'll move the barrow and join you inside."

"Thank you, Mr Hawke. Leave it by the wood store."

He hadn't even known there *was* a wood store, let alone one with a new felt roof and a stack of dry logs.

"Did Ramsey fix the roof on the store?" he asked, stepping into the sitting room, but the words died on his lips.

The last time he looked, the cottage was a pit. Dust thick as ash. Curtains stained yellow from damp. But now? Now the space was clean.

Not polished to perfection, but cared for. The windows were open, the air laced with woodsmoke and something citrus. The curtains were new to the room, but not new to the world. Likely salvaged from another window. Another life.

A worn leather wing chair sat angled by the hearth, its arms softened by time and use. And on the small table beside it, a vase of white roses.

His mother's favourite.

Fresh from the garden. Their third flush.

"The gardener's boy fixed the roof," she said, unaware he was relieved it wasn't Ramsey.

He wasn't angry she'd cut the roses. He was strangely grateful. He didn't care that she'd taken his grandmother's pink porcelain teapot. The one his mother cherished, decorated with a courting couple.

He almost felt at home here. Which was ridiculous.

Shadowmere was his home, yet it often felt like a prison.

"You can sit in the wing chair. It's quite comfortable. I believe it was yours once, before you had the study redesigned. I'll fetch the stool from upstairs."

"I'll fetch the stool."

He mounted the narrow staircase before she could object, driven by a stubborn need to know where she slept.

The chamber was smaller than his boot room. She hadn't used her charm to convince Ramsey to dismantle the best bed in the house. She'd slept on an old trundle bed, pushed beneath the window.

She hadn't insisted on luxury. She took meagre things and made do. He didn't know whether to be furious or impressed.

He crossed to the corner, lifted the candle lamp from the stool she used as a nightstand, and went back downstairs.

"You need a proper bed," he said, setting the stool down and sitting on it. "Drawers. A nightstand. Choose what you want from the house. I'll arrange to have them moved and assembled."

Her hand trembled slightly as she poured the tea into the matching pink cups. "I'm quite happy on the trundle bed. And I'm not sure how long I'll stay."

He felt her words like the prick of a pin.

Guests did not come and go as they pleased. He made the rules. He was master here.

"I meant what I said. I'm holding you hostage until your father's killer is in gaol." No sensible man would let her leave.

Not when she might be the culprit … or the next victim.

Her gaze moved to his spread thighs, then returned to the pretty teapot. "If I want to leave, Mr Hawke, I will. You may like to think you have dominion over me. You don't."

He might have been tempted to overrule her, but he wasn't a tyrant. "A man should have dominion in his own home."

"Over your possessions. Not over me."

I could possess you in a heartbeat.

All it would take was one kiss.

Yet taking from her held no appeal.

He'd find a way to make her give it freely.

"I could throw you over my shoulder and carry you to the gate. You're here only because I allow it."

She handed him the cup with a smile that might fool someone into thinking she was simple. "I've no sugar. Though you strike me as a man who likes everything sour."

"What is this? An attempt to civilise a brute?"

He pinched the handle of the teacup and drank like a lord accustomed to every refinement.

She raised a brow. "A brute would have sat in the wing chair, not on the stool."

He couldn't help but grin. "I adapt to suit my purpose."

She sipped her tea. "Which is?"

"To decide whether tidying the cottage is a necessity or a distraction." He watched her. She'd not been crying today. It was partly why he'd accepted her offer. "Do you need my protection? Are you hiding here? Or do you need time to consider your options?"

She stared into her tea as though searching the leaves for a sign.

"You refused to tell Ramsey the name of your suitor."

"Which suitor would that be?" Her voice was cool, detached. "Both are willing to pay a small fortune to bed me. One out of desperation. The other because you dressed me up like a prize."

Someone had already approached her?

He gripped the delicate china handle so hard it was likely to snap. "Let me guess. There's a house in Mayfair, and an allowance that would make Croesus weep. Who made you the offer?"

He wasn't sure why it mattered. But it did.

She sat, lips pursed, defiant.

"You're not going to tell me?"

She tilted her head. "You have the means to find out, as I do when it comes to your act of vengeance. So why don't we save time and be honest?"

She made it sound absurdly simple. "This isn't a game of riddles, Miss Harland. If you want honesty, start with yourself."

"Very well." She set her cup on the side table, no longer needing the shield. "I'm glad you asked me to dance. Not so glad you wrote a letter and handed it to Lord Templeton. He's currently awaiting my reply to his scandalous offer."

Templeton?

A swell of rage rose in him. He'd expected offers to come pouring in. He'd not expected to feel so damned angry that he could whip every man within ten miles.

"Why the hell didn't you refuse him?"

"I couldn't. He had a tight grip of my arm and said he'd more than match any other offer." Her voice sharpened. "It's why I went to Lady Soanes. Now I understand why you told me to carry a weapon."

"I'll speak to him on your behalf."

"There's no need. I shall deal with the problem myself. What you can do is tell me something that's true. You owe me that, at least."

What did she want to know?

That he'd never taken tea with a woman?

That he liked the idea of her in breeches?

That her white shirt showed the shape of her breasts?

"Your father was my mother's lover. By necessity, not choice." He might have used a more cutting term, but remembered she was grieving.

"That much I gathered." Her gaze drifted to the gold locket resting on the mantel. When she spoke again, her voice wavered. "May I ask when?"

"Eleven years ago."

She closed her eyes as if the answer were a blessing. "After my mother died, then. That's one consolation, I suppose." She paused, a faint crease forming on her brow. "Why wait until now to shame him? You could have ruined me during my first season."

"You had a season?" Why was she not married?

"Of course. I'm three and twenty. My father was a baron." She glanced at her hands resting in her lap. "And I'm a dreadful disappointment."

How? For the life of him, he couldn't see it.

Suspicion flared.

"What did you do to deter your suitors?" He used the plural deliberately. He was a good judge of men's tastes and habits.

"Insulted them. Drew attention to their flaws." She sounded quite proud. "I told Lord Wimborne I'd developed a terrible gambling habit that began at the races. Told Mr Smith-Turbot that I sometimes slipped into a Whitechapel twang when among friends."

"Do you have friends?"

"Not really, but I gave a stage-worthy demonstration." A giggle escaped her—like the one she'd bestowed upon Ramsey yesterday—before she dropped into a perfect slum accent: "'Ere, gov'nor. Can you spare a poor love a penny?"

Dominic laughed. A sound a privileged few got to hear.

"No wonder you're content with a trundle bed. I'm lucky you didn't lure me onto the terrace and make off with my purse."

She leaned in slightly, as if sharing a secret. "In a gown, I'd have few places to hide it."

He fell silent.

He'd fought bare-knuckled. Walked ten paces at dawn. A woman had once come at him with a pearl-handled blade while high on opium. And yet here he sat, drinking tea in a quaint cottage, and had never felt so disarmed.

Miss Harland was a damn sight more dangerous than her father. And just as bloody devious.

"I believe it's my turn to share an honest observation." The blood chilled in his veins as the memories rose. Diving deep into a mire of hatred was the only way to avenge the one person he'd loved. "Your father hurt my mother in ways you couldn't possibly imagine."

She heard the venom in his tone and leaned back. "Hurt her more than you planned to hurt me? I hope so, otherwise that makes you a hypocrite."

That was the trouble with clever women. They always found the bruise.

"I never professed to be a decent man."

"That's just as well. There's nothing worse than lying to oneself." She drew a deep breath. "Tell me what he did, and I shall tell you what he said after you left the ballroom."

He firmed his jaw, ready to say cruelty wasn't a game. But that *would* make him a hypocrite. And he was beyond desperate for answers.

"Do you have anything stronger to drink than tea?"

"No, but I can wait while you fetch a decanter from the house. Though I sense you'll never tell me if I let you leave."

She wasn't wrong.

Already, every muscle had tightened.

His tongue felt thick in his throat.

"I don't suppose there's anything else we might barter. A bottle of *Rosée du Matin* from Floris?" Though nothing smelled better on her than that mysterious scent she wore. "A sapphire brooch from Woodcroft's?"

She fell silent, blinking as though a lash had caught in her eye. "I'd prefer a daisy picked from the place where we might share our first picnic. Or a waltz in a cottage while you hum a tune. Other than that, there's only one thing I want, Mr Hawke."

He braced himself.

Whatever it was, it would cost him dearly.

"I'll tell you everything I know. I'll risk my life to uncover the truth. In exchange, you'll agree to accept me as your partner."

"Partner?" Though he was unsure what she meant, the blood pooling low in his loins made its own assumptions. "You want me to bed you?"

It would be no hardship.

Perhaps then he could be free of her.

She glanced at his spread thighs. "A tempting offer, but no."

"Then what?" He narrowed his gaze, fighting disappointment. "Surely you're not referring to Shadowmere. You want to help organise parties for the depraved?"

She laughed. "Heavens, no. Besides, we'd argue at every turn. And in case you hadn't noticed, I'm something of a romantic."

Guilt settled in his chest like a weight. There was a reason she'd ruined her own season. Miss Harland wanted to marry for love. And now, it would take a man who loved her to the ends of the earth to ignore her dire situation. For that, he was sorry.

"Just tell me what you want, Miss Harland."

At this point, he might agree to anything.

"I want us to work together. To discover who killed my father. And I hate to be the bearer of bad news, but I'm not entirely certain he's the villain you were after."

CHAPTER SIX

Although Mr Hawke had reluctantly agreed to her proposal, Daphne refused to answer him until they were seated in his carriage, rattling along the road to London.

Perhaps he thought the new bed and armoire his men had assembled in her chamber would serve as a fitting bribe. Or that having the gardener clear the pebbles and weeds might win her favour.

But a week had passed since she'd made her pact with Lady Soanes, and playing enquiry agent meant the rest would pass just as quickly.

He sat across from her on the black leather seat, filling the space with his indomitable presence, his eyes locked on her. His prey.

While he appeared immaculate in a charcoal grey frock coat and matching trousers that hugged his solid thighs, she wore the only clean dress she owned. Her dark blue pelisse was fastened to the throat, but her clothing did not escape his scrutiny.

Twice, he'd glanced at the hem brushing her leather half-boots. Now she caught him studying the buttons on her coat. His attention shifted to the curl that had slipped from her bonnet, grazing her jaw.

"Do you have an interest in ladies' fashions, Mr Hawke? Have I torn a seam or left a button undone?"

He stared down his nose, his gaze never faltering. "I was deciding whether a shirt and breeches might suit you better. As for fashion, I suspect you've owned that coat since your first season."

She smoothed her hand over the fine wool. "I only removed old clothes from the armoire when I packed." She'd not wanted her father to think she'd left town. Shadowmere would have been the first place he looked. "And since you're so used to seeing ladies naked, I didn't think it mattered."

His gaze drifted over her again, slower this time.

She hoped to heaven he wasn't picturing her naked.

Silence settled between them.

She'd counted ten cows, a dozen sheep, and four horse-chestnut trees before he finally spoke. "We should turn back. They'll be looking to pin your father's murder on someone, and we both had motive."

"Then we'll move through London like wraiths in the night."

"It's almost noon." From his tone, his patience was a band stretched thin. "We'll be in London in two hours. We don't have a plan, mostly because you still haven't told me what you know."

She stalled. If he deemed the snippets useless, he might dump her on the side of the road. "Did you bring the coroner's report as agreed?" Her gaze slid to the leather portfolio on the seat.

"Must we barter for everything, Miss Harland?" His

expression was carved from stone, but his voice carried a whisky-rich edge.

He enjoyed this game. If he didn't, she'd be sweeping the cottage path, not sitting close enough to catch the scent of his bergamot shaving soap.

Her mother's warning had never felt more apt:

Trust a man's actions more than his words.

"Bartering makes things more interesting." As he placed a large hand on the portfolio, she gave him a crumb. "What my father said won't please you. But I'm only repeating his words."

"Just tell me, woman."

"Call me angel and ask nicely."

He gritted his teeth. "Tell me what you know, angel."

The warm flutter in her belly confirmed what she already suspected. She'd barter with blood just to hear him utter the endearment. Seeing him on his knees might work just as well, too.

She took a fortifying breath. "My father said he wasn't the only man courting your mother."

As predicted, he looked feral when he growled, "The bastard wasn't courting her. He used her for his own gain."

She held up her hands in surrender. "I'm merely the messenger. The one person you can trust to dig until the truth is uncovered. May I see the report now?"

"That's not all he said?"

"No. He said he wasn't the only villain, and if he'd known you bore a grudge, he would have dealt with it years ago."

What had her father done?

It amounted to more than a love affair. If only Mr Hawke would tell her. But he guarded the truth as fiercely as he did his own heart.

Mr Hawke cursed at the window. "A grudge? Is that what you think this is? Some schoolboy resentment? That I'd have those degenerates in my home because I'm aggrieved?"

"I don't know what it is. You won't tell me."

He barely looked at her as he handed over the portfolio. The anger had drained from him, replaced by a sadness so heavy she feared she might drown in it too.

She opened the folder, bracing for gruesome details, her fingers brushing over the crisp parchment as though the paper itself might flinch.

One line had been underlined twice in the coroner's hand.

No water in the lungs.

Daphne stilled.

He hadn't drowned.

Her father had been dead before he hit the water.

She lifted her gaze to meet Mr Hawke's. His expression had changed, the hard mask softened by sorrow. Something in his eyes reminded her of the warmth of his embrace.

For a moment, the burden didn't feel like hers alone.

She read on.

Another line caught her attention.

"A blow from behind. Object smooth and cylindrical. Possibly metal." A shiver rippled across her shoulders. She looked up again. "It wasn't a fight. He never saw it coming."

Mr Hawke leaned forward, eyes narrowing on the page. "A cosh. Or a length of pipe. Something quick. Quiet."

"Used by someone who knew where to strike. Someone close enough to approach him without raising suspicion."

She pictured the scene. Her father. The tyrant who haunted her days and ruined her sleep. The man she'd prayed might wake one morning and be kind.

Tears welled. Not for him, but for the opportunity lost.

"Have you ever wished you could change someone?" She

sniffed, dabbing her nose. "That you could mould them into the perfect parent? That life would be better then?"

He surprised her by answering.

"I wish my father hadn't been a complete wastrel. His reckless behaviour was the catalyst for every tragedy that followed."

She swallowed down her misfortune. "Where is he now?"

"In a grave at All Saints Church. The plot suits the life he led. Neglect for himself, and for everyone who depended on him."

There was no bitterness in his tone, only a tired kind of truth. A man taking stock of the wreckage.

She wondered if he saw that life was a mirror. That necessity had shaped him into someone just as neglectful. Neglectful of his morals, his happiness, his peace.

"When it comes to rotten fathers, we have that in common."

She turned back to the report and read the line about faint ligature marks found on his wrists, though his hands weren't bound when they pulled him from the Thames.

"My father's signet ring was missing. He owed money to the Moseley brothers. They might have taken it in payment."

"No." His reply came too quickly. "They would have tortured him first. Ransacked your house in the dead of night and taken everything of value." He paused. Something dark passed over his features. "Including you. You're not safe until the debt is paid. We need to know how much he owed them."

She froze on the carriage seat. Suddenly, going to London felt like a dreadful mistake. "I can't pay them. I haven't a penny to my name."

"I'll deal with it."

"That's not how bartering works. I'll find a way—"

"No. We'll barter for everything but this."

"But—"

"Miss Harland." His voice gentled. "Please. My mother found herself in a similar predicament. Let me do this for her, if not for you."

She fell a little in love with Mr Hawke—just for a moment. The urge to slide onto his lap and smooth the frown from his brow was nearly unbearable.

Do you like that, Hawke?

You know I do, angel.

"What?" he said. "You're looking at me like I've just been canonised a saint. It's a practical decision. We can't move freely around London with the Moseley brothers on our backs."

Strange how practical felt like protection.

"Still, I shall find a way to repay you."

Or a way to settle the debt herself.

Neither spoke again for a mile.

While she scoured her mind, imagining all the things she might do for him, he seemed oddly preoccupied with the upper buttons on her coat.

Perhaps he was assessing how warm she was because he intended leaving her on Lady Soanes' doorstep, without so much as a backward glance.

Was the trip a ruse? A way to force her out of Shadowmere and avoid the kicking and screaming?

She stilled.

No. His actions said otherwise.

He'd brought her new fire tools last night, and a thicker wrapper to guard against the cold. Why go to such trouble if he meant to evict her?

"Who will we visit first? The witness? Mr Beattie's old comrade thinks he lives in Southwark."

Mr Hawke regarded her in silence, as though measuring

her mettle. "We'll visit the witness before we return to Kingston tonight."

She sagged in relief.

He planned to take her home with him.

"I need to visit a friend in Seven Dials. She's the only person who can broker a meeting with the Moseley brothers without them shooting us first."

He glanced out of the window as they passed a cart laden with barrels, but his gaze lingered at some point in the distance.

"You might charm her into disclosing a secret, Miss Harland. You have a talent for achieving impossible feats."

If there was a compliment there, she didn't dwell on it.

Who was this woman? An old lover? A dear friend?

Jealousy twisted in her stomach.

Absurd.

Since when had a flutter of desire overridden all common sense? She was a thorn in his side. She spent the rest of the journey repeating it like a prayer.

It took the better part of an hour to travel from London Bridge to Seven Dials, the streets growing noisier and more chaotic with every turn of the wheels.

The woman Mr Hawke knew had clearly fallen on hard times. Daphne's fate might not be so different. Once the house was sold and the creditors paid, she'd be lucky to have threepence in her purse.

"There but for the grace of God." Mr Hawke watched a barefoot child cling to her mother's skirts as she sold flowers from a broken wicker basket. "Many on these streets won't survive the winter."

He rapped on the roof, vaulted from the carriage as it rolled to a stop on the crowded street, and crossed the road without a word to his coachman.

Daphne wasn't sure how much money he gave the woman, or what he said to the child as he crouched and pressed something shiny into her hand, but he returned with the entire basket.

She might have commented on the kind gesture, but she was too busy trying to breathe evenly and ignore the ache in her heart.

The scoundrel.

Why could he not be cutting and cruel?

Why offer a glimpse of the man beneath the facade?

To make matters worse, he said, "A gift for Mrs Haggert."

Just as she felt the prick of rejection, he found the only white rose in the basket, brought it to his nose, and handed it to her. "For you, Miss Harland."

Warmth bloomed in her chest. She should toss it back and accuse him of mockery, but her fingers closed around the stem.

Good Lord. He was the devil.

An enticing devil.

One who knew how to soften a romantic's heart.

"No man has ever given me a rose."

"Perhaps they feared you might slap their face with it."

"Only if the gesture were insincere."

He smiled, but it faded as the vehicle turned into Little Earl Street and stopped at the entrance to Monmouth Court, a narrow passage hemmed in by smoke-dark walls.

He took her arm, not her hand, and helped her alight. "What's said here remains between us. If you want to live at Shadowmere, trust is the only currency that counts."

She nodded. To profess too much might make her sound desperate for his approval. "Of course."

The two boys blocking the entrance to the passage knew

him. Though they stood firm in their boots, like soldiers guarding a general's tent, they doffed their caps.

"Looking sharp as ever, Mr Hawke," one said with a cheeky grin.

Daphne silently agreed.

The other was already wiping his sweaty palm on his trousers, anticipating the sovereign Mr Hawke would toss his way.

"Give this basket to Mrs Haggert and tell her I request an audience. It can't wait. I need to leave London today."

The warning note in his voice had her curling her hands into fists against her skirts. She scanned the street behind her, the rowdy laughter from the drunken men outside the tavern setting her nerves on edge.

Had she been in the company of a gentleman, she might have slipped her hand into the crook of his arm. As it was, she didn't dare touch Mr Hawke. Not if she hoped to keep her sanity.

The older of the two boys narrowed his eyes at her. "Mrs Haggert will want to know you've brought company. Pretty company, at that."

"Tell her I'm here with Miss Harland."

That sufficed. The younger boy scampered away with the basket, careful not to drop the flowers, and disappeared into a house at the end of the passage.

That's when Mr Hawke touched her again, his long fingers grazing her elbow as he bent to whisper in her ear. "Mrs Haggert won't mince words. Hold your nerve. But be respectful."

Beneath the lingering trace of bergamot was the warm, clean scent of his skin, and it unsettled her more than the chaos in the street.

She turned her head a fraction. He was so close her heart

galloped. So close she could see slivers of gold in his dark green eyes, the faint crease beside one brow, the tension in his jaw.

"I've waltzed with you and survived, sir."

His gaze dipped to her lips. "Our dance isn't over, Miss Harland."

"It's not?"

"You know damn well it's not."

He released her, stepping away as the boy returned.

"Mrs Haggert will see you now, Mr Hawke."

His words echoed through her mind as they followed the boy to the house at the end of the grimy passage. A thin, skeletal man in a pristine coat opened the door and showed them into a comfortable drawing room. The dark walls and velvet chairs reminded her of Shadowmere, rich, worn, and full of secrets.

They sat beside each other on the settee, waiting as the mantel clock ticked amid the silence. She clasped her hands tightly in her lap. He lounged with his legs spread wide, a picture of casual dominance.

She couldn't take her eyes off his knee, its nearness a maddening distraction. Every time he shifted in the seat, anticipation curled tighter in her belly.

Our dance isn't over.

It's not?

You know damn well it's not.

What did she know? That he found peculiar reasons to visit the cottage. That there was weight to their silences. That something unspoken hovered between them. That she looked forward to the carriage ride home. Even if he slept the whole way.

The door creaked open.

A woman's voice, dry as kindling, cut through the quiet.

"Well. Well. What have we here? A murderess on the run, is it?"

Mrs Haggert kept abreast of all London gossip.

Running a criminal organisation required staying one step ahead of the peelers. Which meant she already knew of Harland's death, and that they were both potential suspects.

A cold hollow opened in Dominic's gut.

He could take care of himself. But Sergeant Carter seemed too eager to see someone behind bars, and Miss Harland was a convenient target.

"She's innocent," he said, rising to greet the woman who'd come to his aid when he was a boy. Her hair was grey now, not black; her cheeks pink with rouge, not a healthy blush.

She had more secrets than Shadowmere.

He'd long suspected she worked for the Crown and wasn't the villain most people feared. But he never asked questions. Never pried.

"Aren't we all?" Mrs Haggert beckoned her closer. "Let me take a good look at you. I'll know if you did it, mind. If you tossed your poor papa into the Thames."

Miss Harland met her gaze without flinching. "I would have done anything to escape his clutches. Anything but kill him."

He didn't expect her to cower, but damn if he didn't feel a flicker of pride.

"We'll see, deary. We'll see." Mrs Haggert took hold of her chin and peered into her eyes. "Has he touched you? Has he used that rugged charm to have his way? I wouldn't blame you if you'd succumbed. There's few what could resist him."

Miss Harland blinked. "Who?"

"Hawke. Who else?"

Had Dominic been drinking coffee, he'd have spit it out.

"He's never brought a lady to the hen house."

Miss Harland frowned. "The hen house?"

"This is the coop," Dominic said, wondering if the world felt vast to her now that she'd lost her only anchor. "A haven for Mrs Haggert's chicks, children without parents. The ones left to wander the streets alone, often blind to the dangers."

"Foxes are ten a penny in these parts," Mrs Haggert said with a world-weary air, "and they don't just roam the city at night."

"They often congregate in London ballrooms," Miss Harland replied, which earned a chuckle from their hostess. "I hear White's is overrun with them."

"Likely you've met your fair share." Mrs Haggert's gaze fell to the full bosom Dominic was having trouble ignoring. "You've a figure men would easily admire. Including Hawke, I'd wager."

"Mr Hawke and I are barely friends," she countered.

"Ah, so you have thought about bedding him."

He stilled, eager for the answer, but Mrs Haggert was done playing games. "Sit down, the pair of you, and tell me why you're here. It ain't as if I'm short of problems already. I may as well add another to the list."

Dominic revealed nothing but the necessary details. His deal with the enquiry agent, the letter naming Harland as his mother's lover, the waltz, the kiss. Acquiring a new maid, though he had never expected to see Miss Harland again, let alone house her in a cottage.

Mrs Haggert tutted. "I hope you paid Daventry for the

information. He'll have you by the danglers till you do." She looked at Miss Harland and gave a toothy grin. "You've got some pluck, girl. I'll give you that."

"What else does a lady have but her wits, ma'am?"

"You've got more than enough to recommend you. Tell her, Hawke. She could have her pick of the plums."

"Not her pick," he corrected. "Some men like the docile types."

Mrs Haggert gave the air a nudge and a wink. "Not you, though. It'd take someone with gumption to stir your pot."

"Enough about plums and pots," he barked.

Mrs Haggert snapped her spine straight. "Watch your tone, laddie. You ain't too tall to get a clip round the ear." She turned to Miss Harland. "The week I took care of him, he never said boo to a goose."

Bloody hell.

Coming here had been a mistake.

Miss Harland was on it like a terrier sniffing out a burrow. "Mr Hawke stayed in the hen house? When?"

"How old were you?" The matron pursed her lips. "Eight?"

"Ten," he said reluctantly. "I was small for my age."

Mrs Haggert cackled. "You wouldn't credit it, would you, deary? Look at those thighs. Thick enough to make an oak look spindly."

"I can't say I've noticed," Miss Harland lied.

Best he rectify that. She'd be pumping the water the next time he washed. It was only right she earned her keep.

Mrs Haggert glanced at the mantel clock. "You'd better get to the point. I've somewhere else to be this afternoon."

Miss Harland spoke up, tucking that distracting dark curl behind her ear. "My father owed money to the Moseley brothers, and we wondered if that's who killed him. We were hoping you might arrange a meeting."

The comment was met with a high-pitched whistle. "Happen you should visit the coffin-maker on Monmouth Street, unless you've got ten thousand sovereigns hidden in a chest."

The colour drained from Miss Harland's face like water from a cracked glass. "Ten thousand?"

He'd known the number would be steep. Men like Harland never gambled small.

"That's what he owes, deary, give or take."

Miss Harland's fingers curled into the plush velvet of her seat. He noticed the tension in her grip before she spoke. "I haven't a penny. My aunt is my only living relative. But I'm sure—"

"You can't visit your aunt," he said. The Moseley brothers would round up all family members. "Sergeant Carter will have a man watching her house."

Mrs Haggert gave a slow, pitying shake of her head. "Happen you *should* visit your aunt. The only way to save your neck is to clear your father's debt. There's a ship that docks down near Fobbing Marshes. I'm told many young women find themselves aboard, bound for distant shores."

Mrs Haggert wasn't exaggerating.

He had seen girls vanish before. Spirited away in the dead of night, sold into god-knows-what by desperate kin or scheming debt collectors, always too late to stop it. Miss Harland would wish she'd married her merchant suitor.

"I'll pay the debt," he said sharply.

Mrs Haggert grinned like she'd found a silver sixpence in the plum pudding. "You? But Miss Harland hasn't a hope of repaying you."

"She can consider it recompense for her part in the plan." A man needed a clear conscience to sleep at night.

"Well, well. That's mighty generous. And you're barely friends, too. I'd keep the news close to your chest before there's a stampede of ladies hoping you'll ruin them."

He was glad he couldn't hear Mrs Haggert's thoughts. She knew firsthand how generous he could be to those facing hardship. He contributed to the upkeep of the hen house whenever he was in town. But this gesture might be easily misconstrued.

Mrs Haggert gripped the arm of the chair and stood. "I'll see if the Moseley brothers are willing to parley. Until then, you'd best lie low. There's a costume shop in Long Acre, deary. Maybe think about getting a disguise."

Dominic rose, as did Miss Harland.

But he wasn't quite ready to leave.

"Miss Harland has concerns regarding her father's involvement. That he wasn't my mother's only lover." The last word lodged in his throat. "I know my mother confided in you."

The slight twitch of the matron's brow was a mild reprimand. "If I've told you once, I've told you a hundred times. My word is my bond. I never break a confidence."

Anger flared. "Not even when Miss Harland's life is in danger?"

"I can't be accountable for everyone's mistakes." She clasped Dominic's upper arm with her bony fingers, her rings dull with age but worn like weapons. Only a fool would mistake her for frail. "You've the strength to take on a Roman battalion. Maybe it's time you called in a few debts."

"Are you suggesting I blackmail the good men of the ton?"

"Lives are in danger, you said. You've not welcomed the debauched into your home for nothing."

Dominic held Mrs Haggert's gaze for a moment, recognising the truth in her words.

Those who partied at Shadowmere paid handsomely to indulge their sins. He knew their wicked deeds, their scandalous secrets. He kept the worst of them on paper, locked in his study.

Power was a currency.

And he intended to spend it.

CHAPTER SEVEN

"You've been quiet since we left Mrs Haggert." Daphne watched him from the opposite carriage seat, too many questions flitting through her mind. "Were you expecting more from her?"

The formidable woman clearly had a fondness for Mr Hawke. It was there in the softening of her wrinkled lips and the warmth of her gaze, woven into her words and the fabric of their history.

Mr Hawke didn't answer right away. He gazed out the window as buildings passed in a blur, his mind somewhere far from the interior of the elegant carriage.

What was he picturing, she wondered.

Something grim? Someone precious?

But she knew what those pursed lips meant. She'd paid attention during the waltz. They bore the strain of plotting revenge. The tightness that came when one denied themselves pleasure while in pursuit of a cause.

He was both a victim and a perpetrator. The hero of his mother's tale, the villain of hers. So why should comforting him be a priority?

She wasn't here to soothe his conscience.

Her own was trouble enough.

"We got what we came for," he finally said, but the nonchalant comment told her that was not what plagued his thoughts. "She agreed to speak to the Moseley brothers."

She seized the moment to probe further.

"Mr Ramsey said you've always lived at Shadowmere. Why would your mother send you to stay with Mrs Haggert?"

He glanced at her, and she could almost hear his feral growl. She wasn't afraid of fangs. The beast she'd lived with had torn strips off her while wearing a feigned smile.

"Ramsey should rein in his loose tongue. I'll remind him where his loyalties lie when we return to Kingston."

"That's not an answer."

"It's the only one you'll get."

She smiled to herself as she imagined rummaging through a box of munitions and picking the one most likely to secure his surrender.

"We could barter. The name of my suitor in exchange for the reason you went to live with a known criminal."

His head shot up. "Why should I care who offered a king's ransom to bed you?"

Oh, he cared.

He'd asked three times on the journey to town.

She shrugged. "Because he may have killed my father and tossed him over Blackfriars Bridge. He's desperate enough to drive to Shadowmere and kidnap me in the middle of the night."

"He'll be dead before he reaches the gate."

"I didn't know you slept with one eye open." She pushed her fingers firmly into her gloves, quickly banishing the image of him in bed. "And the dratted lock on the cottage door is broken again."

He braced his foot on the seat beside her, half caging her in. "Then I'll have it replaced. And shoot the next man who tests it."

She pictured him shooting his own foot, considering how often he lingered nearby.

"Would it be easy to smuggle a woman aboard a ship?" It was a genuine question. A scenario she needed to prepare for. "I don't suppose my suitor will care about the law. Not when he planned to whisk me away to Bengal."

His foot brushed her thigh, accidentally, perhaps. "No one is taking you from Shadowmere. They wouldn't get as far as Wandsworth, let alone Bengal."

She offered an uncertain smile. "As long as you're sure. I've spent sleepless nights worrying about the lengths he might go to."

It wasn't a lie.

She'd woken in a cold sweat last night, heart hammering like a warning bell as she tried to shake the nightmare. Mr Irving's breath had been hot against her neck, his fingers plucking the pearl buttons of her gown with clinical patience.

"You promised your father," he murmured, slipping a wedding ring onto her finger—a band of cold iron that burned her skin.

She'd looked into the mirror and found no reflection.

Only him. Smiling. Rotten cabbage between his teeth.

As the carriage bumped through a rut in the road, she clutched her middle and closed her eyes. She hadn't killed her father, but she would kill Mr Irving if he so much as—

"One of Mrs Haggert's boys found me crying in the street."

She opened her eyes and glanced his way, but it wasn't satisfaction tightening her chest. He had wavered. Wavered when he thought she was afraid. Confessed to something most would not, and she could see how much it pained him.

Mr Hawke was indeed a complex man.

And complexity was a dangerous thing to admire.

"Where were your parents?"

"My father brought me to town to visit Tattersall's. A friend persuaded him to look at a stallion at Aldridge's Horse Bazaar. We were separated en route. I searched for him for hours. Mrs Haggert sent word to Shadowmere."

He spoke with an air of detachment, as though the memory belonged to someone else, as though the boy left wandering the streets was far removed from the man before her now.

But the truth was there, in the stillness of his hands. In the faint tension that pulled at his jaw. In the way he failed to meet her gaze.

Whatever wound he'd buried had not healed cleanly.

Whatever defences he raised, she kept finding cracks in his armour. And each one unsettled her more than the last.

"Hardship brought its own kind of wisdom," he said. "Mrs Haggert taught me something valuable. Something I've never forgotten."

Daphne knew it wasn't that retribution came at a price.

Perhaps it was how to wound and protect a woman in the same moment. How to make her believe he cared for her and disliked her in the same breath.

"What did she teach you?" she asked, hoping to peel back one more layer of the man who kept so much hidden.

"That doing what's right doesn't always look noble. Sometimes the right path runs straight through the gutter. Not every man born of a wastrel has to become one."

He spoke with pride and an edge of defiance. He was not

a man others held in high esteem. The ton feared him. Many loathed him. But she couldn't bring herself to do either.

"Mr Irving is the man who hopes to settle a fortune on me." Saying his name made her skin crawl. "I believe he planned to have me in a pew minutes after the ceremony. Such is his desperation to sire an heir."

Mr Hawke went still. His eyes narrowed. "He wished to buy you like livestock at Smithfield Market?"

She gave a curt nod. "For a sum greater than ten thousand pounds, I imagine. My father would have insisted on enough to line his own pockets." And to treat his mistress to a trip to Brighton. Mrs Foster enjoyed dipping her toe in turbulent waters.

A muscle ticked in Mr Hawke's jaw. "If Irving so much as looks at you again, I'll put him in the ground. Where might I find him?"

"He owns an ammunition firm. There's a warehouse down by the Limehouse docks, and others in Birmingham and Manchester. He won the contract to open a factory in India."

He didn't speak right away. He just turned his signet ring once on his finger. "Irving won't get his grubby hands on you. Not while I live to draw breath."

The carriage felt smaller, and not because his threat loomed large. It was him. The idea that he might die to keep her safe. A cruel exaggeration, surely. So why did she believe him?

"Perhaps we should visit Mr Irving together." They were already suspects in one murder. Heaven forbid they were charged with another. "Tell him we were married by licence yesterday. That should put an end to his plans."

All that mattered to Mr Irving was siring a legitimate heir.

Mr Hawke arched a brow. "Let him think I've had you?"

"Just when you rise in my estimation, you say something to remind me you're a beast." When he frowned, she added, "Call me naive, but doesn't making love require two participants?"

"And your point is?"

"I might do some having of my own."

Mr Hawke's thumb dragged along his jaw, mirroring the focus in his gaze. He leaned back, his wolfish eyes pinning her in place as the silence deepened.

"I have a feeling you'd devour me, Miss Harland."

Heat rose to her cheeks, then spread like fire beneath her skin. "We'll never know. Only a fool would make love to a man who wished to ruin her."

The challenge in his eyes was unmistakable. "Indeed."

Nelson Square
Southwark

"This doesn't look like the home of a humble witness." Mr Hawke glanced at the scrap of paper in his hand, then at the Georgian square with its neat oval garden, and back to the elegant row of brick-and-stucco townhouses. "I imagined something less refined."

Daphne looked at the polished windows and prim façades. "Mr Brown might be a servant." But what would a servant be doing near the river past midnight? And if he was the owner, perhaps he'd been travelling home late.

"He's not a servant," he said, those hawk-like eyes glinting with suspicion. "I've seen the witness statement.

Brown claims to be a clerk. How does a man earning fifty pounds a year afford a house like this?"

He'd read the statement and not told her? Mr Hawke clearly didn't grasp the meaning of a partnership.

Why was she surprised? He distrusted everything and everyone. Had the seed been planted during his time at Mrs Haggert's, or had it taken root later, during the dark days at Shadowmere?

"An inheritance?" she suggested.

"The witness was walking along the riverbank. That's why he claimed not to have seen the perpetrator." He spoke like a barrister addressing a jury. "Men who live in houses like this don't walk shadowy footpaths alone at night."

"Perhaps we should knock on the door and put the same questions to the owner." She'd noticed the curtain twitching in the lower window. It was hardly surprising, given the ominous black carriage parked outside.

Mr Hawke's coachman didn't help. He had the grim stillness of a hangman waiting for the bell to toll.

"If we have any hope of Mr Brown answering our questions, we need to appear professional," she said. "I'll be the grieving daughter. You can be the agent I hired to help solve the case. Everyone knows constables are incompetent."

"You're hardly grieving, Miss Harland."

"No. Grieving implies sorrow over a loss."

Mr Hawke studied her as a naturalist might study a rare beetle. "Does your hatred of him stem from being offered to the highest bidder, or is there something else you've not told me?"

The question struck where every woman was weakest. How could he know what it was like to be denied a voice?

But then she remembered the child lost on the street.

"Based on what you told me about your time with Mrs

Haggert, you know what helplessness feels like." Few men would admit it. "You escaped that life. I was still trapped in its cage."

"Was? You still have one foot in the cage, Miss Harland. I sense there's more you haven't said."

She wasn't about to tell him his eyes reminded her of forbidden forests and twisted fairy tales, where the girl saved the prince.

"In that, we're kindred spirits, Mr Hawke. Perhaps that's why bartering for information is such an engaging pastime."

The man gave an amused snort as he regarded her pelisse for the umpteenth time. As if needing to test the fabric, he took hold of her sleeve while helping her to the pavement.

The front door opened before they could knock. A young maid peered out, her lips pinched, her gaze wary. She eyed the carriage as if it were the Bedlam cart come to collect the master.

"Can I help you?" Her knuckles whitened around the doorjamb. "If you're calling for Mr Brown, he ain't home."

Daphne studied the comely woman. Even an amateur sleuth could tell she was terrified. Not just that. Her vowels were polished, her skin scented with expensive soap, not tallow.

"We're investigating a murder on the bridge last week." Daphne considered asking to come inside but chose a different approach. "We seek answers to a few questions. We're happy to converse on the doorstep."

The maid's chin quivered. "I didn't see anything, ma'am. You'll have to speak to Mr Brown. As I said, he ain't here."

"Is there a Mrs Brown we might speak to instead?" Daphne asked gently.

The girl shook her head. "No. Mr Brown's a bachelor."

"We're trying to corroborate his statement." Daphne

leaned in slightly. She didn't want to frighten the girl, but urgency crept up her spine. "A witness is often considered a suspect, and there are already whispers at Bow Street. I'm quite confident Mr Brown is not the killer."

The last word caught in her throat, and she fumbled in her reticule for her handkerchief. Merely stage directions to fool the audience. What she hadn't expected was Mr Hawke handing her his instead.

It was black, his monogram stitched in gold, the scent so enticing she nearly sighed aloud. Her knees went weak, which rather suited her performance.

"Forgive me." She made the mistake of sniffing into his handkerchief—an act that felt far more intimate than staring at his firm calves in the shower-bath. "The victim was my father." She gestured to Mr Hawke, whose cologne ought to be labelled a dangerous substance. "I've hired an agent recommended by the Home Secretary."

She contemplated giving him a ridiculous name like Mr Crabbit, but he spoke before she could introduce him.

"I'm a thorough man, miss. I'll not see an innocent hanged just because those fools at Bow Street know no better."

The maid glanced along the street before opening the door and welcoming them inside. She closed it firmly, sliding the bolt, as if Napoleon might come knocking.

"Come into the drawing room."

The drawing room? Not the servant's parlour?

Daphne exchanged a knowing glance with Mr Hawke before stepping through.

The room bore the hallmarks of genteel wealth: a Persian rug softened the floors, carved shelves flanked the marble fireplace, and sombre military prints lined the walls. But among the masculine touches were subtler clues—violets on the escritoire, lace on the chairs, and a silk fan tucked behind a vase on the mantel.

The maid gestured to the sofa and sat in the fireside chair.

One thing was certain. Her duties here amounted to more than sweeping out the fireplace and turning down the bed.

Mr Hawke began with an important question. "Can you confirm that Mr Brown was out on the night in question?"

The maid nodded. "He said he was delivering a client's accounts, though he never mentioned who. He also helps at the church, handing out food parcels to the poor in the squalid houses by the river."

"The church hands out parcels at midnight?" he asked.

The maid's chin quivered. "I don't know, sir. That's all he told me."

"Did you wait up for him to return?"

"Yes." She pressed her hand to her throat, as though trying to calm her voice. "I did that night. But I assure you, Mr Brown wouldn't hurt a fly. He's the kindest soul."

She was in love with Mr Brown. That much was clear.

"Where does he work?" Daphne asked.

"Here, ma'am." She fidgeted with her hands in her lap. "He's a scrivener. He writes up legal documents and contracts for all sorts of clients."

Daphne didn't miss the vague phrasing. All sorts of clients. But were they respectable men of trade, or the sort who ran protection rackets like the Moseley brothers? And if Mr Brown bent the rules for them on parchment, what else might he be willing to do?

Mr Hawke must have read her mind, though she hoped his talent for doing so was limited to their current enquiry.

"Has your employer ever mentioned the Moseley brothers?" he said, his voice measured. "They're moneylenders who work out of a premises in Covent Garden."

The woman pursed her lips and blinked as if she had grit in her eye. "No. I can't say he has. But I'm only the maid."

What tosh. There was a sherry glass beside the brandy snifter on the side table.

"But you can confirm he was agitated when he returned home the night he witnessed the murder?" She didn't give the woman time to reply. "Did he come here first, or summon a constable?"

The maid looked overwhelmed. "I … erm. He found a watchman and visited the watch-house. It's just around the corner on Charlotte Street. From there, I think they took him to Bow Street."

"In Mr Brown's statement, he claims he was on the river-bank." Daphne leaned forward and gently squeezed the maid's hand. "I have to ask, could he have seen the killer and been too afraid to say so?"

Mr Hawke added a sprinkle of menace to the pot. "It's important you tell us, miss. His life may depend on it."

That's when the first crack in the dam appeared. A tremble swelled into a wracking sob. The maid dropped her head into her hands, shoulders shaking.

Daphne knelt beside her, rubbing the poor girl's arm. "We only want the truth. Where is Mr Brown? There's a reason you bolted the door behind us."

"I don't know," she blurted.

"When did you last see him?" Daphne tried to sound concerned, but couldn't help thinking Mr Brown was involved in the crime.

"Two days ago." The maid glanced up through bloodshot eyes, her distress impossible to fake. "A carriage stopped outside. There was a row. He climbed in, and I've not heard a peep from him since."

Daphne looked at Mr Hawke, who wore suspicion like an old coat. She lifted her brows in silent question: *What now?*

He stood, dragging his palms down his thighs, the fabric pulling taut over the muscle beneath. "We'll need to search his study."

The maid whimpered but was quick to refuse. "I can't let you look through his personal papers. Not without his say-so."

"Don't you want to help us find him?" Mr Hawke's tone could have frozen the fires in hell. "If he saw something that night, there's a chance the killer means to silence him."

That earned more tears, along with a lifted brow from Daphne.

He ignored her silent plea.

"We don't care that you're lovers. A man was murdered. Your employer knows something he's not told Bow Street."

"He doesn't. Edward would have told me."

Well, that confirmed they were close.

The maid straightened, wiping her cheeks with the edge of her sleeve. "I'm sorry, but you must leave now." Her voice was steadier than before, though her hands trembled. "You can return tomorrow. If Mr Brown's back by then, he'll speak for himself."

Mr Hawke stood rigid. He was a man accustomed to getting his way. "If Brown is in trouble, every hour counts. At least let us search his private rooms."

Daphne feared he might charge upstairs regardless. She crossed the room and laid a hand on his sleeve. "That's enough for one day."

She meant for herself and the maid.

They had a long ride back to Kingston.

"Please," she added softly.

He looked at her, gaze sharp as a blade, and she felt the jolt deep in her belly. "Fine. But you owe me."

The words rang like a forbidden promise. What worried her most wasn't what he'd demand in return. It was the thought she might be tempted to pay.

She faced the maid. "Thank you. We'll return tomorrow."

The maid gave a shaky nod and ushered them out, nearly catching their heels as she slammed the door.

Mr Hawke wrenched the carriage door open. "Either Brown killed your father, and the Moseleys are hiding him, or he's already dead in a ditch."

For a clever man, he'd overlooked the obvious.

"Have you considered that your own actions might have been the catalyst? What if the man you're seeking is part of the ton and knew my father could expose him?"

Mr Hawke had saved her life by storming into the ball-room. But the cost to her father had been steep. Whatever the cause, it was her father's wickedness that got him killed.

"The sins of Shadowmere began long before I hosted decadent parties." He extended his hand, more a challenge than an invitation. "We're standing here because your father's cruelty knew no bounds."

She slipped her hand into his, ignoring the sudden rise in her pulse. "Yes, but you can't discount the possibility someone else is involved."

He glanced at their joined hands, then at her. "We'll discuss it later, at the party. It will keep your mind from the guests' lewd antics."

She blinked. The party was sooner than expected.

"Mr Ramsey said the Autumn Masque is next week."

"It is. But I'm calling in a debt." Mr Hawke tightened his grip on her hand, drawing her dangerously close.

Her breath caught. She hated that he could do that with a single step.

"You owe me, Miss Harland. We'll enjoy the delights of town before returning home tonight."

She should have asked, *What party?*

But it was the way he said *home* that sent her thoughts scattering like birds in a sudden storm. He made it sound as if they were married, had a past, a future, and something deliciously dangerous in between.

"I have nothing to wear," she managed, but based on the devilish look in his eyes, she doubted it mattered. "We'd be fools to linger in town. Not with eyes on every street."

He seemed to take pleasure in her mild distress. "We'll party where no one dares to look. Among the demimonde. We won't stay long."

The man was a walking contradiction.

"I thought you despised sybarites."

"I do. But we have one more task before we leave."

She was afraid to ask what it was.

That wasn't entirely true. She was more intrigued than afraid.

"Won't people wonder why we're together?"

"Why would they?" The rogue drew her hand to his lips, his gaze holding hers as his mouth brushed her knuckles, sending every nerve in her body sparking to life. "Everyone thinks you're my mistress. Let's give them what they crave."

CHAPTER EIGHT

Someone must have drugged the London air, lacing it with something that soothed a man's wrath, clouded his judgement, and stripped him of every ounce of common sense.

Dominic should have been halfway to Kingston by now, rattling through muddy ruts and contemplating supper. Instead, he stood in the grand hall of a Grosvenor Place townhouse, watching Mrs Flavell's strapping butler rub his palms, eager to divest Miss Harland of her cloak.

Lay a finger on her, and you'll lose a hand.

He was already planning the butler's funeral.

"Allow me." He was behind her before the brute could touch her, a possessive heat stirring in his gut. "As I paid for that gown," he murmured at her ear, "it's only fair I'm the first to see it."

"Careful, Mr Hawke." The minx tugged lightly at the bow at her throat, teasing him. "A lady might mistake you for a gentleman."

"There's no chance of that, angel."

He slipped the cloak from her shoulders, muscles tightening as his fingers brushed warm skin. Too smooth. Too soft for a man like him.

The need to be inside her hit with brutal force.

"Turn around. Slowly." Anticipation clawed at him, though he kept his tone measured. "Let me admire the result of my investment."

She obeyed with maddening grace.

The sight punched the air from his lungs.

He loved her in red. It lit her pale complexion, made her black hair gleam like polished jet, and left her lips looking indecently plump. Too plump for a man trying to behave.

Every wicked word he knew crowded his mind.

He reached into his coat pocket and drew out the ruby necklace he'd bought from Woodcroft's. Stepping closer, he swept aside the wisps at her nape and fastened it around her throat. The curve of her neck did nothing to improve his self-control.

"The look isn't complete without this." It was a lie. She looked complete in old breeches and a dirty shirt, her hair tumbling from flimsy pins.

Her fingers closed over the ruby, but the sparkle in her eyes could dull any gem. "It's beautiful. Where did you get it? I never heard you leave the hotel."

He'd had no choice but to escape the suite at the Carroway. Listening to her singing as she bathed in the next room was its own kind of torture. Almost as cruel as staring at the poster bed and imagining what they might do if they stayed the night.

"No need to excite yourself. It's on loan."

"Oh." The light in her expression dulled.

He would've done anything to bring it back.

But admitting he'd bought it for her was a step too far.

"Never mind." She smoothed her hands over the front of her gown. "It was foolish of me to think otherwise."

Bloody hell.

Now he wanted to empty Woodcroft's cabinets.

Or break into the Tower and steal a crown jewel.

He cleared his throat. "The manager at the Carroway will return it when he handles the gown and slippers."

He'd paid the modiste a tidy sum to part with a dress intended for Lady Belmont. It was the only one close to the right size and could be altered within the hour.

"Of course." She looked down at the marble floor, her disappointment as tangible as the thrum of lust in his blood. "I'm grateful you spared a thought for me."

Merciful Lord. She'd bewitched him. He could almost feel her hands around his heart, squeezing until it hurt. Truth be told, he thought of her a damn sight more than he should.

He needed to master himself.

Dominic Hawke didn't moon over a woman like some green lad, not with half of London's libertines watching from shadowed corners and stairwells.

"You understand what it means if we enter the drawing room?"

It was time for a hearty dose of reality.

She shrugged one shoulder as if resigned to her fate. "It means everyone will believe we're lovers."

She paused on that word, and damned if he didn't cram an hour of imagined sin into those two seconds. He was supposed to be immune to this madness. Cold. Controlled. Yet here he was, burning.

"It means I'll never grace a respectable ballroom again." She gave herself a small shake, brushing off the lapse into melancholy. "No matter. My future lies far from London. Finding the truth is all that concerns me now."

Far from London?

Kingston was less than thirty miles.

"You understand we'll need to play a role to convince them?" He stepped closer. "You'll have to touch me—let them think you're desperate to get me out of these clothes and straddle me in bed."

Her eyes widened. "Act like I want you?"

Why did her phrasing grate?

"Yes. Can you manage it?"

"I'll have to follow your lead."

Good God. He was considered among the best of his sex. It should be no hardship. Most of the women here tonight would unbutton his trousers in the shadows of the maze.

"They must believe I own you. That you're at my beck and call." He intended to make the most of the charade, to shatter whatever illusions she still held about him. "It's the only way to keep lechers at bay."

She nibbled her lip. A rare glimpse of nerves. He wanted to carry her to the carriage and keep her beside him the entire way home.

Damn this woman.

"Come." He slid an arm around her waist, bracing himself. "Hold your breath as we pass the salon. Every fool in there is high on opium. Most are half-naked."

A haze clung to the air, thick with perfume and pipe smoke. Voices murmured in dark corners, some laughing, some panting. The scent of sweat, wine, and something acrid warned this was no place for innocence.

No place for Miss Harland.

"Stay close." If he didn't end up in Newgate tonight, it would be a bloody miracle. "Play coy. Don't act surprised."

"So, the point of us being here is what?" she asked, eyes

fixed ahead as they neared the drawing room. "You still haven't told me."

To threaten Templeton. To interrogate those on his list. To cement his place as the bastard everyone feared. Even if he had gone soft in the head.

"To draw out the villain," he said smoothly.

"The villain who killed my father or hurt your mother?"

"Both."

She tutted. "I'm still none the wiser."

"Just pretend you're in love with me."

Her head snapped in his direction. "In love or in lust? Make up your mind, Mr Hawke. You're confusing the issue."

Had he said love?

He must have inhaled opium smoke.

"Either will do. And for heaven's sake, don't call me *mister*, unless I've tied you to the bedpost with leather straps. Hawke is just fine."

A lull greeted them, like the hush before a kill.

The quartet played Mendelssohn. A piece most people ignored. No one came here for the music. They came to hunt, to feast.

The predators stirred as if waking from a winter's sleep.

Heads turned. Women took the measure of him. Men watched Miss Harland with the keen attention of gamblers studying the table. A few moistened their lips.

"Hawke," Miss Harland muttered through her smile.

"It's all right." He tightened his grip. Word had spread. He recognised the look of men circling their next conquest. "I won't let you out of my sight tonight."

He scanned the room, searching for his prey.

Langridge.

Virginia Passmore.

Templeton.

The last of them lounged on a gold brocade sofa, his mouth at a woman's ear, one arm slung casually around her shoulders, his fingers grazing the swell of her breast. All while his wife lay in bed at home.

"Faithless cur."

As if he'd heard his name on the breeze, Templeton glanced over and paled when he met Dominic's hard gaze. The plan had been to draw him aside at some point in the evening and issue a quiet warning.

That plan changed the moment Templeton's greedy eyes raked over Miss Harland's figure.

Dominic seized her hand, pulling her through the crowd.

Templeton stood, clearly panicked. "Please, Hawke. Hear me out." He raised his hands as if to ward off a blow. "There's been a misunderstanding."

"Damn right." Dominic fought to maintain his usual cool indifference, but he'd not felt a rage like this since—well, it didn't matter when. "Touch her again and they'll be picking your limbs off the Thames foreshore."

Templeton swallowed hard. "From the tone of your note, I thought you were done with her."

Dominic squared his shoulders, ready to grab the fop by the throat, but Miss Harland took offence before he had the chance.

"Done with me? How quaint, my lord. I wasn't aware you planned to pass me around like a calling card." She released his hand and raised her chin in cool defiance. "Let me be clear. I'll tell Hawke when we're done."

Dominic might have applauded and offered a grin as smug as the devil's. But someone laughed behind him, and he couldn't afford to lose the upper hand.

"We both know you can't get enough of me, love."

She turned, her coy mask firmly in place. "And no woman will ever satisfy you as I do."

He cursed inwardly.

Because she might be right.

"Can we forget this?" Templeton almost begged.

"Yes. But you're no longer welcome in my house."

"You're banning me from Shadowmere?" Templeton stared like the bailiffs had come knocking. "But I've paid to attend the Autumn Masque. Hawke, be reasonable. I'm sure we can resolve this in a gentlemanly fashion."

"Yes, with pistols or swords?"

"That's not what his lordship meant." Miss Harland laid a calming hand on his chest. Doubtless his heart thumped wildly against her palm, a truth he couldn't hide.

If he couldn't hurt Harland, he'd settle for this fool.

"Then what did he mean?"

Templeton answered quickly. "That we might agree on a way I can repay the slight. A favour owed still holds value."

Dominic didn't have to think too hard.

"Very well. I want a list of my father's creditors."

His mother had kept their identities from him. Somehow, she'd managed to settle every debt. He'd long assumed it was the work of her mysterious lover—a man whose name she'd taken to the grave.

It wasn't until Daventry arrived weeks ago with a letter that the truth emerged. Lord Harland was the coward. The lover who killed her.

"But your father's been dead for more than ten years."

Shame it wasn't twenty. That he'd not suffered a bout of *temporary insanity* sooner. At least he'd settled Shadowmere on his only son before he loaded the pistol.

"If you want to attend the Autumn Masque, bring me a

name and proof. I won't host another gathering until I have the full list in hand and can verify every last one."

A collective gasp echoed behind him.

Good. Let them scramble for a new den of vice.

Miss Harland slipped her arm through his and tugged lightly. "We should give Lord Templeton time to consider his options. You promised to show me the garden before it gets cold."

"I promised to show you a lot of things."

"Then take me outside. Be a man of your word."

The veiled suggestion wasn't lost on him. He might have groaned aloud but offered Templeton one last look instead. "Enjoy your evening. I know I intend to."

He led Miss Harland through the terrace doors into the cool hush of night, eager to put distance between her and the reckless rabble.

The garden resembled Eden after the fall—perfumed with jasmine and teeming with sinners. Lanterns glowed amber among the trees, casting long, sultry shadows. The box maze had become a bordello of rustling hedgerows, moans drifting like incense.

"A maze. How marvellous." Miss Harland's innocent eyes brightened. "At Lady Huntington's country party last Christmas, I reached the centre first."

"The guests in there are of the same mind—being first to the post, that is. Linger long enough and you'll hear their cries of triumph." And a few colourful curses when they crossed the finish line.

Her eyes narrowed. "You're mocking me, sir."

He pressed a hand to his chest. "Mock you? Never. And I told you, only call me *sir* in bed."

She glanced at the burning braziers and the festoons of

lights strung between the trees. "It's rather romantic, given the circumstances."

Her gaze settled on the polished oak floor laid over half the lawn. She said nothing. She looked up at the night sky, tilting her head as the strains of a waltz floated through the open terrace doors.

What must it be like to live in hope?

To dream and not wake with regret?

To be broken and still marvel at the stars?

"What are you thinking?" He wasn't sure why he cared.

She sighed as she stared at the heavens. "That nothing is as beautiful as the sky above Shadowmere on a clear night."

"I can't say I've noticed."

She turned to him. "Then you must come to the cottage. I've a spare chair and blanket, but you'll have to bring your own brandy."

He pictured her outside, wrapped in wool and innocence. Of all the invitations he'd received, none was more tempting than this.

He offered his hand. "I know my name tops the list of men you're meant to avoid, but would you care to dance, Miss Harland?"

"Dance?" She glanced behind, one brow lifted. "There's not a soul on the floor. Who are you trying to impress?"

"You." He caught her hand and didn't let go, though he told himself he should. "I'm happy to top any list but that one. And since you've confessed to being a hopeless romantic, it would be rude to leave you unsatisfied."

Amusement lit her eyes. "I thought you were in the habit of breaking hearts."

He shrugged. "Not yours, it seems."

"I suppose there's no longer any need to hurt me."

"Perhaps I convinced myself I was saving you."

"In some strange way you did."

He pulled her close, one hand settling at her waist, the other capturing hers with an ease that should concern him. Her warmth seeped through her silk glove into his skin, a silent sort of brand.

This wasn't revenge.

Not anymore.

It felt like atonement. And something far more dangerous.

"Is this the dance that wasn't quite over?" she asked as he swept her into the first turn. "What is it about us that seems unfinished?"

He laughed. Trust her to go straight to the heart of it.

"You tell me. You're the one who lured me out here alone. Do you want another taste of me? Is that it? I should warn you. One more won't be enough."

Her fingers curled tighter in his. "I wished to berate you."

"For not buying you the ruby?"

"I don't care about the ruby. It's the gesture, not the gem."

"So you're not annoyed it's on loan?"

"No. I'm afraid. For a clever man, you've done a foolish thing." She held his gaze, her tone serious now. "You hold the key to a vault of secrets. Once the parties cease, your guests will demand your silence."

He couldn't see the problem. "And?"

"We both know there's only one way to truly silence someone. Hit them with a blunt object and toss them into the Thames."

He might have answered with a quip, but no one had ever looked at him like she did now. As though losing him would leave a mark. As though she might mourn him in her dotage.

He didn't deserve her consideration.

"You don't need to worry about me." He pulled her closer. "You're right. I'm no fool. There are plans in place. Every guest who signs the contract knows exactly what's at stake if they betray my trust. It's in their interests to keep me alive."

She searched his face, and he thought he glimpsed pity there. "There are other ways to hurt a man. You target those close to him. You take away everything he holds dear."

His step faltered, his mother's lifeless body still vivid in his mind. But he recovered. The villain hadn't meant to destroy an eighteen-year-old boy. It had merely been the consequence.

"Why do you think I live like a monk? Keep only a few close friends?" Why the Brethren met in secret and plotted vengeance from the shadows?

Something he said struck a nerve. She drew a sharp breath, eyes shining with sudden tears. She stopped dancing, slipped from his hold, and stared as though he were the devil himself.

"Of course. It all makes perfect sense now." Her voice cracked. She touched the ruby at her throat, then recoiled as if it had burned her. "My father always said I was a naive fool."

Confused, he shook his head.

She stepped back, the space between them a chasm.

"It explains everything. The necklace. The dress." She tugged on the silk as if it offended her. "The kindness you've shown me. If they believe we're lovers, they'll hurt me to punish you." A brittle laugh escaped her. "You didn't kill my father, but you could destroy me instead."

"For heaven's sake, woman. Have you lost your wits?" He edged closer. She edged back. "If I wanted to hurt you, I'd give Templeton permission to pursue you."

"Perhaps you have and he's part of the plan." She

muttered under her breath, rambling like a bedlamite. "That's why you agreed to this partnership. To trick me. To lure me into a trap."

"A trap?" His jaw tightened. "I'd kill them if they touched you."

He meant it. Every word.

But promises from a scoundrel weighed nothing.

"I need to leave." Her voice broke on a sob. "Get as far away from here—from you—as I can. Is nowhere safe?"

"Take a breath," he said, the plea cloaked as a command.

But she turned, hitched her skirts, and ran full tilt towards the garden's edge, towards the wrought-iron gate that led to the mews.

He gave chase, boots pounding the ground, ignoring the gasping couple hidden behind the oak—the man's pale arse gleaming like a ghost in the moonlight.

"Daphne!"

It was the first time he'd spoken her name.

He'd imagined it under very different circumstances.

She glanced back over her shoulder, panic in her eyes, and missed her step. Her foot caught on a root, and she went down hard.

"Daphne."

Even as she fell, something twisted in his chest.

He was at her side in a heartbeat, lifting her gently, brushing dirt from her gown, tugging off her glove to examine her hand.

"You think I planned this?" he said, his voice rough with disbelief. "That I meant to put a target on your back? That hurting you once wasn't enough?"

"What else should I think?"

She tried to pull away, but he tightened his grip on her wrist. Words he didn't want to say clung to his tongue.

"You've no defence?" she asked, her anger palpable.

But all he could see were her lips wet with tears, the leaves tangled in her hair, the dirt smudged across her cheek. He should've let her go. Instead, he was drowning. And something inside him cracked.

"Perhaps I wanted you close so I could protect you."

He drew her in, their mouths just inches apart, her warm breath melting the last of his resolve. "So I could right a wrong. So I could ease this blasted craving."

She didn't move. Didn't blink. Just looked up at him like she already knew he was lost.

One kiss, and he could be rid of this fever.

One kiss might silence the storm inside him.

Then he could be done with this madness.

"What craving?" she asked softly.

"This one."

He kissed her, his mouth brushing hers slowly, giving her time to pull away, stamp on his toes or knee him in the groin.

She didn't. Her fingers curled into his coat and she leaned in, her lips parting beneath his.

That was all the invitation he needed.

He took her mouth with a hunger he scarcely understood, one that had clawed at him for days, growing teeth the moment he'd heard her singing as she bathed. The lazy ripple of water and the low, breathy notes of her voice had driven him half mad with need.

To be in that room.

To be inside her.

He'd imagined her through the door, soap sliding over the curve of her thigh, the creamy swell of her breasts rising from the water, visions that left him aching then and made his need a furious, inescapable thing now.

His hand slipped to the small of her back, dragging her close until he felt the press of her breasts and the maddening heat of her body. He should pull away, throw water on the flames.

Instead, he angled her head and took the kiss deeper, his tongue sliding against hers in a slow, claiming stroke that made him throb with the promise of more.

That's it, angel.

Taste me. Taste me like I know you want to.

She moaned into his mouth, a greedy little sound that nearly finished him. His cock ached, rigid with the want of her, the burn of it almost cruel. God help him. One stroke of her hand and he'd spend like a schoolboy.

He forgot himself.

Forgot she was an innocent, not his rampant lover.

He'd never kissed a woman like this.

Like he wanted to lay claim to her soul, drive a placard into her heart and protect the land with swords and rifles. Like he wanted to part her legs and rut like a beast. Fast and so bloody hard.

He shifted, one knee sliding between hers, the brush of her skirts making him curse the layers that separated them.

Her sweet whimper said she wanted him there.

There was nowhere on earth he'd rather be.

The thought proved sobering.

Dominic Hawke didn't lose himself over a woman. He didn't paw at flesh in the dark. He didn't slake his lust like some depraved libertine. He could control his hunger. He could master his emotions.

So why the hell was he still kissing her?

He dragged his mouth from hers with a breathless curse.

"Tell me that was a mistake," he rasped. "Lie to me. Say you hated every second. Say kissing me turns your stomach.

Makes you sick to the pit. That you'd rather die than do it again."

She blinked, still a little dazed and confused.

Then a woman's sultry voice drifted on the breeze. "*Au contraire*, Mr Hawke. From my vantage point, Miss Harland looks like she delights in sin."

CHAPTER NINE

The flamboyant lady behind them, bathed in the golden glow of the lantern she held aloft, wasn't entirely wrong. She resembled Marie Antoinette with her tall powdered wig and extravagant gown, but Daphne couldn't fault her assessment.

Mr Hawke's mouth *was* a delight. Every sinful inch of him made her think and do wicked things.

Lie to me. Say you hated every second.

Never.

The taste of him still lingered, warm and wet on her lips. Her blood still rushed wild through her veins. She ought to berate herself for being weak, but his confession had been a small victory. A rare crack in a man who ruled with iron restraint.

It wouldn't happen again.

She saw the heat in his gaze chill, the resolve harden his jaw as his hands slipped from her waist and he stepped back.

She should have turned away the moment he touched her. Nothing good came from wanting a man like Dominic Hawke. But the glimpse of vulnerability fed her addiction.

"Mrs Flavell." He faced her. "Searching for stowaways?"

"You know the rules, Mr Hawke. What if I came to Shad-owmere and went romping in the garden without first seeking you out?"

"We weren't romping," he snapped.

"Of course not. I suppose Miss Harland had a fly in her eye. A bit of chicken stuck in her teeth. Thank heavens she hadn't dropped a grape down her bodice. Even chivalry has its limits."

Mr Hawke rolled his shoulders and straightened his cuffs.

"I meant no slight." He inclined his head a fraction. "Miss Harland fell. I was overcome with a need to tend her wounds. Nothing to warrant your attention."

He didn't sound like the man who'd asked her to dance.

That man had been composed, yes, but warm beneath it.

This man sounded like a stranger, his voice flat and dismissive, as if she were already his greatest regret.

Mrs Flavell's gaze shifted to Daphne, and she clicked her tongue. "Red, my darling? He's not even buried. Even I would wear black for a month, and I haven't an ounce of decorum."

"I'm trying to avoid sombre colours, ma'am." Daphne stepped out from Mr Hawke's shadow. "There'll be time for mourning if I end up in Newgate. Or the workhouse."

Mrs Flavell's bright eyes drank her in, as if she were a curious antiquity in a shop window. "With Hawke as your protector? Highly unlikely. Poor Lord Templeton has been on the pot since you left the drawing room."

Mr Hawke gave a mocking snort. "He's lucky I didn't put him through the window. I should tell his father-in-law what he's been up to. Let the fool sue me for breach of contract."

"As much as I enjoy a bit of rivalry, Mr Hawke, no one spoils a good party. At least not while I'm the hostess."

"Is that our cue to leave?" he countered.

"No, it's an invitation to stay the night." Mrs Flavell put the lantern on the ground as though laying down her sword. She reached into her bodice and removed a brass key. "The Egyptian room is empty. I keep it for certain guests."

"We're leaving London within the hour."

Mrs Flavell smiled. "I think you'll want to stay."

"Like hell we will."

Daphne was quick to intercede. "We're grateful for your hospitality, ma'am, but half the constables in town are out looking for me."

And by the sound of it, Mrs Flavell expected her to play Cleopatra to Hawke's Mark Antony. History's great lovers died for passion. Dominic Hawke found it a terrible inconvenience.

"Peel's bobbies won't dare look for you here," Mrs Flavell said before playing her trump card. "Might a golden nugget of information tempt you to reconsider?"

Mr Hawke's shoulders tensed. "You'll not bribe us to participate in your nighttime games. I keep to a strict set of rules, and you damn well know it."

Rules? The word hung in the air.

Had he just broken one with her?

She watched his face. Cold as a stone effigy. Whatever had passed between them in the garden was already buried. Would he mourn it? She couldn't say.

Mrs Flavell chuckled. "Rules relating to liaisons? Clearly a passionate encounter in the moonlight doesn't count."

Mr Hawke tutted, his patience in shreds. "Tell me what you know. I assume it relates to why I stormed into Templeton's ballroom and crossed a line no gentleman should."

"Not quite." Their hostess gave an amused hum, almost dismissing him. "I knew your mother, Miss Harland. When we attended Thornborough Academy together." She raised both hands in a silencing gesture. "It hardly seems possible, I know. I don't look a day over thirty."

Daphne's heart skipped a beat.

No one ever spoke of her mother. Her father would turn brittle with rage. And yet the ache remained, sharp as the day she died.

"Stay the night, Miss Harland. And I shall tell you why your mother came here the week before her passing."

The world fell silent.

The music faded.

The distant laughter dissolved.

Questions flooded her mind. Had the fever not killed her? Had those days of crippling pain and whispered goodbyes been a lie? Had her father's grief been nothing but an act?

Oh, Mrs Flavell excelled at stirring emotions.

Daphne couldn't leave, even if she wanted to.

Not now. Not with the past clawing at her heels.

She looked at Mr Hawke, but he barely met her gaze. His frustrated mutter said he already knew what she was about to say.

"Might we stay?"

"We need to be on the road, unless you want to sleep in a gaol cell."

She felt the familiar tightening in her throat, but couldn't bring herself to nod and agree. Not this time.

"You leave," she said. He was probably desperate to put twenty miles between them, to distance himself from the kiss that had curled her toes. "I shall stay the night with Mrs Flavell and find my own way out of London."

Mr Hawke ground his teeth and scuffed the dirt with his boot. He made the rules. He didn't deal in propositions. And probably wasn't averse to kidnapping.

"Don't make me give you an ultimatum, Miss Harland."

She said nothing as memories surfaced. Times she'd stood before her father, her choices tossed overboard like unwanted cargo.

Perhaps this was different.

Perhaps her safety mattered.

There was only one way to know.

She closed the small gap between them and laid a hand on his forearm. Tension coiled beneath her palm. "I can't leave now. But you could stay with me."

The sky darkened as he stared.

A muscle ticked in his jaw.

He stood like a monument to defiance.

A woman's playful scream echoed in the night, and he nearly snarled. "We leave at dawn. I shall carry you from this house if you break our bargain."

Thank heavens.

She wanted to breathe as if she'd held it for a year.

She gave his arm a gentle squeeze, the power beneath unmistakable. "That sounds like the perfect compromise."

Mrs Flavell clapped as though they were the evening's entertainment. "Excellent. Will you join the festivities or shall I show you to your room? It's exquisite. You won't be disappointed."

"Is Langridge here?" he said.

"He's in the smoking room. Why?"

"What about Mrs Passmore?"

"She's resting. Took two lovers and a bottle of ratafia to the Turkish room and hasn't surfaced since."

"If I stay, you'll give my coachman a bed and send our luggage upstairs," he said, determined to issue at least one command tonight. "And you'll ensure Mrs Passmore receives my note."

"Of course. There's an escritoire in the room. Write your missive there. Shall I have supper sent up?"

Though Daphne's stomach rumbled at the suggestion, Mr Hawke refused. "We'll help ourselves in the dining room. I want a corked bottle of claret. I've no wish to wake up drugged and bare-arsed in a bush."

Not wine, or even the scandalous image of Mr Hawke naked, topped Daphne's list of priorities. "When might we speak about my mother? I doubt you'll rise before dawn."

"I shall pen a note," Mrs Flavell said breezily. "Samson will see you receive it before you go. Should more questions arise, you're welcome to return."

Perhaps she had no intention of sharing anything valuable. Or perhaps this was a ploy to force Mr Hawke's hand.

He agreed, a point he stressed as they piled veal and minted potatoes onto a plate while two other guests made lewd suggestions about the sausages.

"I hope you know what you've cost me, angel."

Goodness. Could he not call her *hoyden*? Something sharp and dismissive. Anything that didn't summon memories of a romantic waltz and a blazing kiss in the garden.

"Your pride?"

He didn't answer immediately. Instead, he drew her aside, away from the table and the ravenous guests, his hand firm at her elbow.

He leaned in, voice low. "You've made me break my own rules. That's no small feat."

The heat of his whisper tickled her ear, sending something tight and traitorous curling low in her belly.

"What rules might those be? A preference for your own bed? A vow to stay dry while your guests drown in sin?"

His thigh brushed hers, deliberate or not, she couldn't tell.

"To stay in control. To keep emotion locked away where

it belongs, because it serves no one but the weak. To resist temptation."

His breath softened on the last word. Then his gaze dipped to the swell of her breasts. Another fracture in his polished discipline.

"So why agree to stay?"

"You know why."

She did. She felt it like an invisible shield. He couldn't walk away and leave her unguarded, no matter how much he might want to.

Voices swelled outside the dining room. A burst of laughter, the scuffle of feet, then a couple spilled through the doorway, flushed and giggling. One clutched a half-empty bottle. The other grabbed it and took a long swig.

Mr Hawke muttered something murderous under his breath and reached for the cutlery, sliding two sets into his coat pocket. "We'll eat upstairs. I've little patience left tonight."

He was already steering her towards the door before she could reply. Two men on the stairs stepped aside without a word, backs pressed to the wall.

"Stay close," he said. "Keep your gaze ahead."

It was easier said than done when curiosity wrestled with caution.

At the top, the corridor pulsed with creaks and breathy moans, the perfume so cloying she had to stifle a cough. One door stood ajar.

Inside, a man lounged naked on a velvet chaise while two women fed him strawberries. One laughed as she licked the juice from his chest.

"Keep moving." Mr Hawke didn't break stride.

Daphne meant to. But a woman looked up, and for a

breathless moment, she could have sworn it was Mrs Foster, her father's paramour.

No. It couldn't be.

Not unless she'd found a new lover in a week.

Mr Hawke drew a key from his coat and swiftly unlocked the door marked *Nefertiti's Palace*, ushering her inside with the efficiency of a man eager to shut the world out.

"The lady in that room—" she began, stopping short when Mr Hawke locked the door behind them. "Good heavens."

It wasn't being alone with him in a bedchamber that had her heart thundering like a racehorse at the gate. Or that robbed her of all sensible thought. Some women might sell their souls to be this close to him.

The room was a decadent echo of a pharaoh's tomb. Gold and lapis-blue columns framed the bed. Hieroglyphs covered the walls. The air held the tang of myrrh and spiced wood.

It was a room made for seduction.

Everything in it whispered yes.

"Hellfire." He set the plate on the nightstand and dragged a hand through his hair. "You know how to punish a man, Miss Harland."

This was her punishment as much as his.

The attraction was inconvenient.

"We've kissed, Mr Hawke. You should call me Daphne."

"I prefer to remind myself you're chaste."

"Because you already broke one rule?"

"Because I don't intend to break another."

She chuckled to herself as she set her plate on the side table by the hearth. Since when had she become an irresistible temptress? One capable of bringing this man to his knees.

"Mrs Flavell clearly thought you needed convincing." She lifted the sheer gold nightgown draped over the dressing screen and held it against her. "This would hardly keep out an autumn chill."

Mr Hawke didn't look at her at first. He stared into the fire like a man reciting commandments to himself. When his gaze slid her way, the flecks in his green eyes glowed like embers.

"That woman is an expert in torture. Shall I strip off my shirt so you can lash me with your allure, Miss Harland?"

"No need. I'll sleep in my clothes tonight."

"You can't." He cursed. "That dress goes back to the modiste in the morning. There's already dirt on the hem. Your shift will suffice." He threw the cutlery onto the bed and scanned the room. "I'll sleep on the floor. Or that chaise."

She felt a flutter of relief, and a strange pang of regret.

"We're adults, Mr Hawke. I'm not going to ravish you if that's your fear. I'm not the one who craves intimacy."

That was a lie.

Desire coiled in her belly. She could school her thoughts, but not the flush of her skin, nor the pulse that thrummed in her throat, nor the ache she dared not name.

"Intimacy is the last thing I crave." He adjusted himself with a subtle shift of his stance. "Sometimes a man has no control over his body's … responses."

"Thank you for being honest." She draped the nightgown over the screen, smoothing her hand over the silk. "You're right. No more garden trysts. You may rule your world, but you could never give me what I need." She had to remember that. She prayed she remembered that.

He swallowed as though his throat were dry. "And what is it you need, aside from someone to save you from the noose?"

She could have deflected. Offered a clever remark. But the truth pressed hard against her ribs. "A home. A family.

Love. The enduring kind. I'd like to be someone's everything, and would rather wander the world alone than settle for anything less."

He exhaled slowly, the moment stretching.

He knew he fell short.

A sharp knock punctuated the silence.

"That will be the wine. And our clothes."

He moved to the door, and she took a moment to breathe.

How was she here?

In a den of vice, with this man. A daughter too numb to grieve her father, yet could kiss a scoundrel in a moonlit garden. A runaway hunted by the law.

Her life was nothing but a fantasy.

An idyllic cottage in Scotland that might not exist. Another at Shadowmere that shouldn't feel like home, but it did. A suitor who kissed as though she were the air he needed to breathe. In truth, he was merely satisfying an itch.

"What the hell do you want?" Mr Hawke snapped, dragging her from her reverie. "Perhaps you have a death wish, madam."

Daphne stepped closer to the door, meeting the woman's harried gaze. "Mrs Foster?" So she had recognised her. "Can we help you? Weren't you attending to the gentleman across the hall?"

Her father's paramour had thrown a wool cloak over her harem costume, clutching it tight to her generous chest. The kohl lining her eyes was smudged, black streaking her cheeks. Her greying blonde hair was a hopeless tangle. Strawberry juice stained her chin.

Mrs Foster made to step over the threshold, but Mr Hawke blocked her way. "If you've something to say to Miss Harland, say it to me."

The woman peered over his broad shoulder. "Your poor aunt thinks you're dead," she whispered, trying to push past him, but he had no intention of moving. "She believes the man who harmed Jacob hurt you too. She's been out day and night searching. Even hired a retired runner from Bow Street."

Daphne doubted her aunt cared in any true, maternal way. Not after pushing the match with Mr Irving. She was likely hunting her down now, ready to drag her to the altar and collect her ten thousand pounds.

"I left a note." A note saying she couldn't marry Mr Irving. She had a gift for endurance. Just not enough to suffer that slobbering fool.

Mrs Foster crouched slightly as she tried to peer around Mr Hawke's frame. "She never mentioned a note. Only that something dreadful must have happened to you as well." Her wary gaze shifted to Mr Hawke. "It seems she has every reason to fear the worst."

Mr Hawke gave a mirthless chuckle as he looked down at the woman. "Typical. Save her, and I'm the villain. Try to sell her off, and you're mourned like a saint."

She couldn't argue with that.

Not when he was prepared to pay the Moseley brothers an extortionate sum. And she had the odd suspicion he'd thump Mr Irving if their paths crossed.

"Save her?" Mrs Foster's unladylike snort rang through the corridor. "You've dragged her to a pariah's pit. Her dear papa is dead, killed by you no—"

"I have an alibi. A handful of witnesses who can vouch for my whereabouts." He reached for the doorknob. "Good night, madam. Enjoy your strawberries."

Mrs Foster sprang upright and shoved at the door, forcing herself between the frame and jamb. "Please, let me take you home, Miss Harland. We'll leave together. Lord Ainsley will protect us. We can—"

"Ainsley?" Mr Hawke gave a dry laugh. "Fetch him. Let's see if he plays the intrepid hero once he sees the mark."

Daphne intervened. She stepped to his side, her fingers brushing his arm to gently move it aside.

"Mr Hawke is my protector now." It sounded absurd, like she'd soon be feeding him grapes while he lounged in a milk bath. "My father has been dead a week, Mrs Foster, and I can only assume you're here for the same reason."

Mrs Foster had the decency to blush. "What else was I to do but seek assistance? Your father left me in a terrible predicament. He hasn't paid the lease on my townhouse in months."

Daphne looked at her, suspicion rising.

What if Mrs Foster saw this as a chance to abandon her strawberry dessert and seize something sweeter? To deliver Daphne to Mr Irving and claim the bounty herself?

"I'm sure Lord Ainsley will cover any arrears." Daphne slid her hand around Mr Hawke's solid arm. Heavens. Since when did granite radiate heat? "Just as my benefactor will protect me."

His green eyes warmed as they found hers. "Always."

She stared, transfixed.

And, dare she admit, a little confused.

"Good night, Mrs Foster." He straightened to an intimidating height. "Don't interfere in my business again."

He closed the door, forcing Mrs Foster out, but not before she cried, "I shall find a way to rescue you, my dear. You may count on it."

The echo of it lingered, as did the silence that followed.

He turned to her, the click of the latch sealing her fate. "It seems I'll have to fortify my defences if I want to keep you, Miss Harland."

Her breath caught. Not from fear, but from the look in his eyes. Like she was a treasure unearthed by accident. One he had no business coveting, but could no longer ignore.

"I belong to no man, Mr Hawke." Her voice came steadier than she felt. What must it be like to belong to him? "The truest measure of a woman's affection is that she stays when she's free to leave."

He inhaled too sharply.

Something shifted in the room.

"Am I to wake one morning and find the hearth cold, the cottage empty, the armoire bare?"

She held his gaze. "Perhaps."

He didn't step back, but she felt the steel return to his spine. He would seize control the only way he knew how.

"You have fifteen minutes to undress." He moved to the door, fingers already on the lock. "To slip beneath those gold silk sheets and build a fortress with the pillows."

"Where are you going?"

Several scenarios flashed through her mind. She pictured him striding through the crowd, women reaching for him, their hands on his chest and his jaw, drawn to him despite the danger.

She could stomach him fresh from a brawl but not the thought of his mouth on another woman's skin.

"To fetch our clothes and the wine. Try not to miss me too much."

The door shut with a click. The lock slid home.

He'd left her behind.

Locked in. And he'd taken the key.

The devil.

She might have stood rooted to the spot in a fit of rage, or plucked a pin from her coiffure to pick the lock. She could hammer on the door, call for Mrs Foster.

But in truth, she didn't want rescuing. She wanted to return to her quaint cottage at Shadowmere and continue living her fabricated life.

An icy fear twisted around her heart.

What if she didn't want to leave at the end of the month?

What if she accepted Lady Soanes' gift, stood alone on the windswept banks of Loch Tay, and realised she'd left her soul in a ramshackle cottage in Kingston upon Thames?

There was no time to dwell on it now.

Getting into the gown had been hard enough. Getting out of it might prove impossible. The only alternative was letting Mr Hawke loose on the hooks, though she doubted she'd survive the strain.

With a contortionist's grit, she managed.

The veal and minted potatoes offered ample incentive, as did her rumbling stomach. She'd eaten, combed her hair and climbed into bed before Mr Hawke returned.

He entered without looking at the bed. He noticed her empty plate and she could have sworn he smiled. It died the moment he saw the red gown draped over the dressing screen.

"Tell me you're not wearing that scandalous nightgown?"

"No. Just my simple shift."

"That may be worse." He set the crystal glasses on the dressing table and uncorked the wine. "Claret?"

"No, thank you."

Tension tightened the air between them. She felt like a virgin bride on her wedding night. Well, she was chaste. But he most definitely wasn't groom material.

"Do you mind if I drink?"

"Of course not. Where are my clothes?"

His eyes found hers, lingered, then drifted to her loose

dark hair tumbling over one shoulder. His jaw tightened; he muttered something under his breath and drank straight from the bottle.

She watched his tongue trace his lower lip.

Who knew she would envy a devilish drop of claret?

"Mrs Flavell is gathering a few things she thinks might be useful. Her maid will press your old dress. She insists it will all be sent up by dawn."

"Probably a safeguard to prevent us from leaving."

"Probably." He took another long swig of wine, then shrugged out of his coat and hung it on the hook in the gilded armoire. "The damned thing reeks of opium."

She'd seen him in an untucked shirt before, dishevelled and rakish. But not like this. Not in his shirtsleeves, his waistcoat fitted snug to his frame, every button a threat to her composure. The flicker of candlelight across crisp linen, the tension in his shoulders, the easy power in the way he moved —it all made her far too aware of him as a man.

Life had just become a little more complicated.

He crossed the room and took his plate from the nightstand.

"Your food will be cold," she said, desperate to talk about anything but where he might sleep tonight.

"I don't mind." He sat at the dressing table and ate in silence.

She shifted, trying to get comfortable.

The silence stretched, thick with things unsaid.

"Can I ask you something?" she said when it all became too much.

He paused mid-bite. "Ask. I can't promise I'll answer."

"If you could turn back the clock, knowing me as you do now, would you still have asked me to dance at the Templeton ball?"

He inhaled so deeply she thought he might not stop. Then he stood, took the long bolster, and laid it between them in the centre of the bed.

The cushion felt both merciful and cruel, a reminder that he was close enough to touch, and yet entirely out of reach.

He stretched out beside it, crossing his arms behind his head, eyes fixed on the hieroglyphics etched into the ceiling panels.

"Well?" she asked softly. "Would you?"

"Go to sleep, Miss Harland." He turned his back to her, and the space between them grew colder by degrees. "Trust me. Neither of us want to hear the answer."

CHAPTER TEN

"What do you think it says?" Miss Harland held the sealed letter in her hand, her finger tracing the red wax. The carriage bounced through a rut in the road, and she gripped it like the last piece of wreckage in a volatile sea.

In truth, he didn't know. And didn't want to care.

He was simply glad she was speaking again.

She'd barely said two words since posing that damnable question last night. A question he'd mentally wrestled while his body lay stiff as mortuary stone.

He hadn't answered because he didn't dare.

If he had, he wouldn't have stopped at words. He'd have kissed her senseless, rolled her beneath him, and given her the only answer his body knew.

He'd woken first, harder than he'd been in years, only to find them facing each other, their hands brushing across the bolster. Ramsey would flay him alive if he'd witnessed the cosy scene. Dominic Hawke did not lace fingers with a woman, let alone stroke them in his sleep.

But by God, she'd looked beautiful.

Lashes dark against porcelain skin. Lips parted, breathing slow, sinfully slow.

"I believe Mrs Flavell wanted you to open it," he said, though last night's question lingered between them like the ghost of their kiss. "Preferably before we reach Kingston."

"Do you think Mrs Flavell spoke the truth?" She stared at the letter as if the contents might answer a centuries-old mystery. "I find it hard to believe my mother would call at Grosvenor Place. That she would trust a woman with Mrs Flavell's reputation."

"Mothers keep secrets too." He thought of his own, of how she'd died protecting hers. "She may have turned to an old friend to spare you pain."

Yet his mother had confided in no one.

Why would she, when she didn't trust a soul?

She met his gaze for the first time in an hour. "Do you know, when you're not playing king of the underworld, you can be quite thoughtful."

"Keep it to yourself. Tell Ramsey and I'll deny it."

She smiled. "Let it be our secret then."

In the space between breaths, he felt it again. That trace of connection. That odd affinity with a woman who should hate him.

"Keep our kiss a secret, too," he said.

She nodded, not from embarrassment, it seemed. "And that you called my name in your sleep last night."

Bloody hell. "A nightmare, most likely."

"I'm not sure. You made a strange sort of hum."

"There must have been a bee in the room."

"At Grosvenor Place? In late September?"

"Just open the letter, Miss Harland, before you die of curiosity."

She chuckled. "So formal? You called me darling Daphne in the dark last night."

"Now I know you're lying. 'Darling' isn't in my vocabulary."

She glanced at the letter again but didn't break the seal. If she didn't stop nibbling her lip, she'd make it bleed.

"Would you like me to read it first?" Cursed saints. Was he destined to become her hero? Would he lay his coat on the ground so she could avoid the mud?

She handed him the letter. "Would you mind?"

He'd expected her to refuse. That she trusted him with something so personal was more than he deserved. "Be assured, I shall keep your confidence."

"I know. You may be many things, but you're not an idle gossip."

He broke the seal. A waft of perfume made his nose itch as he peeled back the folds, his heart racing. He read slowly at first, then faster, the words blurring as the pattern emerged. The pallor. The cramping. The barely concealed fear.

He swallowed hard, willing his hand to steady.

Despite armour of steel, the words pierced clean through.

"What is it? Tell me." She clapped a hand to her mouth. "It's something terrible. I can see the horror in your eyes."

Horror was the right word.

But he wasn't reliving a nightmare.

He was understanding it for the first time.

"How did your mother die?" He fought to keep the desperation from his voice, but he needed answers as much as she did.

"Dysentery. That's what my father said." She shifted to the edge of the seat. "Does Mrs Flavell suggest something else?"

Panic flickered in her eyes when he didn't answer.

She grabbed his knee as if needing an anchor. "Tell me."

He cleared his throat. "She went to see Mrs Flavell to ask how a lady might avoid conceiving."

Miss Harland firmed her grip on his knee, though he was grateful for the distraction. "That can't be right. My mother desperately wanted another child. My parents tried for years."

"Mrs Flavell feared it was already too late," he said. "Your mother looked pale. She clutched her abdomen and had to rush to use the pot."

He'd seen those signs before. In his own home. Though his mother had blamed the damp, bad meat, or the water from the well.

Both women. Both sick. Neither surviving the year.

He knew what killed his mother.

He had never spoken it aloud.

He braced himself before reading the next line.

"She asked Mrs Flavell for a loan. Your father kept a tight grip on the purse strings." Gamblers always did when the money was gone. "She said she needed to repay a debt but refused to name her creditor."

He tried to breathe deeply without alerting her, but the hollow look his mother had worn in her final days haunted him still.

His suspicions had been correct.

She'd been using her body to settle the debts.

Lord Harland had forced both women into impossible predicaments.

Now all three were dead.

Had the Moseley brothers killed him?

Or was there another player in this damned game?

Perhaps he should hire an enquiry agent, but he wouldn't drag his mother's memory through the dirt.

"Why did your mother struggle to conceive?" he asked, though he couldn't tell her why the answer mattered.

"My—" She shook her head as if dazed. "My father had a riding accident years ago. His physician seemed certain that was the cause."

Cold crept through Dominic's chest.

Then who the hell had fathered his mother's unborn child? He needed that physician's report.

"Did you ever see strange tinctures at home?" His tone was too sharp, like some overeager Bow Street runner. But he needed to fill the gaps in his mother's story. "Pennyroyal? Savine? Anything meant to bring on her courses?"

"I—I don't know. I was young. Naive to such things. Why are you asking?"

He gathered her hand. "My mother would take a tincture when things got desperate. Pennyroyal, a splash of rue, mixed in gin. She claimed it was for her nerves, but she always took it after my father came home drunk. She'd not have another child suffer for his addictions."

She looked down at their clasped hands, firming her grip, and he clung to it like a lifeline. "You think the story about the riding accident is a lie? That my mother took a tincture for the same reason?"

He watched her closely. "I don't know what to think. But the answer is buried in the past. We'll keep digging until we find it."

He needed to know why Harland was in debt to the Moseley brothers, how long he'd been gambling, and whether his own father had owed money to the same men.

She nodded, tugging her hand free. "We both deserve peace. A chance at happiness. To leave this bitterness behind and start anew elsewhere."

Was there no end to her romantic notions?

Could she not see that life was cruel?

"I'll never leave Shadowmere."

It was a vow, not a choice.

He wondered how she imagined her future. Perhaps walking hand in hand through a meadow with a devoted beau, picnicking beneath the summer sun, making love on the grass. A dream far removed from the world he knew.

"You mean to host wild parties forever?" She looked at him as one might a shoeless urchin.

"Not forever." He folded the note and handed it to her.

"Good." She slipped it into her pocket. "You deserve a better life. One that doesn't chip away at your soul."

It was too late for him.

The die had been cast long ago.

They settled back in their seats, watching the countryside roll by. His thoughts were fixed firmly in the past, and he suspected hers were too.

Peace was the only thing he craved.

Not the only thing. He cast a glance at her mouth, at the swell of her breasts in the fitted pelisse, the soft thighs he didn't need to imagine. He had already admired them in breeches.

But he'd be over it soon.

Vengeance was the only constant left.

Shadowmere's grand iron gates came into view. Beyond them rose his house, weathered grey walls and ugly spires. The heaviness in his chest returned.

Damn this place.

Ramsey was on the steps, hands braced on his hips, before the carriage reached the portico. His grimace could put the gargoyles to shame.

"Don't expect a warm welcome," Dominic said.

Ramsey yanked open the carriage door, inclined his head

to Miss Harland, then growled, "Where the hell have you been? You didn't say you'd stay the night. We've been worried sick."

"We had no choice." He alighted, boots crunching the gravel. He could hardly admit he'd stayed for Miss Harland. "Mrs Flavell had information we needed. The woman made it impossible to refuse her hospitality."

"You stayed in Grosvenor Place?" Ramsey glanced between them like they'd been caught in a naked clinch. "And it never occurred to you that might not be wise? Miss Harland has no hope of returning to society now."

Good. He'd not see her handed back to wolves dressed as gentlemen. At least he was honest about his intentions.

She let Ramsey help her down, much to Dominic's chagrin. The sight of her fingers wrapped around another man's hand stirred something dark and territorial in him.

"It was my idea, Mr Ramsey." She smiled sweetly. "The world is a big place. I don't need to confine myself to London. I've long considered a tour of Bath."

"Bath?" Dominic scoffed. "Full of gout-ridden colonels and simpering widows. You'd be bored within a week."

"Oxford then."

"Full of boys who think learning Latin makes them men."

"Where do you suggest I go, Mr Hawke?"

He shrugged. "I'll think on it."

Kingston was the last place he should suggest.

Ramsey frowned at their exchange. If he was jealous, he could bugger off. Helping her fix the cottage all week didn't give him any claim on her.

"Did you get what you needed in London?" Ramsey said.

Dominic ought to have recited their list of accomplishments, but all he could think about was her tongue tangled with his.

No. He hadn't got what he needed.

He doubted he would until she was beneath him in bed.

"Mrs Haggert has agreed to arrange a meeting with the Moseley brothers. Expect her letter. Alert me the moment it arrives."

"The witness has been kidnapped," she added, though all Brown had done was step into a carriage. "His maid is almost certainly his lover. It's all rather intriguing."

"What did Mrs Flavell tell you?"

"Can we discuss it inside?" Dominic gestured towards the steps, where he'd found his father sleeping on occasion, too drunk to reach the door. "We haven't eaten since supper."

Ramsey shifted his stance. "There've been some developments here since you left. Best you hear them before you walk through that door."

Dominic inwardly groaned.

If this was about the Masque, it could wait.

"A man named Irving called last night. Brought a big brute with him. Asked for Miss Harland by name."

She clutched her chest and glanced around as though the fiend lurked behind the topiary. "What did he say? You didn't tell him I'd been here? You didn't mention the gardener's cottage?"

"I told him I'd never heard of you. That Hawke was out of town." Ramsey sniffed. "There was a scuffle, but Beattie marched them down the drive with two rifles aimed at their arses. Reckon they'll be back."

Irving clearly had a death wish.

"Make sure the footmen are armed. Keep the gates chained until the Masque. Hire more men if necessary."

He didn't look at her, but he felt her fear as keenly as if it were his own—her shallow breath, the stillness in her limbs.

It roused something fierce in him.

Something he had no right naming.

"Could you not have told us that inside?" Dominic said.

Ramsey gave an exasperated sigh. "We've another unwanted visitor. Lady Sanders arrived at dawn. She says she's not leaving without—"

"My aunt is here?" Miss Harland paled.

"She's come to take you home."

Dominic tensed. Like hell she would.

"Sell me to Mr Irving, more like." Her voice shook with fury. "She only lived with my father because she was broke. Uncle Samuel left everything to his secret family in Norfolk."

"The Moseley brothers will expect her to repay the ten thousand pounds," Dominic said. He knew exactly why Lady Sanders was here. Desperate people did foolish things.

"Don't tell her you've agreed to pay the debt on my behalf," Miss Harland replied. "She's been running up credit herself, with no thought of who will settle the bills. She'll be looking for a way to line the coffers."

Dominic caught Ramsey's widening eyes.

"You're paying Harland's debt?"

"It's a trifle," he said flatly. He didn't owe anyone an explanation. "The only way to keep Miss Harland from being marched aboard a ship in Fobbing Marshes."

"And I shall find the means to repay your kindness, sir."

"No need," Dominic said. "Perhaps it will earn me a step towards the pearly gates." Though he doubted he'd ever reach them. "I only wish someone had done the same for my mother."

There. Let Ramsey call him a fool now.

"Where is Lady Sanders? Beattie had better be her shadow."

Ramsey jerked his chin towards the hall. "In the drawing room. Taking tea. Beattie brought out the Sèvres."

"Then let's get this over with."

Miss Harland leaned closer as they mounted the stairs. "I'm not leaving with her. I'm of age. She has no claim on me."

"Trust me, Miss Harland. You'll not leave here unless it's of your own free will."

He felt her gaze on him as they crossed the dark oak hall.

"If ever the day should come and you find I'm gone ..." Her voice was quieter now. "Know it wasn't you. I'd change nothing about the night you stormed into Lord Templeton's ballroom and asked me to dance."

It wasn't the first time she'd mentioned leaving.

Why did he feel her slipping through his fingers? He fought the urge to reach for her hand. To hold it tight. To anchor her to him.

He'd change one thing.

He wouldn't have left her to find her own way. To face the gossip alone. To shoulder it all without him.

My God. He was a mess.

Maybe it would be easier if she did leave.

"I gave you little choice," he said.

The truth sat bitter on his tongue.

"Don't you know me by now, Mr Hawke?" Her laugh was almost playful. "I danced with you because I wanted to. The decision was entirely selfish."

He wasn't sure whether to feel flattered or fleeced.

"I suppose you kissed me to secure your ruin."

"And because I suffered a brief bout of madness."

If he were any other man, he'd pull her close and kiss her senseless. Say things he'd never dared admit, not even to himself.

"And I kissed you last night for precisely the same reason."

"Then we're even, Mr Hawke. We need never think of it again."

He nearly laughed.

He'd thought of little else all morning.

Lady Sanders' tea sloshed over the rim of her china cup when she laid eyes on her niece. Dressed in full mourning, her steel-grey hair scraped into a severe knot beneath a black bonnet, she thrust the saucer at Beattie, splashing drops across his pristine coat.

"Daphne! Thank heavens you're alive." She rose from the velvet chair in a rustle of stiff skirts, ignoring Dominic entirely. "I feared you were lying dead in a ditch … or worse. Mr Moseley is said to favour ladies of fine lineage."

Miss Harland didn't cross the room to greet her aunt. She remained at his side. "I'm perfectly well. Did you not receive my note?"

"Note?" Lady Sanders' eyes widened in horror. "Your father was murdered and tossed in the Thames, and you're worried about a missing letter?"

"Don't pretend you're not relieved. He left you his worldly possessions. Surely there's enough to rent a town-house somewhere."

"South of the river. What on earth am I to do in Bermond-sey?" She gave a delicate shudder, as though she'd been banished to the Arctic. "And really, it's no way to talk about the man who raised you."

Miss Harland stiffened. "The man who planned to sell me to that decrepit, cabbage-loving oaf? Who made our lives an utter misery? Who dined at White's while we ate bread and Cook's tasteless jam? The man who—"

"Yes, yes. Your father was a wastrel. Of that there's no doubt." The lady acknowledged him with a grunt. "And if you had Mr Hawke kill him, I daresay no one would blame you."

"I have an alibi," he said coolly. "Let me remind you, you're in my home and will show me the respect I'm owed."

Lady Sanders gave a mocking snort. "Mr Hawke, you run a bawdy house. Shadowmere can hardly be considered a respectable abode."

Dominic almost smiled.

"On the contrary. I lease rooms to the elite. What they choose to do behind closed doors is their affair, not mine."

Lady Sanders waved a hand at Miss Harland. "And is seducing my niece just another one of your rented entertainments? Or do you plan to offer her to your friends when you tire of her?"

The vein in his temple pulsed. His vision narrowed on the matron with a serpent's tongue. Slowly, he withdrew his watch. "You have two minutes to say what you came for before I toss you out."

Lady Sanders' mouth opened and closed like a startled fish. "I—I came to take my niece home. Away from this perfidious den."

"Home?" Miss Harland stepped forward, one hand settling on her hip. "Or straight to the docks and a ship bound for Bengal?"

The matron's cheeks flushed. "Don't be ridiculous. The best I can offer is a townhouse in Bermondsey. You will have to lower your sights. A solicitor or a banker perhaps. But we'll find you a respectable suitor."

Miss Harland was undeterred. "My place is at Shadowmere now. In whatever capacity that may be. Mr Hawke might be so eager to keep me, he'll propose."

Maybe in some other life. One where he wasn't jaded and

half the ton wasn't out for his blood. Sooner or later, he'd fall short. And she deserved better.

"Propose? Mr Hawke?" Lady Sanders sneered. "They'll have you in Bedlam, girl, with such crazed notions."

Even Beattie couldn't stomach the absurdity. He coughed, nearly choking on his own spittle.

"Was there anything else, Lady Sanders?" Dominic nodded towards the hall. "Unless you'd care to stay for the Masque. I'm sure we could paint you as Pomona and pin a few leaves over what's left of your modesty."

The old vulture stiffened under her mourning bonnet, lips pinched. "Filthy swine. My niece will come to her senses soon enough." Her hand swept the room and stalled, as though she'd expected tawdry excess and found refinement instead. "She was made for better things than … this."

Better? Four months crammed aboard a rat-infested steamship, bound for Bengal? Playing broodmare to a red-faced merchant eager for heirs and a pliant young wife?

"What's better than freedom?" He was on a similar journey himself—to shed his father's shackles, to seek retribution so those closest to him might finally rest in peace. "Perhaps you should focus on finding out who killed your brother. Name a suspect, and I'll investigate."

"Sergeant Carter is more than capable," she countered. "I expect he'll want to know what happened to Daphne."

He didn't take kindly to veiled threats. "By all means, tell him. Your next move will determine whether you're sincere or just another greedy wretch with a despicable plan."

He'd stake a fortune on the latter.

Had anyone in Miss Harland's life not sought to profit from her? No wonder she hadn't wept for her father. No wonder she wasn't scrambling to start afresh with that cold-blooded relic of an aunt.

"I think that concludes our business." He flicked a hand towards the door. "No need to finish your tea. Beattie will see you out."

Lady Sanders drew back as though struck. "Daphne, will you stand there and allow him to speak to me in this vile manner?"

"After your cutting remarks, Mr Hawke is well within his rights."

Lady Sanders snatched up her reticule. "I expected better of my brother's daughter." She drew herself up. "When you decide to behave sensibly, my door remains open."

It was hardly surprising he felt the urge to shield her from these fiends. And he was beginning to forget that it was vengeance, not devotion, that had brought him here.

Guilt settled heavily in his chest. He was losing sight of the plan. Forgetting the woman and child whose pain had set him on this path.

He didn't care who had killed Harland.

This was never about his own suffering.

It was never meant to be about her.

It was about making someone answer.

Happiness had never been the prize.

Daphne Harland was not meant for a man like him.

CHAPTER ELEVEN

Daphne stood beside Mr Beattie in the upper gallery, watching two maids polish the vast ballroom until it gleamed. A footman balanced on a ladder, trimming the wicks of the chandelier with quiet concentration.

Preparations for the Autumn Masque were underway. Gilded mirrors lined every wall. Crimson curtains framed the terrace windows. A colour that spoke of passions Mr Hawke preferred to keep hidden.

Mounted above the grand fireplace, a pair of oversized Venetian fox masks watched the room, one snarling, the other leering. Trust Mr Hawke to choose menace and mischief. A testament to his conflicting nature, no doubt.

"As you offered to help, Miss Harland, you may begin here." Mr Beattie spoke with the gravity of a general on campaign. "Take this list. Check the maids' work. There's no room for error. Precision is key."

She accepted the list with a nod of regret.

The tasks for the Masque filled both sides of the page. Still, it was better than spending another hour alone in the cottage, thinking about Mr Hawke. She'd hardly seen him since he escorted Aunt Augusta out under a storm of theatrical protests two days ago.

He'd left Shadowmere on foot yesterday, just before dusk, two white roses in hand. Mr Ramsey claimed he'd gone for a walk, but the man who returned looked dreadfully solemn.

"Do you have any questions, Miss Harland?" Mr Beattie asked.

She did. Too many to mention.

Who wanted her father dead? That should have been the most pressing. Where was Mr Irving now? Abroad, she hoped. Would Mrs Foster appear in the dead of night, toss a sack over her head, and bundle her out of the house?

But only one thought consumed her.

Would she ever feel the warmth of Mr Hawke's lips again? The weight of his body against hers? The murmur of his voice in her ear?

Fickle fool. Read the list and forget about him.

How could she, when his scent clung to the air?

When every room hummed with his presence?

"Ensure screens are decorated and positioned in every shadowed corner of the ballroom," she read, dragging her thoughts back to the task. She looked up to find Mr Beattie twisting the ends of his moustache into perfect points. "Screens in a ballroom? Whatever for?"

"It's not for us to question the guests' habits, Miss Harland." He turned and barked at the footman below. "Careful, Emery! That's Italian crystal. One slip on that ladder and you'll bring the whole thing down."

"Italian crystal." She hummed in appreciation. "Mr Hawke knows how to host a lavish party."

She thought of the red crystal flutes that had arrived that

morning. The silk-lined marquees in the garden. Each one complete with a velvet daybed draped in expensive furs and the thick scent of incense in the air.

"One gets what one pays for, ma'am."

"How much *are* the tickets for the Masque?"

Mr Beattie glanced behind him and lowered his voice. "At five hundred pounds a head, the guests expect both privacy and spectacle."

"Five hundred pounds?" Daphne gripped the balustrade. Her aunt would have reached for a vinaigrette. "How many attend?"

"Anywhere up to fifty."

"Good heavens. That would buy a townhouse in Mayfair. Or a small kingdom abroad."

Mr Hawke must be wealthier than Midas. So why host parties for people he despised? It had to be about owning secrets. About holding power over London's elite.

"How long does he intend to host these events?"

How much money did one man need?

"Mr Hawke keeps his plans close to his chest. That's all I shall say on the matter." Mr Beattie tapped the parchment in her hand. "Back to the tasks. I expect them completed before day's end."

She glanced at the sheet. "Apple garland safety?"

"Make sure they're trailed through the balusters. We'll not have some drunken lord tripping over greenery and tumbling to his death."

"Of course."

They discussed a host of ridiculous points, the most shocking being a plan to station violinists outside each tent so guests wouldn't have to hear their own debauchery.

Daphne was still absorbing that when Mr Ramsey burst

into the ballroom below, clutching the base of a marble statue as if he'd wrestled it from a museum.

"Where do you want her? In here or on the terrace?"

Mr Hawke had the other end. He was in his shirtsleeves, his cravat missing, his shirt open at the throat. One hand gripped the head. The other was planted firmly on Venus' bare marble breast.

Daphne drew a sharp breath.

Every nerve in her body sparked to life.

Her gaze fixed on his hand, the way his thumb brushed over the stone peak. A shiver chased down her spine. Her nipples tightened, a maddening ache beneath her corset.

He wasn't touching her. Not even looking at her. Yet somehow she could feel the heat of his palm. The warm stirrings of arousal.

"In here," Mr Hawke said, adjusting his grip without a hint of shame. "We'll drape her in chiffon like a goddess of autumn."

That's when he looked up, as if her soul had called to him. Their gazes met and he almost lost his footing.

Every intimate moment they'd shared passed through her mind. His hand at her back, dipping so low her pulse raced, every muscle in her belly tightening. His tongue so deep in her mouth she'd forgotten her own name.

His heat. His scent. The weight of his body against hers.

The scrape of his jaw against her neck.

The way he growled when she bit his lower lip.

She might have dreamt that part.

He blinked. Just once. As if the memories struck him, too.

Mr Ramsey tugged at Venus' base, too preoccupied with the weight to notice the charged silence. "I'll drop her if we don't move."

Mr Hawke didn't answer right away. His gaze remained locked on hers, one hand still planted on the statue's breast.

Slowly, his thumb circled the peak.

The scoundrel.

She forced herself to look away, muttered something about inspecting garlands, and turned for the stairs. Anything to escape that gaze before it burned through her stays.

She needed air. She needed a safe place to calm her pulse. And to maybe hit herself over the head with a skillet.

The cottage was hardly a sanctuary.

The valise Mrs Flavell had given the coachman was still on the chair and contained the oddest assortment of things: a red oriental wrapper with pretty gold orchids, a wool shawl, and a tin of Earl Grey tea. Warm stockings with sweet little ribbons. Plain undergarments. A mahogany case containing a set of pocket pistols, complete with dangerous accessories.

Perhaps she was meant to seduce Mr Hawke, drown him in tea, shoot him, and wrap his body in a cotton chemise. The stockings and shawl were for warmth while she dug his grave.

She'd need one more taste of him first.

She wasn't a complete martyr.

"Are you talking to yourself, Miss Harland?"

She stilled.

Good God, he was here. In the cottage.

She daren't turn around, not when her traitorous eyes would seek the glimpse of dark hair at his open collar.

"Are you sickening for something, angel?"

His voice was smooth as treacle. The endearment a blade to cut the strings on her stays. To strip her bare.

She swung around, words dissolving in her throat.

He filled the doorway, his hands braced on the lintel

above, a devilish smile dusting his lips. "Are you going to invite me in?"

From him, even a simple comment felt ruinous. "You're supposed to wait outside and knock at the front door. Not assume admittance."

His forest-green eyes trailed over her. "I've never been one for etiquette. Everyone knows I'm rude and uncouth."

"What do you want, Mr Hawke?" She forced her spine straight, and his gaze drifted downward, lingering where the fabric stretched over her breasts. A look as potent as a caress. "I've no time to waste. I must finish this list for Mr Beattie, or risk a court-martial."

He laughed at that.

Oh, he was most dangerous when happiness glimmered in those intense eyes. She couldn't bear to look at the man crippled by two white roses.

"You invited me to see the stars, remember."

She frowned, annoyed he felt he could pick her up and put her down whenever he pleased. "You're seven hours early. I presumed you'd found a better offer. You left the house at twilight carrying flowers."

Was there a woman in the village? One stronger than her, able to shrug off his charm? Perhaps she'd never dared to taste the devil's lips. If she had, he'd be trudging through the dark most nights.

A shadow crossed his face. His shoulders dipped, just slightly. There it was again, that rough sigh that sounded as though it had clawed its way up from deep underground.

"They were for my mother's grave."

The air chilled, as if his mother had reached through the veil to smooth the hair from his brow. Just as she longed to do now.

Inside she crumpled.

She knew that haunted look.

She'd seen it in her own reflection too many times.

"Few people pay their respects at night," she said through a tightening throat. "Grief feels heavier in the dark."

Like a cloak made of lead.

He straightened. "Perhaps I needed a reminder."

"A reminder?"

"Of whose soul I must set free."

It took a few seconds to make sense of his thoughts. He feared he was losing sight of his goal. He was his mother's champion, not hers.

"No one would question your devotion to her. Everything you do is in the name of justice."

His gaze roved over her. "Not everything."

He didn't need to say what he meant. It lived in the space between them. An attraction so compelling they both behaved like fools.

"Why are you really here?"

"You know why."

"I want to hear it from your own lips."

He looked at the open valise on the chair. "It's not to see what delights Mrs Flavell packed for you, though I am intrigued."

"It's not what you think. Merely practical things. No whip or shackles. No elixir to loosen a lady's inhibitions."

He stepped into the room, and the space closed in. "I don't want to fasten you to the bed, Miss Harland. I don't want you submissive."

Her breath hitched. She could feel his gaze on her skin, like sunlight through a windowpane, warm and inescapable.

"What do you want, Mr Hawke?"

He advanced, a predatory gleam in his eyes. "To remind

you there's nothing to fear from Irving, the Moseley brothers, or Templeton."

"You make those assurances daily." He was so near, her heart pounded. A strange tingling traced the length of her spine.

"I'm yet to mention the true danger."

"If it's to mind the apple garlands, Mr Beattie told me."

"It's not the apple garlands, though the same warning applies." He reached for the tendril of hair brushing her cheek, stroking it and letting it slip through his fingers. "You should avoid the main staircase. You should avoid me, as one might a lone wolf on the plains."

She could no more avoid him than a moth could a flame.

"Is that your way of saying you're hungry?"

His tongue skimmed his lips. "Not hungry. Ravenous."

She swallowed hard.

"But you know that," he murmured.

"How could I, when you avoid me?"

His fingers trailed along her jaw. The pad of his thumb swept across her mouth. "Perhaps I don't want you to regret the things we might do. I can't have you without offering the protection of my name. And I'm the last man you should marry."

Marry.

The word struck harder than his touch.

She had not asked for vows. Had not asked for protection. She wanted him as he was. Dangerous, unrepentant, hers for a stolen hour.

His hand drifted to the hollow of her throat.

The list slipped from her grasp and fell to the floor.

"I know what desire looks like on a woman, Miss Harland." His palm skimmed the curve of her breast, as though acquainting himself with its shape. "You want me. The question is … do you want a lesson in sin?"

She understood him well enough. He feared binding her to a future she might resent. Feared waking one day to find her gone and himself damned for it.

But she would not be pitied into safety. No man would decide her fate.

"We were never meant for vows and hearth fires," she lied. She had imagined both more than once. "Still, there's no pain in pleasure. And my troubles vanish when I lose myself in you."

The slow curl of his mouth was pure satisfaction. "Do you need time to consider what comes next, or shall I show you?"

Whatever it was, it would be unforgettable.

But she recalled Lady Soanes' warning:

Be yourself. Refuse any other role he gives you.

She lifted her chin. "As a consummate romantic, I'll require more than physical fulfilment, Mr Hawke. Perhaps you're the one who needs time to consider whether you wish to play this game of lovers."

He captured her hand, bold as sin, and guided it to the rigid proof of his desire. "Does that feel like the body of a man who needs time to think?"

Her breath caught. He was impossibly hard, the strength of him a heady, terrifying promise straining in his trousers. And heaven help her, she wasn't afraid.

"I want one night beneath the stars. Hot chocolate. And a secret you've never told a soul." She met his gaze, already imagining the night sky as their canvas. "For that, you can touch me. Anywhere."

He dragged his teeth over his bottom lip. "You barter with skill. I see no reason we can't both be thoroughly satisfied. Tomorrow night, then."

"Why wait? The stars should be out tonight."

His gaze dropped to her lips, then away as though fighting some internal war. "I have a prior engagement. There's no avoiding it." He didn't give her time to air her disappointment. "If you'd permit a late call, I'll come to you the moment I return."

She smiled to herself. He wanted this. Wanted her. The certainty of it eased something sharp and restless inside her. "Until tonight, then. I'll make the chocolate and have chairs and blankets ready."

He nodded, then reached for her hips, drawing her flush against him. "I'll need a parting gift. Something to convince me you're as eager as I am. Something to tame the beast until—"

She silenced him with her mouth.

There was no hesitation. No coy retreat. She didn't wait for him to coax her lips apart, for the gentle brush of his tongue against the seam.

She claimed him.

Her arms looped around his neck, her fingers sliding into the dark waves at his nape. She kissed him like she meant to drown in him, her tongue urgent, searching, matching the slow, desperate roll of their hips.

He groaned, deep and guttural.

There was nothing quite like the sound of Mr Hawke lost. It curled through her like silk drawn over bare skin, an intoxicating reward for every kiss, every tease of tongue and teeth.

His hands smoothed down to her bottom, gripping tight, pulling her closer still, letting her feel every inch of hard, unyielding muscle.

The pressure built low in her belly, a delicious throb pulsing between her legs, as heady as strong wine. Her body arched, desperate for more friction, more of him.

One kiss wasn't enough.

It would never be enough.

The thought ought to terrify her. No other man had ever made her feel like this. So desirable he could barely control himself.

"Hawke!" Mr Ramsey's sharp voice cut through her fevered thoughts.

She tore her mouth from Mr Hawke's, but he pressed a finger to her lips and whispered, "Hush, love."

She could barely catch her breath. Fire smouldered in his eyes, the same fire that scorched every inch of her skin.

"We should be grateful for the interruption," he murmured at her ear, then swept his mouth across hers. "Else we'd have skipped the stars and chocolate."

She slowly unlinked her arms from around his neck, her hands trailing over his shoulders before settling on his chest.

"I like this game," she said, telling herself that's all it was, that this connection between them would fade. "And I look forward to the next round."

He stepped back, his wry smile mirroring her own disappointment. "I knew you'd be trouble before we reached the dance floor."

"You seem to like trouble."

"Perhaps a little too much."

"I imagine you tire easily. This should be no different."

He studied her, perhaps trying to determine if her feelings matched her words. They didn't. They were as far apart as London and Bengal.

"Hawke. Are you there?" Mr Ramsey again, though he didn't enter the cottage.

Could he sense the tension from outside? Was he afraid he might find them flushed and straightening their clothes?

Mr Hawke should have been striding out the door. Yet something kept him in the cottage.

She felt it too. The unwillingness to part. That quiet fear this moment might be the only happiness either of them would ever know.

He kissed her again, a firm, lingering press of lips, like a soldier heading off to war. Little did she know how true that would soon feel.

Mr Ramsey called once more. This time his voice pierced through the haze of heat and hope, chilling her to the bone.

"Mr Irving is back. He brings a contract."

CHAPTER TWELVE

Dominic strode from the cottage, his pulse kicking like pistol fire. Ahead, Ramsey loitered on the path, no less irate.

"Tell me Irving is in his carriage, and you didn't let him through the blasted gate," Dominic snapped. "If I get within three feet of the fool, I'll throttle him with his own cravat."

Ramsey scrubbed a hand over his mouth. "Crocker had no choice, but he made them walk up the drive."

"Them?"

"Irving's not alone. He brought the magistrate."

Dominic stopped dead. "Sir Lionel?"

Ramsey gave a grim nod. "Seems the contract is binding."

"The devil it is." Fury surged through him. "Remain with Miss Harland. Lock the doors. I'll handle this."

Ramsey caught his arm. "Sir Lionel would love nothing more than to see you swinging from the gallows. Take Beattie with you. He's the voice of reason."

Sir Lionel Deane was a puritan who'd loathed Dominic's father. He would burn Shadowmere and all its sinners to ash, if the law allowed.

"Whatever happens, Miss Harland mustn't leave these grounds."

"Understood."

Dominic gripped Ramsey's arm. "She'll want to face Irving and curse him to Hades. Neither of them must know she's here."

"You're asking me to restrain her?"

"No." He was the only man who'd ever put his hands on her. "Just convince her it's wiser to stay out of sight."

He didn't envy his friend the task.

"Tell her I'll pay for her obedience. She may name her prize." She'd want something more precious than money. A piece of his soul.

Ramsey's brow shot up. "Dominic Hawke cowing to a woman?"

"You know how I am when faced with injustice," he said. "She doesn't deserve any of this. An honest man uses whatever means he has to make it right." If he could free her from Irving, perhaps the weight he carried would ease.

Ramsey gave a measured smile. "You can depend on me to do whatever you ask."

"I've never doubted it." He gripped Ramsey's shoulder in silent thanks, then turned and entered the house.

He passed through the hall, his pulse in time with his strides. The scent of Sir Lionel's sickly cologne lingered in the air. He was tempted to tell the man his wife brayed like a donkey in bed, that her lover was forever demanding her silence.

At the study door, Irving's coarse voice carried through the panels, insisting Beattie account for the delay. Dominic cricked his neck and flexed his fingers, though instinct urged him to curl them into fists.

"Sorry to keep you waiting." He sauntered into the room

keen to look upon the blackguard who'd chosen the wrong adversary.

Beattie made to move. "Shall I fetch refreshment, sir?"

"No. These gentlemen are leaving. You'll remain until they do."

"I'll leave once I have what I came for," said the pudgy man in the ill-fitting coat, easily sixty if he was a day. A sheen of perspiration clung to his upper lip.

The sight of him made Dominic's jaw tighten. This was the man who meant to claim her. What in God's name had Harland been thinking?

Dominic allowed himself a faint smile. "Tickets for the Masque are reserved for the well-bred. I'll need proof of your lineage if you mean to take part in the frivolities."

Sir Lionel scoffed. "You know full well why we're here."

"Do I?" Dominic replied. "Last time you came with unfounded allegations. I indulged you then. I won't today."

Today, he would not rely on violence, but on the skills he had honed while playing host to the depraved.

Irving reached into a leather satchel as creased as his brow. He pulled out a bound document and brandished it as though it were a royal decree. "I've come to claim my property. It's all here in the contract. Signed by the girl's own father before he passed."

Dominic fell silent, though his blood roared in his veins. "Did Sir Lionel not offer counsel?" he said smoothly. "Did he not quote from Blackstone's *Commentaries on the Laws of England*?"

The men shared confused glances.

"Explain the problem with the contract, Beattie."

Beattie stepped forward. "At three and twenty, a lady has full legal capacity and is not bound by her father's authority. The courts look unfavourably on marriages arranged for financial gain. With the father deceased, any supposed obligation lapses. And no money ever changed hands."

Dominic gave a smug grin. "Even if Miss Harland were here—and let me be clear, she is not—you have no legal right to enforce the contract." He tipped his chin at Sir Lionel. "As magistrate, you know that."

Irving was undeterred. "Here's a document dated the day before Mr Harland's body was pulled from the river." He thrust it at Beattie. "Miss Harland accepted Bank of England notes to the value of three thousand pounds, the balance payable upon exchange of vows."

"By accepting the notes, Miss Harland agreed to the terms," Sir Lionel added, his tone thick with self-satisfaction.

A cold suspicion slipped beneath Dominic's composure.

Ink had ruined more lives than bullets. These men were capable of far more than petty contracts. He didn't doubt Miss Harland, only the hands that drafted the paper.

He took the document from Beattie and scanned it, noting the date and signature. She couldn't have visited Irving after the ball. He'd already examined the timeline. And had she fleeced the fellow, she would not be living in a small cottage on an estate steeped in sin.

One detail stopped him cold.

The clerk's signature. Edward Brown.

The missing witness?

A common enough name. Too common.

Yet coincidence had a habit of circling him like a vulture.

Brown had drafted the contract. Witnessed Miss Harland's signature. Sworn he'd seen Harland murdered on Blackfriars Bridge.

Dominic said nothing.

He would let these men dig their own graves.

"If Miss Harland has any sense, she'll be miles away." He

crossed the room, fixed the merchant with a hard stare, and thrust the document back into his hand. "Take it to Bow Street. They're better at chasing shadows than I am."

"We need to search the house," Sir Lionel said.

"Do you have a warrant?" Dominic folded his arms across his chest. "You presume a great deal. I met Miss Harland but once. We shared a waltz. Why would she come here?"

"You shared more than a waltz," Irving countered, his face darkening like a bruised plum. "After the debacle at the Templeton ball, the girl ought to be grateful I'm willing to take her."

"Why are you?"

How did the bastard know?

Dominic braced himself. One coarse word about her and he'd forget every lesson in restraint.

"I have business in India and won't depart without securing my legacy. Her reputation is of no consequence. The arrangement serves my purpose."

"Oh." Dominic turned to Beattie. "Tell Mr Irving what we learnt about his licence for those ammunition factories in India."

Beattie inclined his head. "The latest dispatches from London ensure the Governor-General in Council will find reason to deny the application. Mr Hawke has secured a promise from a friend on the Secret Committee; should Chairman Sterling whisper a word of concern, any contract signed in India will be vetoed before the first pound is spent."

It wasn't set in stone. But he trusted Virginia Passmore to repay her debt to him, and mention her reservations to the Chairman while entertaining him in bed.

Irving stilled. Just for a second. Then he scoffed. "You wouldn't dare interfere in Crown interests." His fingers creased the edge of the contract.

"Wouldn't I? I'm capable of causing a damn sight more trouble than that. Consider it a matter of protecting the realm. The Crown must guard itself against vile vermin."

Beattie gave a discreet cough. "You omitted your recent dinner with the Lord Lieutenant, sir."

"Ah yes. I mentioned to Lord Bromley that our magistrate has a habit of bending the law when it suits him."

"You tread on dangerous ground," Sir Lionel snapped.

"As do you. You stand here without a warrant or lawful cause. Leave, before I give you a reason to regret lingering."

Sir Lionel held his gaze for a beat too long. Then he gathered his gloves from the desk with stiff fingers.

Irving stuffed the contract back into his satchel, the only proof of Edward Brown's involvement.

"After you, gentlemen." Dominic stepped aside, one arm extended towards the door. "I'm sure you'd appreciate an escort to the gate."

They didn't argue.

Hands clasped behind his back, he kept pace as they moved through the hall like condemned men.

On the steps outside, Irving muttered under his breath.

Dominic did not ask what was said. His voice cut through the murmur. "I'll see you broke and destitute if I have cause to look upon you again."

He did not slow as he escorted them down the sweep of gravel. Beyond the avenue of limes, Irving's carriage waited on the lane, dwarfed by the iron gates. Crocker was already out of the gatehouse and unfastening the chain.

Sir Lionel paused, as if he expected a final word.

Dominic gave him one. "Next time, bring a warrant."

He waited until the gates clanged shut behind them, and the carriage wheels rattled back along the lane.

Only then did the pressure ease.

St. Alard's Priory
Near Headley Heath, Surrey

The light was failing by the time Dominic reached St. Alard's Priory, the last smear of sunset fading behind the black ribs of the broken nave. Autumn had crept in without permission; the air carried that thin, metallic chill that sharpened the lungs and stilled the blood.

He pictured Miss Harland beneath a blanket, chocolate warming her hands, her eyes lifted to a sky not yet dark enough for stars. Had this been a summons from the devil, he would have ignored it. But these men were not so easily dismissed. They were brothers by circumstance, not blood.

His boots struck old stone as he crossed into the roofless chapel. The saints had long since lost their faces, worn smooth by rain and neglect. Men were easier to trust when their virtues had eroded.

He wasn't the first to arrive.

But they remained in the shadows, behind crumbling columns and fractured arches, standing among the ghosts of the past.

Saint-Clair would be the last to show himself. He was dead to anyone who had once known him by that name.

Not to Dominic. Nor to Montfort or Stanton.

This monthly meeting proved two things. The bond had not been severed. The oath was as strong as the day they made it. Eight years, and still the ton clung to the scandal like carrion birds to bone.

Seconds stretched.

Then he saw it—the glint of a coin in the darkness. Montfort moved without breath or footfall. Pale hair caught what little light remained. His expression was composed, almost scholarly, if one ignored the cold calculation in his eyes.

"You could divest a nun of her drawers and she'd be none the wiser," Stanton said as he entered the chapel. The Devil of Fleet Street never minced words. His greatcoat hung open, inky hair falling across his brow, eyes sharp and appraising as a barrister sizing up a liar.

Montfort chuckled softly. "As a man devoted to facts, you should know they wear none. Did you not study liturgy?"

Dominic emerged from the shadows. "We were spared the refinements of Oxford, forced to make do with experience."

"Oxford teaches more than refinements. How to creep past a snoring brute. How to refuse certain invitations after midnight."

"How a tragedy can unite men as brothers," came Saint-Clair's voice from the dark. "Toss your coins on the ground, gentlemen. After all, what's a pact without a little pomp and ceremony?"

Dominic cast his coin first. He had nothing to prove to these men.

Stanton flicked his with careless precision.

Montfort's barely sounded as it landed near his boots.

Saint-Clair stepped into view, the gentleman they had hanged in all but name, composure polished to a dangerous sheen. He flipped his coin through his fingers as he had the day they were forged. "*Veritas Vincit*," he said in his usual mocking tone. "Truth conquers. If only it could be relied upon."

They all stared at their bronze discs. The wolf stamped into the metal was Saint-Clair's idea, a reminder a man must be savage when protecting his own.

Daphne Harland slipped into his thoughts.

Irving was no different from the predators they'd once faced. And Dominic would not hesitate to bare his teeth.

"Business first," Saint-Clair said.

These meetings always began with a report.

Stanton retrieved his coin and slid it into his waistcoat pocket. He raked a hand through hair as dark as Miss Harland's. Dominic doubted it smelled of roses.

"There was a sighting of you on Hounslow Heath in last week's *Satirist*. Lady Askew claimed you held up her coach and stole her diamond and demantoid garnet pendant."

And Hounslow Heath had since become a fashionable haunt for ladies with restless imaginations.

Saint-Clair's mocking snort echoed through the ruins. "The *Satirist* likes to rake the dirt for truth. I may be an Englishman, but my blood once guarded the gates of Normandy for Viking jarls."

Dominic picked up his coin, rubbing his thumb over the motto that haunted his dreams. "I read the article. I found the lady's dissolute brother at a demimonde party."

While Miss Harland undressed for bed, he had dulled his thoughts the only way he knew how—dragging the sot into the hall and shaking a confession from his scrawny frame.

"Lady Askew lost a small fortune at cribbage and was afraid to tell her husband. I sent a note to Montfort."

Saint-Clair arched a brow. "You, at a demimonde party? I'm almost tempted to check you're not wearing a mask."

"I'll explain when we discuss personal affairs." He would trust these men with his life. They'd be astonished to learn he'd agreed to watch the stars and drink chocolate.

Montfort must have used sleight of hand to take his coin. One moment it lay between them, the next it had vanished.

"I did what I do best. Entered Lady Askew's house while they were at Vauxhall. Found the receipt of sale from a pawnbroker in Covent Garden, tucked inside her stocking drawer."

Saint-Clair smiled as he faced Stanton. "You published a rebuttal along with the broker's statement and informed the authorities?"

Stanton nodded. "Lord Askew published an apology. Bastian Saint-Clair remains a myth."

"And so we ride on, culling liars."

They fell silent, the lies that bound them never far from their thoughts.

"How is Adrienne?" Dominic asked.

The faint amusement in Saint-Clair's eyes died at the mention of his sister. "Still afraid to sleep, even after all these years."

Dominic often lay awake reliving that night. The dawn appointment that marked them all as outcasts. They had been witnesses. Still allowed to walk as free men. Saint-Clair had not been so fortunate.

"Anything else to report?" Saint-Clair said, though he was rarely hopeful these days. "No gossip? No rumours? Or will the truth forever elude us?"

"Mallory's brother is considering a return to England," Dominic said. Debauchery loosened tongues as easily as it loosened morals. "There's still talk you stole into the house at night and abducted their sister. That you keep her prisoner in a stairless tower."

"Vienna Mallory." Saint-Clair scoffed. "I'd wager she eloped with a pirate, threw him overboard, and now captains the deadliest ship on the high seas."

"The Mallorys never forgave you for surviving," Montfort said.

"They got justice. I'm a man in invisible chains."

The bronze wolf lay between them, amid dust and fallen

mortar. A reminder that none of them had walked away unscathed.

Saint-Clair took his coin and turned it once across his knuckles before catching it. "Adrienne is restless and longs to return to town. I cannot allow that. She resents it." He slipped the coin into his pocket. "Enough about me. Stanton?"

"*The Sentinel* continues to print facts, not fiction. Work remains my only indulgence."

Dominic cleared his throat. "That's no longer true for me."

They looked at him like he'd stepped from the ruined cloisters in a burial shroud. Their expressions did not soften once he'd explained his predicament.

"Harland may not be the villain?" Saint-Clair gave a curious hum. "Interesting. There's hope for me yet."

"You've moved Miss Harland into your home?" Stanton spoke like he wished he could print it in the morning *Sentinel*.

"Into a cottage on the estate." One he visited more than he should. One he did not leave easily. "A temporary arrangement. Until I'm convinced she's safe."

The word temporary rang thin.

Saint-Clair laughed. "It's worse than we thought. Lying to one's friends is bad enough. Lying to oneself is a mortal sin."

"Do you need anything from us?" Montfort asked. "You have more resources than the devil has souls. Still, we have our uses."

Montfort was right. Dominic's ledger of favours was thicker than a cathedral Bible. All it proved was men could be bought. Most men. Not these ones.

"If Harland was incapable of siring a child, then I want proof. Who was his physician? Can he be trusted?"

Someone had fathered his mother's unborn child.

If it wasn't Harland, who the hell was it?

"I can gather that information," Stanton said. "I have my sources. I doubt the report still exists, but I can dig deep enough to draw marrow from bone."

Dominic grinned. "Have you thought of working for the Crown?"

"Who says I don't?" Stanton replied.

"For Lucifer's sake, don't tell them you meet with a suspected criminal." Saint-Clair rubbed his wrist like he could feel rope burn. "I'll not be hauled out of here like a friar at the Dissolution."

"After eight years of celibacy, that's a tightly drawn distinction," Montfort said.

"A fugitive becomes accustomed to his own company."

Despite Saint-Clair's amused tone, Dominic recognised the sound of a man resigned to solitude. Yet he would not be alone tonight. He'd be watching his angel drink chocolate while she coaxed his secrets free. He would not dwell on what might come after.

Keen to be on the road to Kingston, he said, "I need a list of every property Irving owns in London. Warehouses. Town-houses. Leases under other names."

"I can find a crumb in a haystack," Montfort said, accepting the task. "You suspect this missing clerk may have been abducted?"

"If Edward Brown signed that document, he's either a fool or a prisoner." No man about to enforce a marriage contract would allow a witness to roam London unguarded. If Irving meant to secure a bride, he'd secure the witness first.

Just the thought of her with that old fool fired his blood. The notion of her with any man had his hands curling at his sides, violence whispering through his veins.

Saint-Clair was right. He had lied. There was nothing temporary about his craving for Miss Harland.

He told himself it would pass, but the signs were there. He hadn't slept. He'd spent an hour watching her cottage from an upstairs window. He could smell her, taste her, sense her before she stepped into a room.

Instinct urged caution.

The only woman he'd ever loved had been taken from him. Why did he feel Miss Harland would leave him too?

CHAPTER THIRTEEN

Daphne wasn't sure he would keep their bargain.

When it came to Dominic Hawke, doubt was her constant companion. Oh, she never doubted how he made her feel. Like she was the only woman in the room. Like she was some rare bloom whose scent could undo a man.

But desire was not devotion. And Dominic Hawke gave nothing freely. Perhaps it wasn't her he craved, but the satisfaction of taking what once belonged to his enemy.

With her father dead, was she the retribution?

Should she play the game, pull out Mrs Flavell's red wrapper and act the coquette? Should she use Mr Hawke to secure her place for the month?

But she was not her father, nor her aunt. Not mean. Not manipulative. Not so obsessed with maintaining a facade that she'd sell her own kin.

Yet that wasn't what made her face the truth.

She wanted him.

She wanted his mouth on hers.

She wanted the breathless rush she felt only with him.

Her body had already made the choice.

So she would do the only thing she could. Trust him.

She gathered the wool blanket around her shoulders and lifted her gaze to the heavens. The world was quiet, the night a vast inky ocean. It was a sight she'd admired countless times. To her, nothing was more beautiful than the sky above Shadowmere.

"You waited." His voice was a slow stroke down her spine. "I wasn't certain you would. Though you should have locked the cottage door."

She glanced over her shoulder to find him filling the threshold. Strong. Masculine. Hers for the night.

No wonder people feared him. The collar of his greatcoat framed the hard angles of his face. The heavy wool exaggerated the breadth of his shoulders, and he seemed so impressively tall in the doorway.

"The adventurer returns," she said playfully.

But there was nothing playful in the way he looked at her. It was the look of a man with one thing on his mind. Not chocolate. Not stars.

Her pulse stumbled as he closed the gap between them.

His fingers closed lightly around her wrist before she could step away.

Oh, she was in danger. In danger of acting on every wicked thought she'd had since meeting him. In danger of surrendering more than her pride.

"I rode as fast as I could. If it's too late, we can meet tomorrow."

The road dust clinging to his greatcoat made him look like he had chased the horizon to reach her door.

"It's not too late." She released the edge of her blanket and rubbed a smudge of dirt off his cheek. "Though you shouldn't have hurried." The knowledge that he had, warmed her more than the thick wool ever could.

"The devil himself wouldn't have kept me away." He drew her hand to his mouth and pressed a lingering kiss to her palm. "You're cold."

The tenderness of the gesture caught her off guard. "I was waiting. I didn't know when, or if, you'd come."

"I've thought of little else since I left you."

Heat traced up her arm, curling tight in her chest and belly. She could spend every night like this, his hand wrapped around hers beneath the stars, his voice softened by the dark.

"You're different tonight," she said. "You're only ever this honest when we're dancing."

"Perhaps I can hear music." His thumb grazed her knuckles. "And it's impossible to deny what exists between us when I'm holding you."

The words settled somewhere deep inside her.

"Then let's dance while we study the stars." She slipped off the blanket and let it fall onto the grass, then slid her arms around his waist. "We can keep each other warm."

"That's all the invitation I need."

His mouth claimed hers before they moved. His fingers threaded into her hair, anchoring her to him. Their bodies aligned without thought, as though the steps had been decided long ago.

The kiss was not gentle.

It was a collision of impatience and longing.

Whatever war he'd been waging with himself was over.

She felt it in the firmness of his mouth, in the way his hand held her steady. There was nothing uncertain in him now. Only a depth of want he no longer tried to disguise.

Her hands tightened at his waist, fingers pressing into the hard line of him beneath wool and linen. He tasted of night air and brandy, and something unmistakably male. When his tongue brushed the seam of her mouth, a soft sound escaped her before she could swallow it.

"I know we were supposed to drink chocolate," he murmured against her mouth. "But I'm accustomed to taking what I want."

His hand slid from her hair to the curve of her neck, thumb stroking the sensitive hollow beneath her ear, and she felt the tremor pass through him as surely as it did her.

"Another truth shared and we're not even dancing."

"We are." He bent to her throat, his breath grazing her skin. "You can feel the rhythm where we touch. The unmistakable sway between your hips and mine."

She could. Her heart thudded against her ribs, her breasts strained against the fabric, and his unmistakable hardness pressed against her, firm and insistent.

There was only one problem.

This wasn't the dance she'd bargained for.

She would not have him mistake want for weakness. If Dominic Hawke wanted to touch her, he'd pay the price.

"We had an agreement, Mr Hawke." She pushed against his chest, putting space between them. "I want chocolate and stars and secrets. Only then will we dance."

His mouth curved. "Fine."

She had not expected him to concede so easily.

"I'll not touch you again until you beg."

She smiled. "That almost sounds like a bet, sir."

"Dominic," he corrected softly. "It is. I like the odds, and I'm prepared to place a wager."

"What's the wager?"

"That we'll kiss again before the chocolate cools."

She lifted her chin, though she feared he was right. "That's a foolish thing to say to a woman intent on proving a point."

"Perhaps I'm confident in my ability to please you."

And that would not do.

"Good. You can begin by shaking the blankets and setting out the chairs while I warm the chocolate on the hob grate."

She didn't want to linger by the fire when she was hot enough to crack the mercury, but she left him to play the hero.

There was a knack to creating the froth on top; it meant constant stirring with the *molinet*. The chocolate thickened slowly, rich with the smell of cocoa and spice. Her attention strayed, and she stole a glance around the doorjamb.

Either Dominic Hawke was cold now he'd removed his greatcoat, or he liked the scent of her blanket. He'd drawn it close, his hand moving over the softness as though committing the texture to memory.

He drew it around his shoulders and lowered himself into the chair, his legs set wide, claiming the space without apology.

Daphne hurried back to stir the chocolate, convinced she held the winning hand. All she had to do was resist him, until he learned she could not be handled at will.

She returned, balancing two cups of chocolate on porcelain saucers. "I added a little cinnamon to chase away the chill."

He stood, his thumb brushing hers as he took the saucer and examined the pattern with mild curiosity. "Did you take all my grandmother's china from the house?"

She kept her hand steady by force of will. "Forgive me. I didn't know it was an heirloom. You did say to take whatever I wanted. And I've never seen a prettier set."

He coughed, then pursed his lips, but a chuckle escaped.

"What's so amusing? It is a pretty set."

"Without doubt the prettiest I've seen." His gaze dropped,

though not to the porcelain. "Shall I hold yours while you sit, Miss Harland?"

"Certainly not. Your fingers are trembling. And if you mean to kiss me again tonight, you should call me Daphne."

"If I call you angel, will I earn more than a kiss?"

Why did that endearment weaken her resolve?

"Such a word should be saved for a special moment." A moment she was not ready to surrender. "A touch for a secret? That was our agreement."

"A touch anywhere," he reminded her.

"You play by the rules when it suits you, I see."

He drew her saucer from her hand and placed it on the old wooden chair. "I make the rules. You know that."

"Does that include stealing my blanket?" She drew it from his shoulders and wrapped it around her own. She could no longer smell rosewater, only his darker, masculine scent.

"I needed something to keep me warm while you were gone."

They would kiss again. The air thrummed between them. A slow ache settled in the cradle of her hips. Despite the open sky, she could scarcely draw breath.

But she steeled herself.

He would need to earn it.

"Have you thought about what secret you might tell me?" She took her seat and accepted the chocolate drink from him, sipping as she waited for his answer.

He settled beside her, stretching out his legs, the breadth of his thighs a devious distraction. "I've no wish to rake up the past tonight. Let's keep it playful. I'll answer the question you asked at Mrs Flavell's."

She prayed he hadn't heard the hitch in her breath. Did he know she had lain inches from him, staring into the dark, wondering what he would say if he dared?

"Which one?" she said coolly.

"If you mean to bluff, do it with conviction." He sipped his chocolate, drew his tongue slowly over his lower lip, and gazed at the spangle of stars.

She couldn't wait while he baited her. "Had you known we'd end up here, would you have asked me to dance at the Templeton ball?"

He didn't look at her. "Yes. No woman deserves to spend her life beneath a man like Irving."

It wasn't the answer she'd wanted.

Her throat tightened. It was her own fault for asking, for not realising this was only an inconvenient game to him. Why had she been foolish enough to fall under his spell?

She shifted in the seat, considering whether to pack her valise and leave under cover of darkness, or sip her drink and bide her time.

"If that's the playful answer, I'm glad you spared me."

Sweet mercy. Get up. Tell him it's late. Send him away.

She drank her chocolate too quickly and burnt her tongue.

"And no," he added. "The plan was simple. Yet it's been anything but."

Tears threatened, but she refused to let them fall. "Really, Mr Hawke, we must work on your delivery. I see now why *darling* isn't in your vocabulary."

He must have heard the fracture in her voice.

He turned to her. "That's exactly the point. Everything about you is a bloody surprise."

She sat in stunned silence, half elated, half convinced she'd misheard.

"A good surprise?"

"A confounding one."

She stood. The blanket slipped to the floor. The cup clattered against the saucer despite her grip. "This is hardly the relaxing evening I had in mind."

"What did you have in mind?" He stood and placed his cup on the seat before holding her stare, giving nothing away. "If you meant to soften my heart, you've wasted your time."

She stepped back. "That was not my intention."

"Then that's a damn shame." He caught her wrist. "You've had my heart in your hand for more than a week. Do you think I'd ride like the devil and risk my neck for anyone but you?"

Her breath faltered. Everything narrowed to the soft brush of his thumb against her wrist, the stutter of her heartbeat, the sweet pulse between her thighs.

Dominic.

The silent call rose from deep within her. He heard it. Answered it. Pulled her hard against him. Wager be damned.

He took her hungrily, kissing her open and deep. It would have been ravishment had she not seized him with equal desperation.

His mouth moved over hers, the silken stroke of his tongue a reminder of the pact between them. He meant to have her pleading before the chocolate cooled.

Her fingers fisted in his coat, drawing him closer, refusing to be overwhelmed, matching every fevered thrust.

Strong, restless hands roamed from her back to her hips, over the curve of her breast before gripping her bottom and hauling her hard against him.

A rough sound escaped his throat.

"You've won," he growled, nibbling the corner of her mouth. "You have me, angel. Any way you want me."

Many women would relish this moment, raise a glass to the victory. But this was never about one besting the other.

"You're the one with the prize to claim."

"Careful," he murmured. The warning did not sound entirely meant for her. "Don't give a man options when he's straining in his trousers."

"One touch. That's what we agreed."

"One touch anywhere." His mouth grazed her earlobe. "You've made a deal with the devil. There's only one place I intend to put my hands tonight. One place I long to explore."

She knew the place. The truth of it was in the slow nudge of his knee between her thighs, in the deliberate brush that stole her breath.

"Tell me you've never felt pleasure from a man's hand."

The words sounded dangerously possessive.

"Never." She doubted she could say that in the morning.

The dark curve of his lips made her skin flush. "Will you let me touch you, Daphne? Slow, intimate strokes that will have you panting beneath the stars. The way I wanted to that night we shared a bed."

Her body answered, a quiver low in her belly, impossible to deny. "You want me to undress out here? In the garden?"

He cupped her face, his thumb sweeping over her bottom lip. "If I undress you, I'll want you." His gaze traced the line of her throat before drifting lower. "More than once. I'm no saint."

Why did it sound like an enticement, not a warning?

"You'll have to show me what you mean to do. I've no wish to fumble in the dark."

"You won't. I'll pleasure you while you watch the stars." He released her, shook out his greatcoat and laid it out on the grass. Then offered his hand. "Come. You'll look at the heavens. I'll look at you."

She slipped her hand into his, a mirror of their first dance. Nothing had been the same since. Nothing would be again once she surrendered to him.

He guided her down onto his coat, warm and scented with leather and him, then lay beside her and drew the wool blankets over them.

"What do you love about the stars?" he said.

She gazed up at the vibrant canopy, relaxing a little, which she suspected was the plan. "Problems seem insignificant against the vastness of the heavens."

He came up on his elbow, his fingers tracing the neckline of her plain blue dress. "Is that why you invited me here? To help me forget about vengeance? Or to seduce me in this celestial setting?"

A shiver ran through her. Whether from his featherlight caress or the ache of anticipation, she could not tell. "Are you seduced?"

"You know damn well I am."

"Do I?"

"My steely reserve is the only thing stopping me from rolling on top of you and forgetting every promise I made."

She had to bite her tongue lest she offer every encouragement. "Have you ever made love beneath the stars?"

"Never. You make me forget who I'm meant to be."

It was a compliment he didn't try to hide.

The secret she needed.

"Then perhaps you should show me the scoundrel I met in Lord Templeton's ballroom. He kissed like he was starved of breath."

"You want to taste sin, angel?"

"You know I do."

He was on her in a heartbeat, claiming her mouth in a savage kiss that sent ripples to her toes. He rolled half over her, the unmistakable hardness of him pressing against her hip.

She felt the breeze whisper over her stockings a second

before his hand followed, his thumb tracing a slow circle at her ankle.

His hand slid higher, that devilish thumb finding the hollow of her knee. One touch. That was all. Yet she felt him everywhere. The taste of chocolate with every glide of his tongue. The burn beneath his fingers. The persistent throb between her thighs.

She thrust her hands into his hair, deepening the kiss as she arched into him. A silent plea she dared not voice aloud.

He heard it.

His hand stilled at her knee, fingers flexing. "Have a care, love. I'm fighting to keep my need in its cage."

She could sense power pulsing beneath his clothes, but there was nothing of the beast in him tonight. Never had she felt so safe, so cherished, with a man most considered lethal.

"Kiss me and I shall try to curb my enthusiasm."

"Don't try too hard. Just be mindful of my condition."

How could she not be mindful when the thick ridge of him pushed against her?

The smile inside her deepened. She had done this to him.

"Any doubts?" he asked.

"None."

He didn't ask twice.

His mouth claimed hers while his hand edged higher, like the sweet glide of steel over silk. He found the ends of the pink ribbon fastened into a bow and tugged gently. Her undoing.

Nothing prepared her for the intimate caress as he slid her stocking to her knee. The skim of his fingers on her bare skin had her shuddering as he traced a path to the place she felt him most keenly.

He paused for a heartbeat.

"If you want me to continue, open for me."

She did. A little nervously.

A moan rumbled in his throat, the sound deepening when his fingers brushed over her, the part he'd promised to explore.

"I knew you'd feel this good."

The rasp in his voice, the lazy heat in his eyes, the ache between her legs, made her forget she was innocent.

"Dominic."

She rocked her hips against his hand and looked at him. Moonlight caught the chestnut in his hair. The steel had left his gaze, replaced by something darker. His breathing deepened, but his touch stayed steady.

It did not change when her breath grew ragged. Nor when her fingers dug into his shoulder.

"Look at me."

She tried. God, she tried.

But the world had narrowed to the relentless circling of his touch, to the unbearable tightening building deep inside her. Each measured movement drew her closer to something she could neither name nor stop.

"Dominic—"

Her voice broke on the second syllable.

"That's it," he said softly. "Don't fight it."

She didn't.

The tension snapped.

Pleasure swept through her in a fierce, blinding rush, stealing the air from her lungs and the strength from her limbs. Her back arched. Her nails dug into him. His name left her in a breathless plea.

He held her through it, his mouth at her temple, his hand never wavering as she trembled against him.

And when the last shudder left her, she realised she was looking at him.

Not the stars.

CHAPTER FOURTEEN

Dominic left Shadowmere before sunrise, the letter heavy in his pocket, the secret weighing more with every mile. The countryside offered no absolution. Daphne's scent clung to him, stubborn as guilt.

He should be at the cottage, not riding to London on a road slick with mist, not breaking his oath before dawn. She would not forgive him, not in this, but he would rather risk her wrath than her life.

London announced itself with smoke and noise and the sour stench of the river. The streets churned with carts and curses. As a boy, he'd learned how quickly the city could swallow you whole. He'd never be that powerless again.

The Moseleys did not deal in dockside shadows. They kept an office in Drury Lane, wore tailored coats, and counted other men's misfortunes. A man given a nine o'clock appointment did not arrive late, nor did he show his full hand.

Dominic tethered his horse in the yard of the Royal.

Hawkers touted their wares as theatre girls drifted home in crumpled clothes. Yet the brothers' brass plate gleamed as though it belonged in Mayfair.

Crooked headstones crowded St Martin's Burial Ground, the dead packed tight beyond the railings. They said many of the Moseleys' unpaid debts lay beneath that soil.

Daphne would not lie among them.

Inside the office, a clerk with a scarred brow and missing teeth looked up before Dominic spoke. He required no introduction.

"I'm sure you know how this goes, Mr Hawke," he said in his broad Stepney accent. "I'm told the guests at Shadowmere submit to the same searches."

"Prudence is a useful habit in any establishment."

Dominic hung his hat and greatcoat on the stand beside the desk, clasped his hands behind his head and let the lanky fellow frisk him.

The man's bony hands worked along Dominic's coat, slid down his ribs, then climbed back to his collar. His fingers slipped beneath the cravat, brushing the gold ring he wore on a chain.

"Touch that again and you'll count with fewer fingers."

The clerk stepped back, palms raised. "Come this way. I'll show you to Mr Moseley's office. It's almost time."

Dominic followed him down a narrow corridor, the boards groaning beneath their feet. Moseley would know of his arrival. The man left nothing to chance.

Somewhere deeper in the building, a long-case clock struck the hour. The clerk waited for the final chime before lifting his hand to knock.

Dominic admired the theatrics. He knew every trick to unnerve a man: the red walls, the dark-stained floor, the drawn shutters. The only thing missing was a coffin in the corner.

Eric Moseley sat behind a bare ebony desk, the elder brother, no taller than a woman and as pale as parchment.

"Mr Hawke." He let the name settle, gold flashing on his fingers as he beckoned Dominic forward. "I'm impressed. Mrs Haggert seldom troubles herself on another's behalf. Her insistence alone was worth the appointment."

Moseley gestured to the leather seat. Dominic sat. He did not dwell on how many men had died in this chair. "Mrs Haggert champions the needy."

"You? Needy? Come now, Mr Hawke. I'm told you could buy half the city if the mood took you."

"I'm not here for myself."

Two women occupied his thoughts. One bound to him by blood. The other by something he would not name.

Moseley watched him over steepled fingers. "Mrs Haggert tells me you've taken an interest in Lord Harland's debt. She mentioned a connection to your mother. God rest her soul."

Dominic gave a single nod. Nothing more. Moseley wanted something. It showed in the sharp glint of his eyes and the slow curl of his mouth.

"Your business is your own, of course," he continued, "but I deal in facts, Mr Hawke. Much like your friend at *The Sentinel*. I'll need more than a nod if we're to come to terms."

"What's said in this room stays here." He met Moseley's gaze evenly. "*The Sentinel* serves its own interests. As do I."

Moseley braced his elbows on the desk. "But you're willing to trade favours, I presume. Else why are we here?"

Favours? Moseley would strip a man to the bone if he scented profit.

"I'll settle Harland's debt. In full. Today."

Moseley's gaze sharpened. "And in return you want … what, Mr Hawke?"

"Your word Miss Harland has not inherited her father's

obligation." A man like Moseley kept his promises. That alone put him above most titled men.

Moseley reached into his desk and withdrew a thick ledger. Dust rose as he turned the pages. "With interest, the debt is fifteen thousand. Are you certain the girl is worth that much?"

The cost was of no consequence. Not where she was concerned. He'd not put a price on her head.

Dominic met his gaze. "My mother died because of debts she couldn't pay."

"She's blood, not your enemy's daughter."

"Miss Harland is in this predicament because of me."

Moseley gave a mirthless chuckle. "She was ruined long before you claimed her as your mistress."

The word hit like a fist to the chest. He kept his expression neutral, but every muscle in him tightened. Moseley had no idea what she was to him. Neither did he, if he was honest.

Still, he admired his instinct for precision.

"A man must make peace with his conscience."

"Paying the balance won't bring her papa back. I'd wager you marked his card when you revealed your little secret to the *ton*."

His throat felt thick. "Secret?"

He'd be damned before he named it.

"That you knew the identity of your mother's lover."

The remark stoked a fire in his gut. "You mean the bastard who used her? Who forced her to sell everything"— he stopped short of saying herself—"to repay my father's debt to him?"

Moseley leaned back in the chair, hands braced across his abdomen. "Your father owed many men money. I believe Harland was just the spawn in the pond."

Every limb felt heavy. He'd been chasing the information

for years and had never found proof. "You know the names of these men?"

The moment the question left his mouth, he knew Moseley would use it.

"I acquire debts for a living, Mr Hawke. Have for almost two decades. I know of every seedy transaction that takes place in this city. Your father took out private loans to claim back his vowels. Personal transactions that left no trail."

Dominic had come to the same conclusion. It was a loan his mother fought to repay, not gaming debts. Harland was the benefactor. But not the only one. Someone else had slipped a noose around her neck.

Moseley wasted no time laying his cards on the table. "Pay Harland's debt and you may do as you please with his daughter. Our claim will be satisfied."

Dominic sensed there was more.

"Of course," Moseley continued, moistening his lips as if preparing to feast, "I can share something I do know. It may put certain questions to rest. Perhaps bring you the peace you crave."

Dominic firmed his jaw. One wrong move and the cost would be high. "And you want something from me in return?"

Moseley shrugged a shoulder and smiled. "That's how bargains are made, Mr Hawke. One good deed for another."

"Then name your price and I'll weigh the odds."

He braced himself. It would be steep. He had no doubt.

"Miss Harland," Moseley began, and the words chilled Dominic's blood, "has an admirer. Let us call him a common enemy."

There was only one man as taken with her as Dominic was. "You speak of Mr Irving, owner of—"

"Irving & Sons Ammunitions. Yes." Moseley's upper lip

curled, baring his teeth. "I dislike men who imagine distance frees them from obligation, Mr Hawke."

He stifled a smirk, keeping the stone mask in place. "Irving owes you money?" If so, fortune had dealt him a better hand than he'd expected.

"Not me. My brother invested in one of his enterprises. I would prefer Irving remain in England until matters are resolved."

Dominic would prefer Irving board the ship and die on the crossing, but Moseley's solution had a certain elegance.

"I also deal in facts, Mr Moseley. What is it you require?"

Moseley removed a leather portfolio from his desk drawer. "A word to your contact on the Secret Committee. Place this before Chairman Sterling and express a few quiet concerns. Any contract signed in India will become little more than waste paper."

Dominic reached for the portfolio but did not open it. He regarded it a moment, allowing silence to suggest hesitation. In truth, Moseley had handed him exactly what he needed. Even so, interference in Crown business carried its own dangers.

"Agree to this, and I'll tell you what connects Miss Harland's mother and yours."

Dominic shifted in the chair, firming his grip on the portfolio. "Very well. I'll ensure the right people see these documents, but will deny all involvement if asked."

Moseley nodded. From his coat, he withdrew a letter and slid it across the desk. The edges were frayed, the paper foxed. "I keep everything, Mr Hawke. In my business, you never know when it may prove useful. It's yours now."

The letter was dated a decade ago, written in his mother's elegant hand. The tone was desperate. He could almost hear the strain in her voice, see the shadows beneath her eyes, feel the weight of the debt.

The ring at his throat felt heavier, and he silently cursed his father to the devil.

"She sought a loan," Moseley said. "She preferred my terms to those of the lord who'd made life unbearable. Unfortunately, she died before I could reply."

His heart pounded so hard it rang in his ears.

"She never named this lord?"

Moseley gestured to the letter. "Everything I know is in there."

"But you mentioned Miss Harland's mother."

"She came to me for a loan to silence a blackmailer. A lord who made her life unbearable." He paused, watching Dominic as the words settled. "Unfortunately, she had no means to keep up the payments. I run a business, Mr Hawke. Not a charitable foundation."

Moseley made his skin crawl.

But then the rogue handed him a boon.

"It's likely a coincidence," Moseley continued, unperturbed. "But it shouldn't be difficult to investigate. Look for those who befriended Lord Harland and your father. Men who had access to both households. I can supply a few names for a price."

Dominic inwardly sighed. "I doubt it's one I'm willing to pay."

Moseley grinned. "It's always good to test the boundaries. Besides, those men will likely be enjoying the delights at Shadowmere tomorrow." His smile thinned. "Evil men often return to the scene of their crimes."

Dominic's fingers tightened on the arm of the chair. Not because he might have poured wine for the fiend who'd harmed his mother. But because the villain was still out there.

A faceless man who vanished in a crowd. And if he had killed Harland to keep his secret, he might turn his attention to Daphne.

She woke to the memory of Dominic's mouth on hers, his hand a teasing glide between her thighs. A sweet ache lingered in her chest. The stars had faded, but his presence remained. The bed beside her might be cold, but a part of him was there with her. Touching a place inside her she was too afraid to name.

She shook herself.

Such thoughts were dangerous.

They ruined debutantes during their first season, made fools of the innocent, filled weak hearts with hope.

She couldn't afford to dream. Even if his mouth was heavenly and he sometimes said tender things. She would earn her keep, not live at a man's pleasure.

She threw back the sheets and climbed out of bed, rubbing her arms against the morning chill. There was work to be done. The timing could not be better. Guests would pile through the doors tomorrow, revellers gathering for the Autumn Masque.

Her mocking snort broke the stillness.

Guests. They did not come by generous invitation.

The Masque was not a party, but a display of Dominic's control. He had nearly drowned in weakness once. He would not do so again.

He had told her his mother took lovers to survive. That she paid for it with her life. And that one man bore the blame. But what had happened at Shadowmere when his father died?

Dominic was not careless with his hatred. Something he had not told her drove it. If she understood that, she might understand him.

She dressed in haste, snatched Mr Beattie's list from the table, and went in search of the taskmaster. She found him talking to Mr Ramsey outside Dominic's study, both men frowning over a sheaf of papers. Perhaps they'd misplaced the gilded fig leaves.

"Since this business with Miss Harland, he's not thinking straight," Mr Ramsey said, sounding rather irate.

She considered retreating before they noticed her.

"Every move he's made follows a logical pattern," Mr Beattie said in clear disagreement. "Have faith. This is another rational step to him discovering the truth."

There was nothing logical about the way he'd touched her last night. Nothing rational about succumbing to this confounding attraction.

"The truth might see him killed. When the Moseleys issue a summons, the sexton sharpens his spade."

The men heard her sharp intake of breath.

Both turned to stare as though she were a spy at Court.

She approached. "Has Mr Hawke heard from the Moseley brothers?"

While Mr Ramsey uttered an expletive, Mr Beattie gave a reassuring smile. "A letter arrived late last night. I'm sure Mr Hawke will explain once we've finished preparing for the Masque."

Last night? He had said nothing to her.

"I see the list in your hand, Miss Harland," Mr Beattie said, a poor attempt at distraction. "If you'd care to walk with me, we'll check the completed tasks."

She looked at the study's solid oak door. "I'll speak to Mr

Hawke first. I'm keen to see the letter. After all, the debt to the Moseley brothers is mine."

She spoke like the mistress of the house, not a fugitive clinging to freedom. But she would not be kept in the dark. And they were hiding something.

Mr Ramsey moved to block her path. "Hawke's not in there. No one enters without his permission." He rattled the brass doorknob to prove it was locked.

"Then tell me where I might find him."

"Who can say? The estate is vast."

Her chest constricted. She'd negotiated enough with her father to know when men expected compliance.

But Mr Ramsey had made a mistake.

"Then I have a wealth of ground to cover, and the air will do me good." She thrust the list at Mr Beattie. "I'm confident you'll find no problems. If you see Mr Hawke, tell him I'm looking for him. It's a fine day. Perhaps I'll begin with a walk to the church."

She turned on her heels and strode along the corridor.

Mr Ramsey followed, boots striking the boards in sharp rebuke. "You can't leave Shadowmere. Mr Hawke gave strict instructions."

Mr Hawke was not her keeper. Nor her master.

She did not slow, even when the burly fellow reached her side. "Direct me to Mr Hawke, and I'll discuss it with him."

"Wait here. I'll see if I can locate him."

Locate him? He had never been difficult to find.

Then it struck her. The letter. The summons.

Had he gone without telling her? Without trusting her?

Cold seeped into her bones.

Had he ridden to London? Alone?

Keen to test the theory, she said, "I'll begin at the stables. One of the hands may have seen him. I expect he's out ensuring there's room to park twenty carriages tomorrow."

Mr Ramsey stiffened. "For heaven's sake, woman. Let me find him."

"Why? I've nothing better to do."

She'd reached the mews when Mr Ramsey caught her arm. One stall stood empty, tack hooks bare.

"Hawke isn't here."

"That much is obvious." She'd known it before she set foot on the cobblestones.

"He went out early this morning to fetch supplies."

"Supplies? You mean he rode to meet the Moseley brothers." She faced him fully. Men summoned by the Moseleys were rarely seen at supper. "You knew, and you let him go alone?"

Mr Ramsey's stern facade cracked. "Maybe you're not aware, but once Hawke makes a decision, there's no turning him."

Oh, she was aware. At Lord Templeton's ball, he'd decided to dance with her whether she agreed or not.

"Could you not have ridden behind and stayed out of sight?"

His nostrils flared. "This house is run on a strict set of rules. If Hawke can't trust me to follow orders, then I've no business being here."

Would it always be this way?

Would he always decide and she'd be expected to obey?

"I'm leaving the house to visit the church and the old housekeeper Mrs Buckley. I'm told she lives two miles from here." She raised a hand to stall him when he tried to interrupt. "Any attempt to stop me won't end well, Mr Ramsey."

She was tired of secrets. Tired of being handled like a child.

Mr Ramsey's laugh was more a bark. "I've a mind to throw you over my shoulder and tan your hide."

Outrage stiffened her spine.

Was every man who lived here a heathen?

"You'll not dare lay a hand on me, sir." She scowled and prodded his chest. "I'm saving my strength for Mr Hawke, but perhaps I should test it on you."

He found that even more amusing. "Give me fair warning. I'd like a seat in the stalls for that."

"Do you know nothing about women, Mr Ramsey? We play the long game. Silence cuts deeper than any blow."

She strode away, lengthening her stride when she sensed him close behind. "Do you mean to shadow me all day?"

"Wherever you go, I'm instructed to follow."

"Then keep up," she called over her shoulder. "We've a fair distance to cover. I pray you've eaten."

Mr Ramsey stayed with her for a mile, whistling idly at her heels. He watched her climb the stile and didn't offer a hand.

She set off down the rutted country lane, dodging farmers' carts laden with turnips, Mr Ramsey's boots striking a steady march behind her. When the grey spire of All Saints rose behind the hedgerow, she angled towards it without hesitation.

She moved slowly through the churchyard, reading the names carved into stones the weather had tried to erase. She pictured him walking this path alone, flowers in hand, the weight of it all pressing down on his shoulders.

Sighing, Mr Ramsey stepped ahead and pointed towards the edge of the churchyard. "Over there. Near the oak tree."

So he'd decided to be helpful.

Perhaps he was tired and wanted to go home.

Benjamin Hawke's grave lay neglected. Coarse grass

forced its way through the cracks. The stone was dark with grime and moss. The contrast with the memorial beside it could not have been more stark. A son's verdict, written in weeds.

"A man's reputation follows him even in death," Mr Ramsey said quietly. "Some say he shouldn't rest in consecrated ground."

She kept her gaze on the stone.

"Others say he was shot in cold blood."

"What's the truth?" she asked.

"No one cares."

She looked at the memorial beside it, two white roses laid upon the grave. The plot was immaculate, the marble polished to a hard sheen.

"Mr Hawke must have loved his mother dearly. He's not forgotten her."

"And never will."

She ran her fingers along the cold edge of the stone.

It would take everything she had not to yield when he returned. But if she meant to reach him, she would have to demand the truth.

"Why two roses?" There were more in the garden.

"That's not for me to say."

She didn't press him. He'd said enough.

She walked out of the churchyard and followed the lane back to the stile, damp earth clinging to the hem of her skirt. She didn't climb it, but continued on, trusting the maid's directions.

"Mrs Buckley won't tell you anything," Mr Ramsey said, still trailing her like an errant ghost. "She swore an oath to her mistress and wouldn't grant the Lord her confession."

She did not wait for him.

"Often it's the things people don't say that prove telling."

Mrs Buckley's tiny cottage sat beyond a bend in the lane, its thatch threaded with ivy, a narrow plume of smoke rising from the chimney. Hardly the dwelling of a secret-keeper.

The woman who answered looked near seventy, her cheeks rosy from the hearth. Warm air, rich with the scent of butter and something freshly baked, met Daphne at the door.

Mr Ramsey cleared his throat. "Mrs Buckley."

The woman's expression brightened. "Mr Ramsey. What brings you here today?" Her kind eyes settled on Daphne. "No need to explain. I can see why you wouldn't want her at Shadowmere this weekend."

"Miss Harland is a guest, not a maid."

Mrs Buckley paled, studying Daphne as though she had sprouted horns.

"Not a guest for the Masque," Daphne corrected. "Mr Hawke allows me to stay in the cottage while we try to prove neither of us killed Lord Harland. My father."

Her fingers gripped the jamb. "I see. Well, you'd better come in. I've just finished baking scones. They should be cool enough to eat."

The cottage was well tended, copper pans polished bright above a scrubbed pine table. Standing in the warmth of it, she had almost forgotten she was furious with Dominic.

Mrs Buckley set the scones between them and poured the tea. They sat for half an hour over refilled teacups, speaking of the Masque: candles ordered, musicians engaged, the house bracing for another spectacle.

"I expect Mr Beattie is ticking jobs off his list, making sure it's all ship-shape. That man would walk through fire for Mr Hawke."

It was good to know someone looked after him. She doubted he made it easy.

"There were over thirty tasks on the list he gave me."

Daphne dabbed the crumbs off her lips with a napkin. "Mr Beattie will be wondering where I've got to."

"I'm surprised Mr Hawke could spare you today."

"He's in London and doesn't know we're here."

Mrs Buckley's frown deepened. "London? The day before the Masque?"

Mr Ramsey excused himself and rose abruptly. "We should return before Beattie sends out the cavalry."

They thanked her for her hospitality, but Daphne paused at the threshold and gripped Mrs Buckley's hand.

"I intend to lock myself in the cottage tomorrow night, but is there anyone I should be wary of? Men I should avoid at all costs?"

Mrs Buckley patted her hand. "Spend the weekend here. Two maids are coming from Shadowmere. You won't be alone."

Daphne glanced at Mr Ramsey pacing the lane, then lowered her voice. "Perhaps I should. But I find myself drawn to Mr Hawke as surely as a compass points north. I must see him in his worst light if I'm to make any decisions about the future. I believe he finds solace in my company too."

Her pulse quickened at the admission.

None of it was a lie. He did not wear his armour so tightly when he was with her.

Mrs Buckley's smile faded. "Mr Hawke carries ghosts heavier than most. I've never known him seek comfort. Only justice."

Justice. As though that were enough.

"Because of his father?"

"Because of the company his father kept."

The journey might not be a waste after all.

"We're seeking his creditors in a bid to find answers. My

father was one. Someone killed him and threw him in the Thames."

Guilt stirred.

She wished she cared enough to mourn him properly.

Mrs Buckley clutched her chest. "The past is best left buried."

Buried men had a habit of resurfacing.

"The past will destroy Mr Hawke. I need to know the names of his father's creditors. One will suffice."

Mrs Buckley hesitated but described a few men she called gamblers and rogues. No one Daphne recognised. "That's all I can tell you. It's all I could tell Mr Hawke when he asked."

"Did his mother not say anything that might help us discover the identity of these men?"

Mrs Buckley shook her head. "No. Mrs Hawke kept her own confidence. She was afraid the truth might damage her son."

The truth had damaged him anyway.

Daphne squeezed the woman's hand. "It's the not knowing that hurts him most." She paused. "If you think of anything that might prove useful, please send word to Shadowmere."

She made to leave, but Mrs Buckley gripped her hand. "There was someone she mentioned once. It's the only time she ever referred to the debts. She kept those secrets, even from me."

Daphne's heart galloped. "What did she say?"

"That Lord Templeton could bleed a desert dry and call it charity."

CHAPTER FIFTEEN

The sky had turned a murky grey by the time Dominic reached Shadowmere. The first heavy drops of rain landed on the sleeve of his greatcoat as he waited for Crocker to unlock the gate, the iron chain rattling against the bars.

"Has anyone passed through here today?" He was keen to know if Daphne had stuffed her clothes into a valise and quit the house in a temper.

Crocker shook his head as he worked the key in the padlock. "First time opening it since before dawn, sir."

The tension in his shoulders eased.

Not the tightness in his gut.

It wasn't Moseley's document tucked in the saddlebag that troubled him. Nor the reckoning that awaited him when he explained his absence to Daphne. He trusted his instincts. They'd been needling him since he left London, since Moseley's veiled warning.

Evil men often return to the scene of their crimes.

He looked back at the road.

Would he dare come to the Masque?

"I'll post two extra men on the gate in the morning. I want every carriage searched. Admit no one who isn't on the list."

"Aye, sir." Crocker dragged the chain through the iron railings. "And if there are strays that can't be accounted for?"

"They remain in the gatehouse under lock and key until Ramsey comes to vet them. No exceptions. No excuses. That includes the magistrate."

Crocker nodded as he stepped aside to let him pass.

Dominic reiterated the same concerns to Duncan, his head coachman, as he dismounted. "Search every boot before the vehicles are parked. Man them night and day. No one leaves here without my permission."

A groom hurried from the shelter of the stable block, steadying the restless horse and taking the reins with a respectful nod.

How often had the same courtesy been shown to the man who destroyed his mother? Had the bastard ridden through the open gate, confident no one would ask questions?

"Shall I post a groom near the footpath?" Duncan nodded towards the cobbled passageway that led to the gardens. "A man could climb the stile on the lane and cross the fields without being seen."

Damn. He'd never had to consider it before.

Guests liked spectacle. They arrived bold and brazen. A man with darker intentions would not.

"I'll speak to Ramsey."

"I expect he's of the same mind, sir. He went that way with Miss Harland some time ago."

Dominic stilled. "How long ago?"

Why the hell were they walking when there was work to be done?

Duncan shrugged. "Two hours, I'd say."

"Two hours, and they've not returned?" He heard the

crack in his own voice. Had she left Shadowmere? Without waiting. Without giving him the chance to explain. Was Ramsey aiding her escape or attempting to bring her home?

Home.

The word caught him off guard. He dismissed it.

"They might be sheltering from the rain, sir."

Or someone had intercepted them. Ramsey would not abandon his post on the eve of the Masque. Not without good reason.

"I'll walk that way. Assess the danger myself."

It took effort not to break into a sprint.

Barely a minute passed before he saw them trudging across the field. Daphne tipped her face to the sky and stuck out her tongue to catch the raindrops.

Ramsey laughed as if he enjoyed her company. He shrugged out of his coat and draped it around her shoulders, tugging it tighter across her chest.

Dominic's world darkened.

The rain turned cold against his collar.

He had never wanted to kill a man more.

Daphne saw him at the edge of the field, eyes blazing. Her laughter died. Her smile hardened into a scowl that slid beneath his skin.

Ramsey wouldn't meet his eye.

"Duncan said I'd find you here." His jaw ached from holding it tight. "He neglected to mention you were amusing yourself in the pasture."

Daphne said nothing. She strode past as if he were a post in her path.

"Miss Harland insisted on walking to the church." Ramsey's answer came a beat too quickly. "We've just had tea with Mrs Buckley."

"We would have invited you," she called over her shoulder, "had you been here. I wouldn't have kept you in the dark."

The comment cut like a lash.

He was cold and tired, wet from the rain. He'd not feel guilty for saving her damn life.

"You could say thank you," he shouted.

She swung around, hands braced on her hips. "Thank you. Thank you for proving I'm nothing but a thorn in your side."

She turned her back on him and walked on.

He rounded on Ramsey. "You showed her my mother's grave?"

Ramsey wiped rain off his face. "She wants answers. You can't blame her for that. I kept our oath, but Mrs Buckley told her something. She wouldn't say what."

"If it concerns my mother, I have a right to hear it."

He had faced down killers without blinking. He would not be dismissed by a woman.

He marched after her. A sensible man would return to the house, shut himself in the study, and let his temper cool. But Daphne Harland was a distraction he could not master.

"You'll tell me where you've been and what you've said." He followed her through the mews, aware of the stable lads pretending not to stare. "Every word. Do you hear me?"

"The same applies to you."

She started running, not to escape the rain but him; her boots slipping on the wet cobbles.

He could have caught her easily. Made a spectacle of them both. But he didn't give chase until she reached the cottage. He wedged his foot in the gap before she could close the door.

"We'll discuss this properly," he said, expecting her to throw her weight behind the wood and force him out.

"Which is precisely what we should have done before you

rode to London at dawn." She marched upstairs, leaving the door ajar.

He entered, braced for what awaited him above.

The boards creaked as he crossed the landing.

He'd prefer pistols at dawn to this.

"Do you have any idea what it's like to be a woman?" she said when he ducked beneath the low lintel into her chamber.

It sounded like a trick question.

"You're not invisible to me if that's the implication. You were uppermost in my thoughts today."

She pulled Ramsey's wet coat off her shoulders and hung it over the wooden chair. "If that were true, you would have woken me. Given me the choice to accompany you. Is that so difficult?"

"Yes, because I know what men see when they look at you." He knew every curve of her by heart. Knew the effect she had on him.

She blinked, her mouth softening, but then she flicked her hand at the spreading puddle at his boots. "You're dripping water all over the boards."

"I'm not leaving." He shrugged out of his greatcoat, opened the small window, and tossed the sodden garment into the rain.

"It's best you do. You've lost your wits."

"I lost them in Templeton's ballroom."

"I didn't ask you to ruin me."

"But you're glad I did."

She snatched a towel from the washstand and pulled the comb from her hair. He watched as the damp locks tumbled loose around her shoulders.

Bloody hell.

"You wore another man's coat today." He'd be the only man to shelter her from a storm.

"Because you weren't there."

He stepped closer. "Mrs Buckley told you something."

She patted the ends of her hair with the linen. "That she adds almond essence when she glazes her scones."

"I know. I settle her accounts."

She paused. "How endearing."

He took another step, forcing her to tilt her chin to meet his gaze. "You'll tell me what she said. I have a right to know." He meant to hold her with a hard stare, but his gaze slid to the raindrop tracing the line of her throat. "Why go to my mother's grave?"

The sharp question did nothing to quell the heat coiling low as she drew the linen over her neck and the slope of her shoulders.

"Perhaps I went looking for your heart."

"I doubt you'll find it."

She looked at him with blue eyes he could drown in. "I glimpsed it in the garden last night. I suspect it's never far."

It had been buried in hallowed ground until he met her.

He wasn't sure who moved first. One moment there was space between them, the next his fingers closed around her wrist as she brushed a damp lock from his brow.

"You'll tell me everything," he said.

"You'll make amends for leaving without a word."

"I doubt you'll be satisfied until you've drawn blood."

"You know me so well."

He looked at her mouth, their breath mingling, his need rising. "We're alike. Both downright stubborn."

"Stubborn and afraid."

He feared nothing and no one.

Except for the way he felt about her.

"And hypocrites," she added, pressing closer.

Panic cut through desire. "I ask nothing of you."

"I was speaking of myself." Her hand rested on his chest before drifting higher to trace his jaw. "I refuse to be owned by any man … but I long to be owned by you."

"Be careful what you ask for. I might give it to you."

"I deserve some recompense for being left behind."

He cupped her face, his thumb pressing beneath her chin as though he meant to steady her.

In truth, he meant to steady himself.

The resolve lasted a heartbeat.

"Then you shall have it."

He lowered his mouth to hers. Her lips were warm. Softer than he remembered. Softer than he deserved. He should pull away. Demand answers. Why had she gone to the grave? What had Mrs Buckley said? What did she think she knew?

Instead, he eased her lips apart with a patience he did not feel. He could taste her without taking. Please her and still master himself.

But her fingers curled at his nape, and the touch undid him. When she sighed against his mouth, his composure slipped. His hand went to her waist and he hauled her against him, kissed her like a man who ached to see her undone.

This thing between them was no game.

Heat surged low and savage. The throb in his trousers refused to subside. His hands slid to her bottom and he crushed her to him.

He needed her beneath him. At his mercy.

He deepened the kiss, driving it until her breath faltered and she clutched at him as though the floor had shifted beneath her.

He should stop.

Give her a moment to reconsider.

He tore his mouth from hers with a rough breath. "You'll

be the death of me before the week is through. Speak now if you've had enough."

"Enough?" The glint in her eyes made him question who was doing the claiming. "I'll not stop until I've found your heart, Dominic."

"You'll be looking for a long time."

"Perhaps that's the plan."

He held her tight against him, searching her face for the slightest hesitation. "You've no idea what you're inviting."

"I believe I do."

"You want me inside you?"

Her breath hitched. "I've always dreamed of living dangerously."

Dominic swore under his breath and lifted her clean off the floor. "Then you'll have no cause for complaint."

She gasped as her back met the mattress, her skirts tangling around her thighs as he came down over her.

God help him.

It took strength not to undo his trousers and part her legs. He strained against the wool, the call to take her pounding through his veins.

She kissed him, their mouths meeting in a heated clash of lips and tongues, her hands moving over his shoulders, into his hair, down the warm line of his neck.

Dominic groaned against her mouth. The slow rock of her hips ground the last of his restraint to dust. He had told himself he could remain distant even in this. That discipline was its own armour. She had made it impossible. Waiting was no longer an option. Every inch of him burned. He had to touch her.

He bunched the fabric in his fists and hiked her skirts, his palm settling on the silk of her stockings, a delicate barrier beneath his rough hands, but he didn't pause at the ribbons. His fingers moved higher, finding the slick heat he craved.

Saints' teeth.

Daphne gasped, her body arching into his touch, just as she had in the garden, when she came apart beneath the stars.

"Have you touched yourself and thought of me?"

He kissed her before she could answer, his tongue stroking deep, matching the slow circles his fingers traced beneath her skirts.

"You're never far from my thoughts, Dominic."

"You'll need a fan when you think of me tonight."

He stepped back from the bed and looked at her. Her dark hair lay loose across the pillow, her lips flushed from his kisses, her skirts tangled around her thighs.

He had never wanted anyone the way he wanted her.

He swore softly and shrugged out of his coat, letting it fall. His waistcoat and cravat followed. Then he dragged his shirt over his head and tossed it aside.

She watched him, mouth parted, swallowing hard as her gaze drifted over the dark hair on his chest and the hard lines of muscle beneath it. Then it rested on the chain around his neck.

"The ring was my mother's," he said, answering her silent question as he set it on the nightstand. He couldn't dwell on it, not when every breath he took tasted of her. "Where were we?"

"You wanted to do something wicked. I know that look."

"You had scones and jam. I crave something sweeter." He caught her ankle and slid off her boot.

"What's sweeter than strawberry jam?"

"You, angel." He tugged off her other boot and dropped it to the floor, never taking his eyes from her. "Bend your knees if you're curious."

She did, her breath catching as he shifted lower on the bed.

His heart hammered as he settled between her legs. "Still curious?"

"Desperately so. But you know that."

He lowered his head.

He'd dreamt of this since that night at Mrs Flavell's.

His mouth brushed the silky skin just above her stocking, the scent of her stirring something dark in his blood.

Daphne.

He kissed his way to the centre of her heat, his breath fanning over the tight little nub begging for his attention.

The moment stretched. Then his lips touched her there, drawn out as though he meant to savour her slowly.

That resolve lasted a heartbeat.

"Dominic."

His grip tightened on her thighs, the need to possess her surging through him. He sucked and circled her with his tongue, her hips lifting to meet the rhythm.

He felt the tremor building in her, heard it in every broken gasp. He did not relent.

She called out, reaching for him. "Dominic."

The sound of her crying his name should have been warning enough. He had spent years building walls no woman had ever crossed—yet here he was, on his knees like a man who had forgotten every rule he lived by.

He lifted his head and rose over her again. For a moment, he simply looked at her. He had faced men who wanted him dead and never once hesitated. Yet this woman could undo him with nothing more than his name on her lips.

"I want you. If you've changed your mind, tell me to leave. I'm losing what little discipline I have left."

She cupped his jaw, the haze of desire alight in her eyes.

"Stay. This is the only thing I want. No one's ever made me feel the way you do."

He didn't argue. Couldn't.

He drew her closer and gave himself over to the moment he had tried and failed to resist.

"I'm a different man with you."

"Not different. A warmer version, perhaps."

He should strip her bare. Take it slow. But he couldn't allow himself time to think. The layers between them were a mercy. Feeling her bare beneath him would break him.

"I need you, Daphne."

"I'm here, though you might need to undress me first."

"We won't waste time with gowns and ribbons."

"At least help me out of this dress." She pushed herself up off the mattress, fingers fumbling with the fastenings at her spine.

Saints have mercy.

The bare curve of her shoulders as the fabric parted stopped him cold. Without a word, he turned her gently and worked the buttons himself. The bodice loosened and he eased it from her, helped her step free of the skirt. Her stays and petticoats remained—enough layers between them to keep his head clear.

"Leave the rest," he said quietly. "If we're disturbed, I'd rather not explain myself to Ramsey."

She laughed softly. "You don't want to see me?"

There was nothing he wanted more. But he was already in deeper than he'd intended. "Yes. When time isn't against us." When he had more control over himself.

He drew her back to the bed, his hands settling at her waist as she sank against the pillows. The chemise was soft against her skin, her blue eyes watching him with a trust that undid him completely.

He lowered himself over her, his mouth finding her throat, her collarbone, the warm curve of her breast through the thin linen. Her breath hitched. Her fingers slid into his hair.

He could tell himself this was nothing more than desire.

He would be lying.

"You're certain you want this?"

The blaze of longing in her eyes said she did.

"I want *you*, Dominic."

He freed himself and pressed closer, guiding himself into her, a groan escaping as she sheathed him in warmth. He had not known it could feel like this. Like coming home.

He forgot every reason he had for resisting her.

He eased forward, rocking slowly into her as she grew accustomed to the size and feel of him.

Her legs wrapped instinctively around his waist, drawing him closer. Her hands settled against the bare muscles of his back, as though she had never doubted she belonged there.

Why had he denied himself that same simple pleasure?

Because he was already picturing how it would end. With her gone. Him ruined. And still, he didn't let go.

He bent over her, his breath warm against her neck as he moved again, careful at first, until the rhythm between them built.

"Daphne," he murmured, his voice roughened by restraint. "I need to drive deeper. Look at me when I do."

She did, her eyes wide but steady, trusting him in a way that made something tighten painfully in his chest.

God help him.

"If it hurts, if you want me to stop, say the word."

She shook her head, one hand sliding into his hair as if to anchor herself. "I don't want you to stop."

He lowered his forehead to hers, breathing her in. For

years, vengeance had been the only thing that burned through his blood. Now there was this woman beneath him, and he craved her more than he had ever craved revenge.

He kissed her deeply. One slow glide answering the other.

He had meant to take his time.

He had meant to maintain control.

But the way she clung to him, the way her breath warmed his throat, the way her body answered his every movement—

He rolled his hips, one long thrust filling her.

"Daphne."

She gasped, her nails pressing lightly into his back as the deeper stroke drew a soft cry from her lips.

"I'm all right," she whispered. "Don't stop."

He searched her face for doubt and found none.

Then she said the one thing no one ever had.

"Please, Dominic. I need you."

Whatever control he had left vanished. The bed creaked beneath them as he gathered her close, the rhythm between them building until neither could hold it back. She clung to him, fingers digging into his shoulders, his name slipping from her in a ragged whisper.

His release broke with brutal force. With a rough groan, he withdrew just in time, bracing himself on the mattress beside her as he spilled over her thigh.

As the tension subsided, he looked at her mussed hair and swollen lips and gave silent thanks for the chemise. Bare skin would have finished him.

"Are you all right?" He eased off the bed, took a handkerchief from his coat pocket, and returned to tend to her.

"I'm perfectly fine." She shifted on the pillow, still flushed from his attentions. Her gaze lingered on him. "A little overwhelmed, but fine."

"Overwhelmed in a good way?" He tucked himself back into his trousers before he succumbed to his baser instincts.

She smiled. "In a way that might tempt me to repeat it."

A laugh escaped him. "You're a dangerous woman. You have a talent for dismantling a man's defences."

She looked quite proud of herself. "Have I managed to sneak past your barricade, Mr Hawke?"

"You've been raising the portcullis an inch at a time."

"Who knew I had the strength?"

"Who indeed."

She had more steel in her than she knew. He only hoped it would prove enough when the guests came for the Masque. Beattie likely had a dozen questions waiting for him at the house, but Dominic had no wish to leave her just yet.

He climbed onto the mattress beside her and lay back against the pillows. Daphne curled against his side, her head settling on his shoulder. He wrapped an arm around her without thinking.

She traced idle circles on his chest, fingers drifting to where his mother's ring usually rested. "I went to see the grave and Mrs Buckley so you'd know how it feels to be ignored."

"It worked."

"So why did you cast me aside?"

"I didn't cast you aside." He thought of Moseley's cold eyes, the way the man had filed her existence away like a debt to be called in. "I was afraid Moseley would find a use for you if he met you. I'd rather risk your disappointment."

"You don't sound sorry."

"I'm sorry I hurt you. I'm not sorry I left you behind."

For a moment, neither spoke.

"Will you tell me what Mr Moseley said?" Her tone had

cooled, though her hand remained on his chest. "I presume you paid him."

"Yes. The fifteen thousand your father owed him."

She shot up on her elbow. "Fifteen thousand? Good heavens. How will I ever repay you?"

His gaze moved over her slowly. "I can think of several ways. Beginning with what Mrs Buckley told you."

"Not until you tell me what Mr Moseley said about my father. Do you think he killed him?"

"No. He would have used it as leverage to frighten me instead of holding me to ransom." The bargain still rankled. Dominic disliked being forced to deal on another man's terms. "Forget I said that."

She sighed, snatching her hand from his chest. "You need to decide whether you want a partner or a prisoner. Partners don't keep secrets."

He reached for her hand, turning it in his palm as though he had no intention of letting her retreat.

"Both our mothers applied to Moseley for a loan to pay a lord who may have been blackmailing them."

Daphne frowned. "Blackmail?"

"Moseley said evil men return to the scene of their crimes. That the villain has likely visited both our houses." That might make the bastard easier to identify. "He may be at the Masque tomorrow." The idea of her alone in the cottage chilled him. He leaned closer and kissed her temple. "If Moseley's right, you should stay with Mrs Buckley."

"If I'm your prisoner, I have no choice. If I'm your partner, I shall remain at your side." She tucked herself closer. "We were separated this morning, and look at the trouble it caused."

"I'm not complaining."

Her sultry smile said she wasn't either. "I'd prefer not to

walk four miles to prove a point, though it wasn't a wasted journey."

His heart missed a beat. "Mrs Buckley knew something? She's always played ignorant with me." Women were better than men at keeping their word to his mother.

"If it's any consolation, your mother told her nothing. But Mrs Buckley did recall something she once said." Daphne draped her arm over his chest as though she feared he might bolt from the bed.

He braced himself. "What did she say?"

"That Lord Templeton could bleed a desert dry and call it charity."

CHAPTER SIXTEEN

Laughter should warm the heart, not chill the blood. Music drifting from the ballroom should stir delight, not dread. Yet a shrill squeal outside the cottage made Daphne clutch her chest, wishing the Masque were ending, not beginning.

She should be celebrating.

Dominic Hawke had made his choice. He would rather be her lover than her gaoler. He wanted a partner, not a prisoner.

It was foolish to want more. Affairs such as theirs rarely endured. She had told herself as much while lying sated in his arms.

Yet she could not quiet the memory of him. The timbre of his voice. The scent of his skin. The weight of him pressing her into the mattress.

She had not slept. She had scarcely eaten.

Desire she could manage. Hope was another matter.

She inhaled deeply, though there wasn't a spare inch in her gown.

Her costume had arrived an hour ago. A daring shade of moss green. The bodice hugged her figure, its neckline sweeping low across her shoulders, delicate lace threaded through the silk like creeping ivy. Layers of gauze fell from her waist in a soft cascade, trailing behind her like forest mist.

It was not the gown of a timid debutante. It was the armour of a woman who had chosen her battlefield. Yet she felt anything but armed.

Her heart lurched at the sudden knock. It would be Dominic. But she demanded he repeat the secret phrase before she opened the door.

"I want you in my bed tonight," he drawled.

The hair on her nape stirred at the thought. "That's not it."

He sighed. "I left my heart in the ice house."

"No, though that might be true."

He paused, though she knew he was smiling. "Nothing compares to the sky above Shadowmere."

"You're supposed to say it with conviction."

"I would if I believed it."

She opened the door and peered around the jamb, though the sight of him stole her breath. He stood there in black. Broad shoulders. Dark green eyes. A mouth made for sin.

She caught his hand, drew him quickly inside and locked the door behind him. Only then did she notice the scent of lilac on his coat.

Jealousy prickled beneath her skin.

"A new cologne? It smells suspiciously floral."

His mouth parted. His gaze dragged over her bare shoulders. "You can't walk into the ballroom dressed like that. I asked Charlotte to send something modest. Every man here will want you."

At his veiled praise, the gown felt indecently tight.

"You're avoiding the question, Dominic."

"I'm the host. I'm expected to greet the guests and endure the occasional embrace." He drew his thumb across his lower lip as he studied her. "You'll tell them you have the plague."

She pursed her lips. "I thought I might play the hostess."

"Not a chance. I'll kill any man who comes near you." He glanced around the sitting room. "You have a shawl. I've seen you wear it."

"It will ruin the costume. Wait until you see my mask."

The mask was fashioned in deep green feathers, layered like the plumage of a hunting bird. A slender black beak curved over the bridge of the nose, lending its wearer a predatory elegance.

She lifted it to her face and did not look away.

She was no one's prey.

Dominic groaned. "Saints' teeth. If I'm not hauled off in irons tonight, it will be a bloody miracle."

"Is that another of your strange compliments?"

His hand came to rest on her waist. "You look beautiful. I don't like how much that matters."

"Matters because you dislike competition."

"Matters because I won't lose you."

She laid a hand on his upper arm. "You won't lose me. Not tonight."

His thumb brushed the inside of her wrist, where her pulse betrayed her. "Still, take this." He drew a small blade from his coat, sheathed in jewelled leather. "Tuck it into your stocking. If only to appease me."

She felt his fear for the first time, stripped of bravado.

She lowered the mask and brushed her mouth against his. He breathed her in before coaxing her lips apart, tasting her as though staking a claim.

When they parted, she took the sheathed blade. "I'll keep it close."

"To frighten. To maim. Nothing more."

He held the mask, watching as she lifted her skirts and slid the blade into her garter. He did not look away.

The air thickened between them. If not for the Masque, they would already be upstairs, undressing, tumbling into bed.

A cheer drifted from the ballroom, followed by the scrape of violins striking up a wilder tune. She'd almost forgotten he had a house full of sinners.

"I presume you have Lord Templeton in the stocks?" she said before temptation could take hold.

Dominic exhaled through his teeth. "I locked him in the study with Ramsey. He swears he could find no proof that anyone owed my father money. He should have searched his own ledger."

"How are we to play this?"

"We'll lie and build the story as we go."

He stepped behind her and fastened the mask, his fingers steady against her temples. His mouth brushed the nape of her neck, a quiet claim before battle.

"Ready?" He took her hand, threading their fingers together. For a moment, he was not the master of Shadowmere, only a man afraid of losing her.

They kept to the shadows and slipped into the house through the servants' quarters. The corridors were quiet and cold, the revelry muffled behind thick doors.

"Any guest found here is barred from future events."

She pictured the maids beside Mrs Buckley's hearth, eating scones and blissfully unaware. "Who waits on the merrymakers?"

"They're expected to bring their own servants." He paused at the top of the stone staircase and gave her hand a gentle squeeze. "Breathe. Then act as though they're here for your amusement. Once the shock passes, it's only theatre."

She swallowed hard, her throat dry as ash. "Nothing here could rival my nightmares of Mr Irving."

She was wrong.

A masked couple pressed against the panelling, the woman's green skirts tangled around her thighs while a man in a stag mask laughed softly against her throat, his hand already wandering where it pleased.

Halfway up the staircase, a woman in crimson silk straddled a masked gentleman too drunk to stand. Her laughter echoed against the red walls as guests flowed around them, as though the display were part of the evening's entertainment.

Yet something other than disgust stirred beneath her ribs. A sadness for the man who still twined his fingers with hers. This was the fortress he had chosen.

With it came another truth. She did not belong here. It had been indulgent to think she might. That she could pretend.

She gripped his hand a little tighter. Not because she might get lost among these degenerates. Because their worlds were farther apart than she had allowed herself to believe.

He mistook the slight tremble in her fingers for a different kind of fear. "They won't dare approach you. I'd have their heads if they did."

The mask concealed the crack in her composure.

"I know."

People parted as they walked through the elegant corridor, moving like restless shadows. Animal masks hid their faces, not the hunger in their eyes or the ruin of their mouths. The house swelled with noise, not all of it music.

Lord Templeton was on his feet before Mr Ramsey closed the study door behind them. The crackle of the fire and the laughter drifting in from the corridor barely disguised the lord's ragged breath.

His eyes were upon her first, like a child at a confectioner's window. Though it would be a mistake to think him innocent. The mask he gripped in his hand was that of a wolf.

"How much longer am I expected to remain here?" the lord said, careful to appear nothing more than mildly frustrated. "I've a friend waiting upstairs."

Dominic invited her to sit in the throne-like chair behind the desk while he remained standing, hands braced behind his back, a monument of stone.

"You were told to name one of my father's creditors and bring proof of the debt. That was the bargain we struck at Mrs Flavell's."

Templeton ran a hand through his hair, exhaling sharply. "I've made enquiries. No one keeps gaming records from over a decade ago. There was no mention of him in White's Betting Book."

The pause stretched.

Dominic began pacing. "You gambled with my father. Surely you know the men who joined you at the tables."

The lord swallowed. "If you haven't been able to uncover it, what hope do I have? If you want the names of men he met in gaming hells, that's most of the ton."

"Give him foolscap and ink, Ramsey. Let him make a list."

Mr Ramsey obliged by gripping the lord's shoulders and forcing him into a chair beside the desk. He took paper from the drawer and pushed the inkwell towards the trembling fellow.

Beads of perspiration formed on the lord's brow.

"I want at least ten names," Dominic said.

The glass bottle rattled on the walnut stand as Templeton dipped the nib. "I don't know why you need this. You know these men are ne'er-do-wells, much like your—" He bowed his head and scribbled a list of names, pausing to steal a sly glance at her bodice.

"Keep your eyes on the paper," Dominic snapped.

When finished, the lord pushed the foolscap away as if he'd signed his own death warrant. "They're the only men I can recall."

Dominic snatched it, his brow creasing as he scanned the page. "I see Harland tops the list. Yet you've omitted the name that should come the easiest to you."

"Whose?"

"Yours."

The lord blinked, his cheeks aflame, as though the burgundy upholstery had leeched into his skin. "Why include mine? I told you we gambled at the same tables."

"You failed to mention my father owed you money."

Like all good gamblers, the lord bluffed. "A few hundred pounds here and there. I can't speak for others, but he settled promptly."

"That's not true," she said, though the last thing she wanted was to draw his attention. "You hounded Mr Hawke's mother. My father said you bled her dry and called it charity." The lie came easily.

"Harland was merely looking for a scapegoat." Templeton's voice rose an octave. "Everyone knows he was the one obsessed. He used the debt to secure a place in her bed."

Mr Ramsey moved like a striking viper, clasping Dominic's arm as if he feared he'd lash out.

"I met with Eric Moseley. He knows of every debt and seedy transaction that happens in the city." Dominic shrugged out of Mr Ramsey's hold and approached the desk. "My mother wrote to him. I have the letter."

Templeton leaned so far back the seat threatened to topple. "I don't know what she said, but it has nothing to do with me."

"But it does." Dominic's words carried a sinister edge. "You're the lord who made her life so unbearable she wrote to a notorious moneylender. She'd rather deal with the devil than suffer you."

"It's not true." He was on his feet, hands raised. "It was a mutual arrangement. I gave her a ruby parure when we parted. She sold it to a broker on Oxford Street. He may still have the receipt."

Dominic's mouth hardened. "You bought her."

His eyes darkened to the heavy green of a hemlock grove. There would be no reasoning with him now.

"You were fifteen years her junior," he barked, flexing his fists. "Not much older than I was then."

Templeton lurched away and darted behind the throne chair where she sat, gripping the carved rail as if it might shield him. She could feel the warm panic of his breath against her neck.

While the men glared at one another, she slipped a hand beneath the desk and slowly raised her skirts, easing the blade from her garter and hiding it in the folds of her gown.

"It was a brief affair. I'll not be hounded like a dog for it."

Dominic must have seen something in the lord's eyes. He stopped prowling. "Step away from the desk."

"Don't test his patience," Mr Ramsey added.

"His patience? I've done nothing wrong."

Dominic drew a slow breath. "Step away. I won't ask again. Touch her and it will be the last thing you do."

Her palm grew clammy beneath the hilt.

This wouldn't end well.

"Enough." The word cut through the room as she rose slowly from the chair, gripping the blade against her skirts. "Backing a man into a corner isn't the way to get answers."

Fury burned in Dominic's eyes. "We have his answer."

"We only have part of the story."

Her mother had been desperate too. She had died with a secret. There were too many coincidences to ignore.

"I've told you everything." The lord remained behind the chair.

"My mother needed money," she said, her voice steadier than she felt as she turned to face the lord. "And she knew Mrs Flavell."

Templeton blinked. "Half the ton knows Mrs Flavell."

"But not every woman goes there looking for help." She lifted her chin. "She also wrote to Mr Moseley, asking for a loan. To escape the same unbearable suitor. You, Lord Templeton."

"Me?" he stuttered. "I barely knew your mother."

"Yet you visited the house." She invented that part.

"I gambled with your father, but we were barely acquaintances." He dared to step from behind the chair. "I don't know anything about these loans. When you find the real culprit, I expect an apology."

Dominic's attention snapped to his quarry. "Was it you?"

"What are you accusing me of now?"

"Were you responsible for my mother's condition?" The question tore its way out of him, stripped of his usual control. "Was my mother carrying your child?"

The room went still.

Templeton's face drained of colour. "What?"

Dominic's fists clenched until his knuckles blanched. "Answer me." His voice cracked on the last word.

"I told you. It was a brief affair. It ended a year before she died."

"I don't believe you." Dominic rounded the desk. "She's dead because of you. The unborn child along with her."

Daphne caught her breath. It made sense now. The two

white roses. The rage that drove him to control every debauched lord in the ton.

Templeton didn't stagger back. He squared his shoulders, determined to stand his ground. "You've got the wrong man."

"You forget I know what you're capable of. You see a woman you want and prey on her weakness. Use money to buy a place in her bed."

The lord's mouth thinned. "I offer a solution to their problems. You make it sound as though I force them."

Daphne cleared her throat. "You do make it hard to say no."

"Careful," Mr Ramsey warned quietly when Dominic muttered a curse. "Give his lordship a chance to explain."

Templeton's gaze flicked between them, calculating now rather than afraid. "If your mother was with child, it was not mine."

Dominic's breath shuddered. "You expect me to believe that?"

"Believe what you like," the lord shot back. "I thought her willing. If you want the man who ruined her, look elsewhere." He drew a hand down the fur trim of his coat. "Ask yourself. Do I appear more terrifying than Moseley?"

The comment gave them all pause.

"Perhaps Harland was your man," Templeton added. "The devil agreed to sell his own daughter to save his neck. He knew both your mothers intimately, and the timeline fits."

"Harland couldn't father a child," Dominic countered. "I have his physician's report. It's why Miss Harland has no siblings."

Daphne thought of Mrs Flavell's letter. Her mother had feared falling with child. She despised her husband. Which meant there had been another man.

Templeton scoffed. "Physicians are not infallible. Perhaps

it was a temporary injury. Or the man made a mistake. Speak to those closest to him instead of dragging me over the coals."

Daphne's mind flicked to Mrs Foster, the woman her father had kept in London for years. And to Aunt Augusta, who knew every sordid detail of the household. If anyone knew the truth, it would be them.

Yet the lord's newfound courage raised suspicions too.

Templeton gripped his wolf mask a little tighter. "The question you should be asking is this: where were you while your mother was being harassed? It's a pity you discovered your courage so late."

Dominic went still. His jaw tightened, but the shine in his eyes told a different story. Perhaps the person he truly blamed was himself.

Was Shadowmere his penance? A place where he forced himself to witness what his mother had kept hidden.

She felt the same prickle behind her eyes, a thickness in her throat. Not for his mother. For him.

But he didn't crumble. He buried his pain and gripped the desk with a ferocity that threatened to splinter the wood.

"Take your mistress and get the hell out of my house. I'll refund the price of your ticket. There's little I can do to restore your honour."

Templeton gave a harsh laugh. "You preach about honour, yet you bedded Harland's daughter just to spite him. She'd have been better off with me. I merely wear a wolf mask."

Dominic lurched forward, murder in his eyes.

Daphne stepped into his path before Ramsey could move, the blade still clutched in her hand. She braced her palm against Dominic's chest, feeling the violent thud of his heart beneath her fingers.

"It's not the same," he rasped, fury roughening his voice.

"I won't discard her when the game grows tiresome. I'll marry her. I know my duty."

The room fell silent.

Her hand slipped from his chest.

Duty. The word her father had used when he bartered her future for coin.

She stared at him. Marry her? The decision had been made without her consent. No proposal. No declaration. Merely a convenient way to repair the damage done.

Tears filled her eyes, blurring the room into a smear of candlelight. The first drop slipped beneath her mask.

Dominic clasped her elbow. "Daphne."

"Don't say another word." Each syllable came in airy gasps that betrayed her effort at poise. "Like every man I encounter, you've forgotten I have a voice."

She pushed past him and hurried from the room, wishing for a carriage to take her anywhere but here. He might have followed, but she was swept into the stream of guests hurrying towards the ballroom.

A small platform had been erected beside the musicians. A masked gentleman stood upon it while a woman circled him, lifting his chin as though inspecting a horse at Tattersall's, as the crowd shouted bids.

This was the world Dominic ruled.

A world she could never call home.

Daphne turned away. The heat, the noise, it all felt suffocating. Before anyone could stop her, she hurried through the terrace doors and into the cool night air.

She took a moment to stop and breathe.

But Shadowmere on the night of the Masque was no place for a lone woman to linger. A man prowled from the depths of the shadows, the beak of his mask long and obscene. He reeked of perfume and brandy.

"Just when I thought the night dull," he said, arrogance etched into his stride, "you appear."

"I'm in no mood for games, sir."

"Neither am I, sweeting."

She could have used Dominic's name as a weapon, certain this wretch would cower. Instead, she drew the dagger from its sheath.

"One more step and I'll gut you like a fish." Moonlight caught the edge of the blade, the sudden glint making it all the more menacing.

The man only laughed and came closer, his gloved hand lifting as though he meant to take her chin. "Temper like that ought to be rewarded. Come claim your prize."

"Back away from her."

The command came from the terrace. Dominic stood there, broad-shouldered and immovable, his expression cold enough to chill the air.

The masked gentleman turned, his confidence collapsing like rigging in a storm. "Easy, Hawke. I meant no harm. Women who come to the Masque know the game."

She didn't wait for him to descend the steps. She hurried down the gravel path toward the gardens and her cottage.

Not *her* cottage.

Nothing about her life here was real.

By the time she reached the door, her breath was ragged. She fumbled inside her bodice for the key, her fingers clumsy with haste.

The lock clicked.

She slipped inside and slammed the door behind her, throwing the bolt just as footsteps pounded up the path.

Silence held for a heartbeat.

A heavy fist struck the wood.

"Daphne."

She pressed her back to the door, her pulse racing.

"Go back to your guests, Mr Hawke."

"Open the door. Let me in."

That was the problem. She had let him in—a self-proclaimed scoundrel—and fallen prey to some foolish notion that he was different from other men.

"There's nothing left to discuss."

"There's everything to discuss. Open the damn door."

She couldn't. One look at the dark torment in his eyes and she would stroke his brow, be the softness he didn't even know he craved.

"I need something to wipe blood off my knuckles."

"You have a handkerchief in your pocket."

He cursed beneath his breath, but tempered his tone. "Let me in, Daphne. Don't lock me out because of something I said in the heat of the moment."

She imagined opening the door, falling into his arms, burying her face in his neck and breathing in the scent she was starving for.

"Are you saying you didn't mean it?"

Nothing. Just the scuff of his boots on stone outside the door, the cries of sybarites and the haunting lilt of the violins.

"I suppose marrying me must seem abhorrent," he said.

"Self-pity is beneath you. You have the strength to own your mistakes. Don't disappoint me further."

"Disappoint you? I've done everything possible to make amends."

Did that stretch to touching her beneath the stars, making love in her bed? Did it include all the beautiful things he had said and done?

She threw the dagger to the floor and pulled the ribbons of her mask free, letting the disguise fall away so she could breathe again.

No matter how fiercely she felt for him, she could not remain here. Not in this house. Not with a man who let the past poison his future.

"I'd like to leave Shadowmere. You can do one last thing and I'll ask nothing of you again." She wrapped her arms around her middle, though it was her heart that ached. "Send for Charlotte."

CHAPTER SEVENTEEN

Mr Ramsey arrived to escort her to Dominic's study and carry her valise. He'd brought a small wooden box and wrapped the pink teapot and cups in broadsheet pages, stacking them neatly inside.

"Hawke says you're to take the porcelain."

She stared at the box. "I can't take it. It belonged to his grandmother."

"They're Hawke's orders, not mine."

Her eyes blurred for a moment. "Leave it. Please."

He ignored her plea. "Hawke's never given a woman anything. Best to accept it with good grace."

A diamond necklace would have suited a mistress.

This felt like he was giving her a piece of his soul.

"Is Charlotte here?"

Part of her prayed the answer was no, that it wasn't too late to change her mind. That they might argue, kiss, and spend the rest of the day in bed.

But the noises of the damned, the howls in the darkness, the heavy heaving of a hundred lungs meant she could not suffer another night at Shadowmere.

"She's with Hawke in the study."

The thought of seeing him made her chest tighten.

For a moment, she could scarcely breathe.

How did you say goodbye to a man you loved? How did you accept this might be your biggest regret?

"We should go now." The sooner it was over, the better.

She left the cottage and couldn't bear to look back.

Mr Ramsey didn't speak until they entered the house. "I know he's not gone about things the right way. He can be a stubborn devil. But you've unsettled him in ways I've never seen before."

She pictured the possessive glint in Dominic's eyes as he entered her, the look of surrender when he came undone.

"It's difficult to know what's honest and what's said to serve his purpose."

Mr Ramsey frowned. "He's been pacing that study like a caged beast all morning. Surely that says something."

"Yes. That he's lost control and despises the feeling."

"There's more to it than that."

He'd used her to prove a point.

To demean Lord Templeton.

She forced the thought aside. Finding the reason behind her mother's need for money might bring her closer to her father's killer. That had to be her focus now.

Her heart missed a beat when she saw him at the window, staring towards All Saints' steeple. His broad shoulders were rigid beneath the black coat.

Charlotte was talking. He paid her no heed.

But he turned when he heard the click of the door, his eyes closing briefly with agonising slowness. "You're ready. Good. You should leave before the guests crawl out of bed."

His frosty tone came as no surprise. The truth lay in the dark circles beneath his eyes, the stubble shadowing his jaw.

"I have no wish to linger," Charlotte said, cool and immaculate in pale blue. "Heaven forbid we encounter a naked stag on the staircase."

"Then you'd best not delay," he said.

The distance between them felt like a chasm. One she didn't know how to cross. No. This would not be her lasting memory of him.

She steeled herself and approached. He didn't flinch when she touched his arm, only sighed when she kissed his cheek. "Perhaps when we've both dealt with our ghosts, we might meet under better circumstances."

Tea at Gunter's. A walk in Hyde Park.

He clasped her elbow, the protector in him missing the emotion behind her words and seizing on what he believed mattered most. "You plan to continue the investigation on your own?"

"My mother needed money too. I'm beginning to wonder if she truly died of an illness. The answer feels within reach."

He drew her closer until only an inch separated them, the heat of his body a parting caress. "I suppose I've no right to forbid it."

"No, but I'll be careful."

He gave a curt nod, a muscle ticking in his jaw as he released her. "Charlotte can be resourceful. I trust you'll stay with her in Wimpole Street."

"Until I uncover the truth." She could linger. Every second with him felt like a gift. But she hadn't been entirely honest. "There's something you should know. The real reason I came here to work as a maid."

He straightened, shifting his chain mail into place. "Yes."

"I thought working here might help me bide my time, and you owed me something for the trouble you caused." She swallowed past the bulging lump in her throat. The truth would wound him. "Charlotte has a cottage in Scotland I might lease. I only had to stay here the month."

Silence stretched.

Dominic swallowed.

He turned to the window, glancing at the church spire before facing her again. "Then leaving is the sensible choice. Whatever I thought we had clearly meant nothing."

No. I love you.

"I told you I had no plans to stay."

"I thought you'd changed your mind."

Charlotte cleared her throat. "Perhaps we should go before we're seen by a guest. I'll not have it said I participate in these sordid gatherings."

"Ramsey will escort you to the mews." He moved behind his imposing desk, opened a ledger and began making notes.

She stepped away.

Her fingers still tingled where she had touched him.

What she would give to return to the cottage and feel the heat of his body against hers, to lie with him in sated bliss.

Mr Ramsey picked up the box and placed it in her arms.

The porcelain rattled softly inside.

"Goodbye, Mr Hawke."

The scratch of his pen never paused.

"Goodbye, angel."

Daphne spent most of the journey back to London staring out the carriage window at passing fields, tears sliding down her cheeks whether she willed them or not.

The memory of him, head bowed, struck like a blade to her heart. She wished she could claim her tears were for her father, for her dire situation, not for Dominic and a far-fetched dream.

Charlotte's comment didn't help matters.

"I've never seen him like that."

Daphne gripped the seat cushion. "Like what?"

"Lost and a little afraid."

Her first instinct was to pound on the roof and tell the coachman to turn around. "What could Dominic possibly have to fear?"

"Feeling something other than hatred."

"Guilt is his constant companion." The truth was clearer now. Lord Templeton had hit the mark with a barbed arrow. "Hatred is something he turns outward to survive."

Charlotte hesitated. "You're in love with him."

Daphne looked down at her hands. In his arms was the only place she'd known true peace.

"I'm in love with the man who comes to my cottage. I'm not sure I know the man who commands Hades."

"Are they not two sides of the same coin?"

"And therein lies the problem."

Charlotte fell silent. Her gaze moved from Daphne to the box on the floor. "Hawke gave you a gift?"

Not a gift. A piece of the life she was leaving behind.

"His grandmother's porcelain tea set."

Even saying the words tightened her throat.

"Something precious then."

"And not at all practical."

"The best gifts rarely are."

The thrum of the wheels filled the silence for the next few miles. They spoke of the weather, London gossip, and Daphne's plans for the coming days.

"I'd go home, but I'm not convinced my aunt won't drug my tea and put me on a boat to India."

"The most wicked betrayals aren't plotted in back alleys, but around the dinner table." Charlotte sounded like she spoke from experience. "You'll stay with me. I insist. At least until it's safe for you in town."

Daphne released a breath she'd been holding since leaving Shadowmere. "It won't be for long. Just while I determine what happened to my father and why my mother needed money so desperately."

She told Charlotte everything on the journey. About the case, the blackmail, and why Lord Templeton's eagerness to name another man troubled her.

Charlotte sat forward. "You think your mother and Hawke's met the same fate?"

"Both wished to prevent a child." Daphne mentioned her mother's visit to Mrs Flavell. "Both wrote to Mr Moseley, hoping to secure a loan. Both were intimately involved with my father."

"His mistress, Mrs Foster, must know something."

"Yes. They've been lovers on and off for a decade."

Charlotte glanced out the window, the grey sprawl of the metropolis coming into view. "And that's why you left Shadowmere? To pursue your own agenda?"

At the mention of Shadowmere, her heart grew heavy.

"No. Dominic told Lord Templeton he would marry me. It was about control. To prove a point. As if the decision were his alone."

Knowing he thought it his duty cut deep.

Charlotte arched a brow. "Hawke spoke of marriage?"

"Yes, as a weapon to attack Lord Templeton."

"And you'd rather he'd made a sweeping declaration?"

Something in Charlotte's tone said she believed Daphne expected too much of a man like Dominic.

"Is it foolish to want him to love me?"

"No," she said quietly. "But you should ask yourself who you love more. The scoundrel or the dream?"

She already knew the answer.

She loved the man who dominated a room with a single look. The man who would break the hand of anyone who touched her. The man who wore his mother's ring around his neck and carried roses to her grave.

"Was I wrong to leave?"

Charlotte shook her head. "It must have been frightening to walk alongside those masked fiends. Sometimes a lady must make a stand. You're allowed a voice, Daphne. Hawke needed reminding of that."

Would he realise it?

Or would he strengthen the barricade around his heart?

"It was hard to think while there," she admitted. And yet leaving had been the hardest thing she had ever done. "I have never witnessed anything quite so abhorrent as the Autumn Masque."

"I can quite imagine." Charlotte adjusted her gloves and considered her for a moment. "What say we attend Lady Parker's ball tomorrow? Mrs Foster will be there. We'll lure her into the garden and you can bombard her with questions."

"Shouldn't I be in mourning?"

Shouldn't she help her aunt arrange the funeral? Should she grieve for a man who didn't deserve her tears?

"You'll be the topic of the evening, regardless. You may as well give the heifers fodder." Charlotte raised a hand. "And before you raise another objection, I have the perfect gown for you to wear."

Conversations died when Daphne entered Lady Parker's crowded ballroom. Under the blaze of chandeliers, every head turned. Their eyes lingered on the deep purple silk of her gown, disapproval plain on every face.

Music drifted from the orchestra balcony, a lilting waltz at odds with the sudden hush.

But she would not stumble. She would not sweat.

Charlotte slipped her arm through Daphne's in quiet solidarity. "Head high. Remember, they're only vultures if you look like carrion. And you look exquisite tonight."

She would have preferred to blend into the cream walls, hide behind the burgundy curtains, or find a quiet alcove and hope Mrs Foster ambled by.

But if Dominic had taught her anything, it was to own her space. To turn disdain to one's advantage.

"If that chin dips, you'll sleep in the coal shed tonight," Charlotte teased. "Remember, walk slowly. Pause before speaking. Elegance comes not from jewels or fine clothes, but from presence."

Charlotte guided her through the throng with practised ease, nodding to acquaintances and ignoring those who stared.

"You're certain Mrs Foster will be here?" Daphne searched the sea of heads, looking for a woman with too much rouge and hair as wild as a bird's nest.

"Her new protector is Lady Parker's brother—Lord Ainsley. He never misses a ball." Charlotte leant closer. "He would rather scandalise the room than be thought dull."

"I suppose she'll follow him around like a lapdog until he's settled her debts." Daphne didn't smile. What would Mrs Foster do for money? Practically anything, it seemed. Did that extend to murder?

They circled the ballroom in search of the woman. Men

gravitated towards Charlotte and looked straight through Daphne. Part of her was almost relieved. Her heart belonged elsewhere.

Charlotte tugged her sleeve. "There, by the terrace doors."

Mrs Foster loitered beside a potted palm, peering through the fronds as though she were invisible. It might have helped had she not worn canary yellow.

Daphne followed the line of her gaze to Lord Ainsley—and stopped.

Dominic stood near the marble fireplace, listening with that same guarded stillness she knew too well. He didn't spare Lord Ainsley a glance. He looked at her as if they were alone in the dark, his eyes slowly stripping away her clothes.

The air left her lungs. She should have looked away. Instead, the music seemed to fade as her thoughts returned to the memory of their entwined fingers and the hope nothing could part them.

Dominic.

For a moment she forgot why she had come.

Lord Ainsley had his own distractions. A curt nod at Mrs Foster and the woman disappeared through the terrace doors.

"We should follow her into the garden," Daphne said, eager to put distance between her and Dominic before her composure deserted her completely.

Charlotte agreed, but her step faltered at the terrace doors.

"What's wrong?" Daphne asked.

"Nothing." Charlotte's fingers tightened briefly on the door frame. "I once learned a harsh lesson in a garden." She released a quiet breath and stepped outside. "Come. I see her heading for the rotunda."

Mrs Foster was not draped gracefully upon a stone bench like a goddess of Olympus. She was crouched behind the garden temple, ducking like a thief avoiding the watch.

"Mrs Foster," Daphne called, leaning around a pillar. She found the woman sipping from a silver flask. "Is there something wrong with Lady Parker's champagne? There's ratafia if you prefer."

"Go away," came the brusque reply. Mrs Foster pushed the stopper back into the flask and slipped it into her reticule. "If Mr Hawke sees me talking to you, he'll have my guts for garters."

"You have greater worries than that."

Mrs Foster jerked as if a rat trap had snapped beneath her feet. "No. Tell me you've not found more. I thought Ainsley was the only one."

Daphne caught the sharp scent of brandy on her breath. "The only one?"

"The only loan amongst your father's belongings."

Daphne shook her head, though she was not entirely confused. Dominic's story rang in her mind like a warning.

"My father's debts are not your responsibility."

Mrs Foster grasped her hand. "They're not?" She sagged with relief. "Thank heavens. You persuaded Mr Hawke to settle the debt, as he did with Mr Moseley. Your aunt received a letter this morning, confirming the account has been paid."

The injustice of it burned.

Her aunt would benefit from Dominic's generosity and whatever remained in the will. Even in death, her father meant to punish her.

"I couldn't possibly ask Mr Hawke for such a favour." Yet the thought of repaying him in kind was tempting. "He believes you know something about his mother's death."

"Me?" She clasped her chest and stumbled back. "I never knew her. I met your father months after he ended his affair with Mrs Hawke."

Questions filled her mind, but she focused on the one that might prove her father's innocence—at least in this.

"You were his lover for a decade, yet never had a child."

Mrs Foster paused. Her throat worked before she said, "After his riding accident, he was incapable."

That was the answer Daphne had hoped to hear.

But why the hesitation? Why the strain?

"You know what was said about my father and Mrs Hawke." She had to tread carefully. It wasn't her place to repeat such a guarded secret, though Dominic had accused Lord Templeton outright.

"He swore it wasn't true."

Daphne needed her to be specific. "You believed him?"

"He had no reason to lie."

"Other than Mr Hawke might kill him for it."

Mrs Foster stepped closer. "We spoke about it at the time. Before Mr Hawke built his sordid empire. Before he stormed into Lord Templeton's ball to ruin you."

Ruin? Daphne remembered Dominic's hand closing around hers, the music fading as he led her from the floor. In that moment he had felt less like a scandal and more like salvation.

She forced the image aside. "You're avoiding the question. Did you believe him?"

"Yes. He blamed Lord Templeton. There was some question about the timing. Your uncle acted as mediator. He took the physician's report to Shadowmere as proof."

She resisted the urge to gasp. "Proof he couldn't be—"

"The child's father." Mrs Foster raised her hands as though calling for calm. "It was a long time ago. The details scarcely matter now."

They mattered to Dominic. More now than ever.

"What did Lord Templeton say at the time?"

Mrs Foster's composure cracked. "I don't know." She gripped the pillar and glanced towards the house. "You need to leave. I'll not give Lord Ainsley a reason to raise the interest."

Interest. "Tell him you won't pay."

"I can't. He's covering the rent."

Charlotte leaned towards Daphne. "If we're finished, we should go. Lord Ainsley has stepped onto the terrace. He's one to avoid."

Still, Daphne had one more question. "There were ligature marks on my father's wrists when they found his body. Was it a game gone wrong? An accident you made look like murder."

Mrs Foster paled. "I hated what that man made me do." She shuddered with revulsion. "But you're looking in the wrong place."

"Lord Ainsley is coming this way—" Charlotte stopped abruptly. "Wait. Hawke has called him back. They're talking on the steps."

Daphne looked at Mrs Foster. "Once I have the truth and my father's killer is in custody, I shall find a way to free you of the debt."

She moved to leave, but Mrs Foster caught her arm. "Your father spoke with Lord Templeton before he left the ball. They agreed to meet privately that night, after he'd visited Mr Irving. I don't know if they ever did. But I can't risk causing trouble."

Daphne went stone-still.

Lord Templeton and her father, meeting in secret the night of the murder. The implications were difficult to ignore. No wonder he'd argued with Dominic. Templeton was up to his neck in the mire.

Charlotte touched her sleeve. "We must go."

"Is Dominic still there?"

"Yes. Ainsley's gone, but Hawke hasn't moved."

She stepped onto the grass and saw him beneath the terrace lamps, his hands clasped behind his back, though she remembered how they felt on her skin. The firm line of his mouth was unchanged, though she knew how it softened when he kissed her.

Her pulse quickened as she drew nearer, unsure how he would greet her. With warmth or the cold civility he had shown the day before?

His gaze never left her as she mounted the steps.

She managed a smile. "Mr Hawke."

He inclined his head. "Miss Harland."

Formality sat between them like a stone wall.

Unsure what to do, she stepped past him, but his hand closed around her wrist. Not roughly. Firm enough that she felt the heat of his fingers through her glove.

"Dance with me."

It was the last thing she should do.

A dance would be a slow, exquisite form of torture.

She lifted her chin. "Is that an invitation or a command, Mr Hawke?"

He held her gaze. "I seek permission, Miss Harland."

That, more than the request itself, undid her.

She should have refused. Thought of her sanity.

Instead, she said, "Very well. Perhaps we might compare notes. I assume you're here to make enquiries."

"Something like that."

Charlotte excused herself. "I believe I see someone I ought to greet. I'll leave you to your enquiries."

Dominic inclined his head, but they did not follow Charlotte into the ballroom. Relaxing his grip on her wrist, he closed the distance between them and every nerve in her body sparked to life.

"Shall we dance here on the terrace?"

"The terrace?" She had to admit the idea was romantic.

"I know you like to feel breathless beneath the stars."

Only when he was the cause.

She glanced towards the ballroom. "Without music?"

"We don't need music."

"We don't?"

"When we touch, we always find a rhythm."

He guided her into the first step, his hand settling at her waist with a familiarity that caught her breath.

Her fingers tightened slightly on his shoulder. "I didn't expect to see you here tonight."

"And I thought you wore that exquisite gown to torment me."

"Charlotte thought deep plum would suit me."

"It does. A little too much."

"You seem to like everything I wear."

"It isn't the clothes."

His thumb shifted slightly against her waist, easing the knot in her chest. He wasn't angry. Not distant or cold.

Yet she didn't understand why he'd asked her to dance. And while she wanted nothing more than to lean into him, their differences still lay between them.

"I didn't lie about my reasons for staying at Shadowmere. I was angry and afraid and had nowhere else to go."

He breathed slowly through his nose. "You should have told me Charlotte offered you an incentive to stay. There would have been no misunderstanding between us then."

"You said I could use the cottage until we'd caught my father's killer. And I told you more than once I planned to leave. We spoke of Oxford and Bath."

"I thought us being lovers changed that."

Lovers. The word settled in a place reserved for him.

He held her so she could feel his hard body.

"I can't read minds, Dominic."

"Yet you live in mine."

The admission sent a ripple of heat through her. She could not have this conversation—not now. Her emotions were too raw, and they had come here to find a killer.

She steadied herself. "Then perhaps we should focus on why we're here tonight. Lord Templeton—"

"I don't give a damn about Templeton." His voice cut across hers. "I told him I'd shoot him if I saw him again."

His fingers gave a brief squeeze as they turned.

"Mrs Foster said my father arranged to meet Lord Templeton on the night he died. A man his size could throw a body over Blackfriars Bridge. And he had motive."

She felt him stiffen.

"Yes. He wished to hide the deplorable way he treated my mother. Templeton knew I'd kill him if I found out. I still might."

Her step faltered, but he firmed his grip on her waist.

"I'm quite sure your mother meant to save you, not see you hanged for ridding the world of a wastrel."

Perhaps the word *might* was important. Vengeance had been his only goal before ... before them. Something had changed.

They turned slowly across the terrace, the lamps casting long shadows over the stone, a faint breeze lifting the hem of her gown. She was reluctant to say more, but he needed to hear the truth.

"Mrs Foster recalled something that happened years ago. My uncle acted as mediator. He took the physician's report to Shadowmere to prove the accident had left my father incapable. That only left Lord Templeton. No other names were mentioned."

He swore under his breath. "That bastard."

He stopped dancing, though he held her tight.

Unsure what he might do, she reminded him of one important fact. "Without proof, it's hearsay. Perhaps if you told me how she died, we might make a case against him."

The answer did not come easily.

"Poison," he said at last. "No one else knows but the physician who attended her. A good man who's no longer with us."

It wasn't the shock that made her heart stumble, but the water gathering along his lower lashes. Whatever they were to one another now, he trusted her with the truth.

"I can see why you stormed into the ballroom bent on vengeance." Why he had not given the daughter of his enemy a second thought. "I'll visit my aunt tomorrow. She will corroborate the story."

He cleared his throat. "You'll not go alone."

"If you appear beside me, she'll say nothing at all. I'll suggest we meet at a coffeehouse." If she went home, her aunt would insist she live under her roof, not Charlotte's.

"I'll sit where she can't see me."

"Dominic, everyone notices you."

"Then take Charlotte."

She touched his shoulder. "Don't worry."

He studied her for a moment, as though deciding whether to argue further. Perhaps he didn't wish to overstep after his careless mention of marriage.

"Very well. I've business of my own tomorrow."

"Business?" She had no right to ask.

"I'm meeting friends. We've compiled a list of properties owned by Irving. We mean to find the missing clerk."

"Will you send word if you do?"

"I'll be in town for a few days. May I call on you at Charlotte's?" He paused before saying, "I need to know if your aunt confirms Mrs Foster's story."

"Of course."

He held her gaze a second longer, as though reluctant to let the moment end. Slowly, his hand slipped from her waist.

The absence left her feeling as hollow as a drum.

She drew a breath. "Is our dance at an end, Mr Hawke?"

A faint smile touched his mouth. "You know it's not."

CHAPTER EIGHTEEN

Dominic stood in Daphne's dark bedchamber, watching the gentle rise and fall of her chest, the soft flutter of her lips. She slept on her side, knees drawn to her chest, clutching the black silk square embroidered with his monogram.

His grandmother's pink teacup sat on the nightstand beside a wilting white rose in a small vase.

She'd been crying. Because of him.

Charlotte had said as much when she tried to prevent him from entering and he'd tussled with her strapping butler. But something fierce in his chest stopped him from returning to the hotel.

"I need to see her."

"You saw her two hours ago."

"I need to see her again. Just for a few minutes."

One glimpse might quiet the craving. He'd raced across town in the dead of night, heart thundering, simply to stand in her room.

"Don't make me call in a debt, Charlotte."

"Consider it already paid." Charlotte had pulled the ties of her wrapper as if tightening a noose. "If she wakes and wants you gone, I shall drag you out myself."

He'd nodded, sworn he wouldn't linger.

Yet here he stood.

He fought the urge to crouch by the bed, brush her hair from her face, prove she was real. To wake her and beg her forgiveness.

He meant what he'd said. He wanted to marry her. Not because he was duty-bound or plagued with guilt. Because he was in love with her.

In the stillness of her chamber, the familiar burn of hatred was gone. The need to make the world pay no longer pressed at his back.

He felt calm. At peace.

Never more certain she was his life now.

He lowered himself into the chair in the shadowed corner of the room and drew the ruby necklace from his pocket.

She'd worn it the first night he kissed her, when she'd driven him half out of his mind with need, only to tell him he could never give her what she wanted.

The list was seared into his soul.

Love—she was wrong about that.

She wanted to be someone's everything.

There was no doubt she was his.

A family—he'd have no trouble there.

He wanted her as surely as he needed to breathe.

A home—ah, there lay the stumbling block.

He'd made a pact with the devil. Such bargains were hard to break.

Shadowmere was built on control. Surrendering it would be no easy feat. Yet there was nothing he wouldn't do for her. He only hoped he wasn't too late.

He closed his eyes, if only for a moment. Her scent and the sound of her breathing were enough to lull him to sleep.

His body surrendered to the quiet, to the warmth of her nearby, as though the world outside ceased to exist.

A hand rested on his knee, rocking gently.

"Dominic," she whispered.

He blinked awake, unsure if he was dreaming. Someone had lit the lamp. An amber glow bathed the room.

Daphne crouched beside his chair, dark hair spilling over one shoulder. The low neckline of her nightgown offered a generous view of her breasts, rising and falling with each breath.

A familiar ache stirred.

Something softer settled in his chest.

"What are you doing here? You gave me a fright."

He rubbed his eyes. "Forgive me. I know it's late. There's something I must give you. Something I want to say that can't wait."

Her gaze moved to the ruby necklace in his hand. "You forgot to return it to the jeweller? Good Lord, you've had it a week."

The chair creaked as he shifted. "It was never on loan. I bought it for you. I've carried it in my pocket ever since."

She looked at the necklace, then at him, and reached the wrong conclusion. "Dominic, we've discussed this. You don't need to make amends for what happened in Lord Templeton's ballroom."

"That's not why I bought it."

"I hear Mr Woodcroft can sell sand in the desert, but you're not a man who succumbs to pressure."

Why did she not see the obvious answer? Because he'd made her believe he was ruled by duty, not his heart.

"I bought it because I wanted to own something you'd

worn." He paused. He daren't confess how many times he'd held it and thought of her. "I have a strange compulsion to buy you the world."

Her breath came a little quicker. "Why didn't you tell me?"

"Tell you I'm not the soulless devil I'd have you believe?"

She smiled. "Your quest for revenge told me everything I needed to know about you. A soulless man doesn't risk his life for a mother who died a decade ago." She gave a small shrug. "And you brought me fire tools. A heartless devil wouldn't care if I was cold."

"Am I so transparent?" His gaze dropped to the open buttons of her nightgown. He'd come to regret never knowing the heat of her skin.

"My mother taught me to judge a man by his actions. I could list the ways you've been kind to me."

"Except when I stole your voice."

He brushed his thumb over the ruby.

"Yes, except then." She winced as though the memory pained her. "You don't know how hard it was for me to leave Shadowmere. To leave you."

"You said the truest measure of a woman's affections is that she stays when she's free to leave." The words tasted bitter on his tongue. "What was I supposed to think?"

"I wasn't free. You put me in shackles when your pride answered for me. But that's not the reason I sent for Charlotte." She stood, pulling her hand from his knee. "I couldn't bear another night there, surrounded by heathens."

He shot to his feet, drawing her up with him. "You don't think I could protect you?"

"It doesn't matter. To stay is to condone it."

He drew a calming breath. "You know my reasons for

hosting them. The house my mother gave her life to save would have fallen into ruin."

She shook her head as if he were a boy who couldn't solve the simplest puzzle. "She didn't give her life to save the house. Everything she did was to save you."

He turned away, her words cutting to the bone.

His mother would not recognise him now.

"I like the power," he admitted, staring at the wall.

"The true measure of power is having command over yourself."

"You think I don't know my own mind? You'd rather I smooth the coarse edges, become a man you could admire?"

She slipped her arms around his waist and pressed her cheek to his back. "I don't want you to become someone else. There's no man I admire more than you."

He closed his eyes. He needed more than her admiration.

"Did you come to give me the necklace? To confess you bought it for me? Is that the news that couldn't wait?"

"Not quite." He faced her.

Perhaps she saw the pain in his eyes, the sorrow he'd carried for years. Her hand lifted before she seemed to think better of it. Then she brushed his hair from his brow and kissed him softly on the lips.

Something in that kiss unravelled the last of his doubt.

He'd been right to come.

His arms closed around her, the ruby necklace still tangled in his hand, and he deepened the kiss, drawing her closer as if he meant to anchor her there.

She opened for him, her hands clutching his coat with sudden fierceness, the kiss turning desperate.

And then he tasted it—the salt of her tears.

He drew back, saw more tears slide down her cheeks.

"What is it?" He searched her face, wiping them away

with his thumb. "I overstepped. This was ill-timed. I shouldn't have come here uninvited."

She cupped his cheek, her light laugh confirming he'd missed the mark. "It's not you. These feelings steal my breath. Dominic, there's something I must—"

He touched a finger to her lips. Though he longed to hear more, she had to know why he'd come. "Let me speak first. Please, Daphne."

She blinked tears from her lashes. "Very well."

"The ruby is yours, though that's not what I came to give you." He tucked the necklace back into his pocket and drew out his mother's ring. "I want you to have this."

She pressed her hand to her mouth, eyes widening as he held the slender gold ring, a pale green peridot set between two pearls.

"No. I can't take your mother's ring."

He placed it in her palm and curled her fingers around it. "It's the only thing I care about, besides you. Why wouldn't I give it to you? I'm in love with you. It will only ever be you."

For a heartbeat she stared at him, lower lip trembling.

"Dominic …"

She swallowed hard, tears gathering on her lashes.

"I love you, angel."

The words left him exposed. There was nothing left to hide behind. Now only her answer remained.

She lifted her gaze to his.

"Dominic, I love you."

The breath left him. His throat closed around the question he couldn't stop. "You love the man who visits you in the cottage? I'm not always him."

She laid a hand on his cheek.

"I love the man who can bring a ballroom to its knees. The man who takes no prisoners. The man who trusts me enough to show me his softer side. I love all of you. The saint and the sinner."

He closed his eyes, sliding an arm around the flare of her hip and pressing a tender kiss to her forehead.

"Come home with me." He brushed his mouth against her temple. "I'm not the sort of man who picks daisies, but you'll have my loyalty and my love."

A breathless sound escaped her, half-laugh, half-sigh. "You're precisely the sort of man who'd pick me daisies. But we can't think about the future until we deal with the past."

He swallowed, his throat dry. "The past could ruin us."

"No, the truth will save us." She eased out of his arms and showed him the ring in her palm. "If you don't avenge your mother now, it will come back to haunt you."

The thought struck like cold steel. Losing her would be worse than leaving his mother unavenged. He had endured a decade of secrets. He'd not endure another day without her.

The tenderness gave way to purpose.

"You search Mr Irving's properties for the clerk. I'll arrange to meet my aunt and see if she remembers my uncle acting as mediator."

Fear prickled the back of his neck. He would leave nothing to chance. "I'll need the name of the coffeehouse and the time you're meeting her. Use my carriage." The creak of the boards on the landing had him glancing at the chamber door. "I should go before Charlotte lets her butler off the leash. You'll send the details to Mivart's Hotel?"

Every instinct said to forbid it.

But she'd not be kept in a cage.

"You'll know exactly when and where I'm meeting her."

His gaze dropped to her mouth. He couldn't leave without kissing her again. Not when every moment might be their last.

He cradled her throat and swept his thumb over her lower lip. There was no need to ask permission. She met him half-way, their mouths colliding in a soft, breathless blur of heat and desperation.

He kissed her as though committing the feel of her to memory, so deep it drowned every thought in his head.

"Get dressed," he said, his body so hard it pained him. "Come with me to the hotel."

Her palms flattened against his chest, fingers curling in the fabric as though she might pull him back for another kiss. "One moment," she breathed. "Let me speak to Charlotte."

The room felt wrong without her. Last night he'd sat in his throne-like chair at Shadowmere, lust and laughter filling the house, and felt nothing but the absence of one woman.

His woman.

She loved him. She'd said so. And still he couldn't believe it. After years spent wielding power, he had no defence against something he couldn't control. Love was a door left unlocked. Happiness a thing that could be taken. He'd not survive another decade kneeling at a graveside.

Perhaps when Templeton had confessed and Harland's killer was caught, he might have faith. When the past was buried, he might think to the future. For now, these moments with her were all he had.

Daphne returned and closed the door gently behind her, as if she feared waking the house. Her smile confirmed they were leaving.

Beneath the glow of the lamp, he could see the flare of her hips through the thin cotton nightgown. He'd seen the swell of her breasts but not their fullness, not the rosy peaks grazing the material now.

The desire to peel it off her was almost unbearable.

"You'll come to Mivart's?" he asked.

"Charlotte thinks I shouldn't be seen entering a hotel."

Sod Charlotte.

"We stayed at the Carroway and spent the night at Mrs Flavell's." A place no more respectable than a bordello.

She closed the gap between them. "Charlotte said you can stay the night here." Slipping her hands beneath his coat, she pushed it off his shoulders.

"In the guest room?"

"In bed with me."

She watched him. Heat flared in eyes everyone said were made of stone. Lips used to giving harsh commands softened. His shoulders had loosened, his rigid stance of authority gone. And lower still, the line of his trousers left little doubt what her invitation had done.

"Should I ask what Charlotte wants in return?"

"Only if you want to spoil the moment." Her fingers moved down his waistcoat, working the buttons free though she wanted to tear it open. "I believe she intends to call in the favour at a later date."

"Of course she does."

"Too high a price to pay for a night with me?" She pulled his shirt from his trousers, setting her palms to the firm plane of muscle beneath.

He hissed through his teeth. "You know the answer."

"Perhaps I'd like to hear you say it." She drew her fingers over the fall of his trousers, heat pooling low as she traced the hard length of him.

He closed his eyes against the slow stroke of her hand. "God, Daphne, I'd sell my soul for one taste of you."

"I suspect you'll have more than one taste tonight."

His eyes opened, dark with a hunger he made no attempt to hide. "Like a true housemaid, you know how to stoke a man's fire."

"I only care about yours."

"I'm burning for you, love."

"Then we'd best get you out of these clothes."

She pushed the waistcoat from his shoulders and drew his shirt over his head, breathing him in as she did. Soap and cedar, and something warmer that belonged only to him.

The pull was instinctive.

Her lips brushed his chest, then drifted higher to the line of his throat, tasting his skin, feeling the steady beat of his pulse beneath her mouth.

His hand closed in her hair with rough possession, tipping her face back. He kissed her wildly, as though every moment of waiting had led to this.

A groan rumbled in his throat, as urgent as her need for him.

There was nothing as magnificent as this man when he forgot to be invincible, when he lowered his guard and let her in.

He broke first on a ragged breath. "I'm so hard for you." His fingers grazed her breasts as he reached for the sleeves of her nightgown. "I need to see you, every damn inch." He stilled. "No. You take it off for me."

It was a plea, not a command, and she was learning to tell the difference. Perhaps that's why she found the courage to step back and draw the gown slowly up her thighs.

His tongue skimmed his lower lip, a dangerous grin forming. "Not the angel now. I think you like punishing me."

"Who knew I could have you at my mercy?" She raised

the material up past her hips, relishing his sharp intake of breath.

"I knew. I knew the second I held you in my arms." His gaze lingered where she ached. "Take it off. Torture me a little more."

"Always in a hurry, Mr Hawke."

"You drive a man to distraction, Miss Harland."

"Yet you made love to me without removing my chemise." She'd wondered why, but a lack of experience had left her guessing. "Perhaps I'll insist you leave your trousers on tonight."

He palmed himself over the fall. "That could be a problem. I'm about to split a seam."

"Well. We wouldn't want you to leave in a state of dishabille."

She drew the nightgown over her head and let it fall.

For a moment, he merely looked at her, his throat working, his eyes wide amid the amber glow, the heat of his gaze scorching her skin.

"You don't know what you do to me." His fingers worked the buttons on his trousers, his eyes never leaving her. "Having you as I wanted in the cottage would have ruined me."

"I ruined you on Lord Templeton's dance floor."

He smiled and her heart constricted. "You're not wrong. You're the first and only woman to have me begging."

"Lie on the bed. Let me hear you beg some more."

When had she learnt to be so bold?

He pulled off his shoes, pushed his trousers down past his lean hips and stepped out of them. He was larger than she remembered. And strangely beautiful with it.

"You mean to own me, love?" He drew his hand down his rigid length, a sensual hum in his throat as he looked at her.

"I learned a thing or two from my first Masque." Her confidence wavered. "Though you may have to guide me."

"I'd do anything for you. But you know that."

"I had an inkling when I saw you at the ball tonight." She felt a flutter in her chest as she pictured him on the terrace. "But one can never be sure."

"You should have had an inkling when I gave you the key to the cottage." He pulled back the bedsheets and settled on the mattress. "What do you plan to do with me?"

Love you.

Ease every painful memory.

She climbed on top of him, straddling his broad thighs. "My father refused to pay for riding lessons. This will be my first."

"Lucky me, though I suspect you'll be an expert."

"There's only one way to know."

She reached between them, closing her hand around his hot flesh and guiding him to her entrance. Their gazes locked as he eased inside her an inch, then a little more, stretching her, filling her slowly.

Their breath left them in a rush.

The hunger in his eyes sharpened, but there was something else there, something softer reserved only for her.

"God." His gaze moved over her face, the slope of her shoulders, lower still. "Everything about you is so damned divine."

His hand closed over her breast, his thumb grazing the peak, and she felt the answering pull of it low where they were joined. She closed her eyes against the feel of him buried deep.

When she moved, tentatively at first, his hands tightened on her hips.

She learnt the rhythm the way she learnt most things: by feel, by instinct, by reading his face for what undid him.

His thumb found the place that made her gasp, circling with the same unhurried patience he brought to everything that mattered. He meant to make her come before anything else.

"Don't stop, Dominic."

He thrust upwards as he stroked and worked her.

"*Daphne.*"

The sound of her name, rough-edged and almost broken, tipped her over. She shuddered, her fingers clutching his shoulders, the pleasure cresting and breaking across her in a long, helpless wave.

"You're mine now." He rolled her beneath him in one smooth movement, his voice dropping to a growl. "And I mean to take you hard."

He was true to his word.

He gripped her bottom, angling her hips so he could drive deeper, filling her completely with each stroke. She wrapped her thighs around him and held on, her fingers pressing into the hard muscle of his back.

His mouth found her ear. "You're mine. Say it."

"I'm yours." She pressed her lips to his jaw, his throat, whatever she could reach. "Only yours."

He groaned against her neck and drove deeper still, as though he meant to make good on every word.

She locked her thighs tighter around him. Whatever awaited them—the past, the danger, the ghosts neither had buried—nothing would part them again.

"God, Daphne." His breath fractured, his rhythm losing its careful edge. "You undo me completely."

She felt him shudder, felt the moment his control broke. He withdrew, his release spilling hot against her thigh as he buried his face in her hair, her name on his lips like the last word of a prayer.

For a long moment, neither of them moved.

"Tell me you want another lesson," he panted.

She held him, tracing lines on his back, loving the weight of him. "You're wrong. I'm a novice, and may need a dozen a week."

"Only a dozen?"

He rolled onto his back and settled beside her, drawing her against him, her back to his chest, his arm heavy and warm across her waist. Outside, London was nothing but the distant clatter of hooves and a drunken lout singing.

His fingers found hers and stilled.

He'd noticed the ring.

He brought her hand closer, turning it gently in the lamplight. She had slipped it on when she went to speak to Charlotte.

"My mother would have loved you." His thumb moved over the peridot. "But I won't ask you to wear her ring. It's a symbol of my devotion. The one thing I cherished … before you."

She couldn't speak for a moment.

Of all the things he had given her, that was the greatest.

"I want to wear it. What's dear to you is dear to me now."

He pressed his lips to her hair. "I love you."

She smiled, nestling closer. "I love you too."

She had his ring on her finger and his heart in her hands.

Happiness was surely within their grasp.

Yet a sudden chill crept across her skin.

Outside in the dark, a killer was still breathing.

CHAPTER NINETEEN

Daphne woke to the solid warmth of Dominic beside her, to the tender ache in her chest, to the knowledge this wasn't a dream.

He loved her.

Dominic Hawke.

A ruthless scoundrel to most. Hers alone in the dark.

He looked peaceful as he slept, nothing like the dangerous owner of a house that catered to sin. The man was a walking contradiction. While his hand rested gently on her hip, the scar on the arm braced above his head told its own story.

She watched him, wondering how they might manage when she could not live at Shadowmere and he would never relinquish the empire he'd built.

Perhaps they could find common ground.

Some arrangement to suit them both.

One of them would have to yield, and she knew who it would be.

But there was little point worrying now. Finding the clerk was Dominic's priority. She would prod her aunt's conscience. If Lord Templeton was a lying toad, surely she would know.

Dominic shifted, his leg brushing hers beneath the coverlet, his fingers firming on her hip. The memory of him inside her had heat pooling between her thighs.

She raised the sheet a fraction and lingered, her gaze moving slowly over him, the dark stubble along his jaw, the hollow at his throat, the broad expanse of his chest, lower still to the lean line of his hips and—

Sweet Mary.

He was already aroused.

"Lost something, angel?"

She dropped the bedsheet. "Yes, my inhibitions."

He pulled her closer. "You won't find them down there."

"No. I lost them in a cottage at Shadowmere."

His hand slid from her hip to the curve of her backside. "Or the garden. You weren't so shy beneath the stars."

"You're entirely to blame, of course."

The squeeze on her bottom stoked the fire in her belly.

"You sound surprised. I am a rotten scoundrel." He rolled her on top of him with ease. "Perhaps I should remind you how wicked I am."

The solid length of him pressed against her. His hands settled on her hips, guiding her over him in a slow, deliberate rhythm.

"Shall we stop?"

"Certainly not."

He kissed her, his tongue moving in long, languid strokes.

"Will you take the lead, or shall I?" The husky timbre of his voice sent a shiver through her. "Well?"

She answered by rising over him and guiding him into her, just as she had last night. They moved together, achingly slow at first, then so fast and urgent her heart thumped wildly in her chest.

They fell back onto the bed, breathless, his arms closing around her. Below, doors opened and closed, voices drifted up, the clatter of the house going about its business, while he murmured something about doing it again.

"Now I know why you insisted I replace the trundle bed." She touched his chest but it only fed her growing need for him.

The sudden chime of the church bells striking noon had them both sitting upright.

"Bloody hell." He groaned, reaching for his trousers, nearly knocking his grandmother's teacup off the nightstand. "I heard the milkmaid and must have fallen back to sleep."

"Charlotte's thick curtains earn their keep." She felt his gaze linger on her bare skin as she crossed to the armoire in search of a clean chemise. "I thought she'd have sent the maid to wake us. We need water for the washbowl and I must write a note to my aunt."

"I'm supposed to be at *The Sentinel* in an hour."

She opened the drawer and took a pair of stockings.

"Is that where you're meeting your friends?" She didn't know he had friends besides Mr Ramsey and Mr Beattie.

"Stanton owns *The Sentinel*. He sent me the physician's report. Montfort is skilled in picking apart legal documents and should have a list of all Irving's properties."

"So you won't be scouring dockland warehouses alone?"

"No." He looked at her, his gaze tracing the line of every curve. "I won't be leaving this room if you insist on standing there like that."

She was tempted to tease him, but pulled on her chemise. "You will be careful? Dockworkers are a different breed, and

Mr Irving pays well enough to buy their loyalty." A thought intruded. "The clerk may already be dead."

He took his shirt and shook it out. She considered pulling up a chair and watching him dress.

"Sergeant Carter suspects the clerk is hiding, in fear for his life. That he can identify your father's killer."

"You spoke to Sergeant Carter?"

She almost said 'without me'.

"I called at Bow Street yesterday and reminded him of the clerk's importance to the case. He's had the watchman monitor the clerk's house, in the hope the maid might lead us to him."

"You didn't tell him you were searching Mr Irving's properties?"

"I mentioned that the marriage contract in Irving's possession is a forgery. And that it bears the clerk's signature." He shrugged on his coat. "He knows I'm gathering a list of his properties but not that I'm scouting them today."

She had barely fastened the last button on her chemise and he was dressed and raking his fingers through his hair.

He crossed the room, his hands settling on her bare forearms before he kissed her as if he meant to bruise her lips.

"Do you mean to brand me, Mr Hawke?"

"I mean to mark every inch. But if I don't leave now, I never will."

"Will you not wait for the water?"

"I'll change at the hotel." His arm came around her, his hand cupping her bottom. "Come to Mivart's tonight. We could bathe together."

She laughed softly. "And I thought you weren't a romantic, Mr Hawke."

Aunt Augusta had agreed to meet her at Pickins coffeehouse in Bishopsgate at four, conveniently close to her modiste. She had refused to pack Daphne's things, stating matters had gone too far and it was time she came home.

She was already waiting in a discreet booth near the back when Daphne arrived and had ordered them both tea and lemon seed cake.

Her aunt muttered under her breath as she glanced at Daphne's old blue pelisse from beneath the rim of her dark bonnet. "Have you no shame, girl? Surely the maids at Shadowmere have something black."

"I'm not in mourning."

"It does no harm to keep up appearances, though your father is still at the morgue pending enquiry."

Daphne slid into the booth. "I'm told Sergeant Carter is looking for the witness who disappeared under suspicious circumstances."

Aunt Augusta made a small puffing sound. "What was he doing, lurking by the river at night? No good, I should think. He could be a footpad in disguise. You know your father's signet ring is missing?"

"Yes, Mr Hawke said the police suspect robbery."

Her aunt scowled. "I warrant Hawke stripped it from his finger before he tossed him in the Thames."

"Mr Hawke did not murder Papa."

"You would say that. You're in bed with the devil."

"He has an alibi."

"Yes, he was at Mivart's gorging on the bones of his victims."

"That's enough, Aunt," Daphne snapped.

Aunt Augusta sighed before nodding. "Let's not bicker. Heaven knows we have enough strife coping with the gossip." She smoothed her gloves and flicked her hand at the teapot. "You pour, dear. My nerves are in tatters since you left."

Doubtless, this was the first of many jibes. Daphne steeled herself and poured the tea. "Have you heard from the solicitor? Has he mentioned the details of the will?"

"Once your father's debts are settled, I'll be counting the pennies in one hand. The fool mortgaged the house."

The news came as no surprise. There was a reason he'd decided to sell his own daughter.

"It wasn't to pay the Moseley brothers. You know they hound the family for the debt. You owe Mr Hawke your gratitude."

Her aunt shivered. "I suppose he'll want blood."

"I'm sure he'll settle for an explanation." She took a long sip of tea, watching her aunt's reaction over the rim of her cup.

"About what?" Her aunt harrumphed. "If it's about your trip to Bengal, that wasn't my idea. The pressure of the loan left your father doolally."

"There's the debt Mrs Foster is working to pay."

Her aunt paled. "For heaven's sake, speak quietly." She glanced about as if the walls had ears. "Look. I see no harm in telling you now. Your father had a particular arrangement with her. She … provided certain services … to ease his financial burden."

Daphne froze. She'd been living with a monster who deserved to rot in hell, not the city morgue.

"I know that Mrs Foster is currently paying Father's debt to Lord Ainsley."

Aunt Augusta leant closer. "It's a dreadful affair. I had to give her some items from the house. The last of the silver. Your mother's pearl earrings and cameo brooch."

The comment landed like a stone in water.

Daphne dropped the cup on the saucer, the clatter ringing through the coffeehouse. A few people turned their heads to stare.

"They weren't yours to sell," she said through clenched teeth. "They were bequeathed to me. Besides the locket, they were all I had left of her."

It was her own fault. She had left the most precious things behind.

Her eyes stung, though whether from grief or the blur in her vision, she couldn't say.

"We'll find a way to buy them back from the pawnbroker." Her aunt took a handkerchief from her reticule and dabbed at the spilt tea, then refilled Daphne's cup. "It was only a temporary measure."

"Did my father have the same arrangement with my mother?" she blurted. "She was so desperate to repay a loan, she begged the Moseley brothers for money."

Aunt Augusta puckered her lips. "Who told you about the loan?" She poured the last of the milk into Daphne's cup. "Your mother made us swear never to mention her … spending."

Why was this the first she'd heard of it?

Why was Augusta not drinking her tea?

"That's not the reason Mr Moseley gave."

Aunt Augusta took a lump of sugar in the nippers and dropped it into her cup. "What did he say?" The spoon clinked against the china as she stirred. "You can hardly trust a moneylender's word."

"He gave Mr Hawke a letter Mother sent him, asking to borrow a considerable sum." The lie came before she could think, though her head felt a little muddled. "It's in my valise. Did you know she was being blackmailed by a scoundrel?"

Her aunt shrank back on the bench. Something in her eyes said she did know, but she was quick to deny it.

"It's not true. We would have known."

"It's in the letter. That's why I asked you to meet." She lifted her cup to her lips, but something sharp and unfamiliar beneath the bergamot made her pause. She only pretended to drink.

"It must be a forgery."

"Why would Mother lie?"

"Foolish girl," she sneered. "Mr Hawke is lying. He killed your father and is concocting an elaborate story to hide the deed. I suspect the tale about his own mother is untrue."

What a strange thing to say.

"You know the story about his mother is true. Uncle Samuel acted as mediator. He went to Shadowmere to resolve the question of who fathered Mrs Hawke's child."

Her aunt stopped breathing for a moment.

She held a distant stare, the colour draining from her face.

What was so shocking about Daphne's uncle visiting Shadowmere?

It sounded like a rather honourable thing to do.

Suspicion stirred. She thought of her uncle's secret family in Norfolk. The children he'd sired while married to her aunt. A will that failed to name his wife.

She shook her head, though it felt as heavy as lead.

Her gaze dropped to her half-empty teacup.

Her aunt hadn't drunk a drop.

Panic fluttered like a trapped bird in her chest.

"You don't look well, Aunt." Daphne slid out from the bench, though her steps wavered, and she gripped the table for support. "I'll ask for a pot of fresh tea. Yours is cold."

Before she could object, Daphne crossed to the counter.

The waiter told her to take a seat and he'd be with her shortly, but it wasn't tea she wanted.

"I need you to do something for me." He must have thought she'd been secretly swigging brandy. Some syllables sounded slurred. "My coachman, Jones, is parked outside the modiste's. If I'm taken ill and helped out by my aunt, you must alert him at once."

His brow creased. She likely looked fit for Bedlam.

"Please."

He gave a curt nod and continued pouring wine into a carafe.

She returned to the booth, glad of a seat.

"I've ordered you a pot of coffee instead." Daphne drew her teacup closer. "I don't mind drinking cold tea."

Cold tea laced with laudanum, no doubt.

What devilry had the woman planned?

She would soon find out.

Her aunt reached across the table and patted her hand. "All that business at Shadowmere was so long ago. I'd almost forgotten until Mr Hawke stormed into the ballroom to wreak havoc."

She blinked quickly. "Is it hot in here? I fear I've come over quite faint."

"It is rather warm, but then I'm in black crepe."

"Forgive me. I don't feel at all well. And I barely slept a wink last night."

That was true.

Her aunt gripped the saucer and gave it a delicate shake. "Have another sip of tea, dear. I find it soothes the spirit. Fresh air will help."

Daphne pressed her fingers to her forehead, as though it pained her. She needed a second to think.

The only way to know her aunt's motive for slipping her laudanum was to play the fool and go along with the plan.

Was she supposed to wake in bed at home, wrists shackled to the bedposts? Or on a ship bound for India?

There was only one way to know.

"Yes, a brief walk outside might help." She rose as if dazed. "Wait for the coffee. I shan't be long."

"Nonsense. I'm coming with you." Aunt Augusta was on her feet, wrapping an arm around Daphne's shoulders. "You've caught something at that dreadful house, I expect. The things that go on there defy belief."

"Men do like their secrets," she said, allowing Augusta to steer her through the coffeehouse and into the small cobbled yard at the back.

"None more so than Dominic Hawke," her aunt snapped.

"I was referring to the thing Mr Hawke said about you and Uncle Samuel." She felt her aunt's arm tighten against her shoulder.

"What thing? Since when did the man indulge in idle gossip?"

Daphne didn't answer. She let her head fall against her aunt's shoulder.

"You need a doctor." Augusta opened the gate and peered along the alley behind. "Like your mother, you've a weak constitution."

They hurried along the narrow passage, avoiding barrels and sidestepping a dead cat half-hidden in a drift of coal ash.

Daphne didn't recognise the carriage parked in New Street, or the jarvey perched atop the box, his tricorn pulled low.

"Father sold the carriage," she muttered.

"It's the hired vehicle I've yet to return."

Another lie. The interior was polished to a high sheen and smelled of new leather, not spilt gin and stale sweat.

Her aunt bundled her onto a padded seat and told the jarvey to hurry, but gave no direction.

Daphne gripped her reticule as the vehicle lurched forward. Beneath the velvet lining lay the pocket pistol Mrs Flavell had given her. The blade was already in her stocking.

Her aunt sat beside her, arm firm around her shoulders. "Do you remember the thing Mr Hawke told you? Think, dear."

She rubbed her eyes and mumbled the words. "Mr Hawke. I'm in love with Mr Hawke." It felt good to say it aloud. Even slurred, it was the truest thing she'd said all afternoon. "Lord Templeton told him about Uncle Samuel's visit to Shadowmere."

"Yes, to act as mediator. We've established that."

Daphne rocked in her seat. What harm would it do to make a wild accusation? "And that Uncle may have fathered Mrs Hawke's child himself."

Perhaps she was over-performing.

She'd never been a natural actress.

Still, it hit the mark.

"That's preposterous. Your uncle acted on your father's behalf. He was too weak to confront the problem." She muttered under her breath. "Your father was barely sober after your mother died."

Yes, Daphne recalled her aunt and uncle living with them for a time. Her father had been short-tempered, snapping at her over small things. She had assumed it was grief. The hostility had never quite left him. He'd been happy for her to live in Bengal.

"I know nothing more than that." She let her head tip

back against the seat. "Mr Hawke mentioned giving the information to Sergeant Carter."

"Sergeant Carter." Her aunt reached for the overhead strap. "Why trouble him over the actions of a Jezebel?"

It wasn't the first time she'd used the term. Every mistress her uncle kept was given the same moniker.

A realisation settled over her, cold as dread.

One she prayed was wrong.

"Uncle Samuel gave Mrs Hawke a loan to clear the debts." She let herself slip on the seat as the carriage turned a corner. "He did the same for Father many times. Mother saved sovereigns in an old Earl Grey tin."

She'd once caught her mother hiding it in the cupboard.

Mrs Flavell had included the same tin in the valise she'd given Daphne. And the other items. A wool shawl—her mother always covered herself when Uncle Samuel visited. The Oriental wrapper. Her uncle had been raised in Canton.

"Your uncle was a generous man. He helped those in difficulty, nothing more. Don't twist it into something sordid."

"Mother was with child and it wasn't Father's."

Her aunt's derisive snort echoed in the carriage. "This family has been plagued by Jezebels. Judging by your recent behaviour, it's in the blood. I've spent a lifetime paying for others' misdeeds."

Only then did Daphne catch the stench of the river. The thud of hammers, the shouts of men. It took a moment to realise they were entering the docks.

She knew where her aunt was taking her. Not home to a warm supper and a comfortable bed, but away from here. Far enough that her uncle's secret would remain buried.

Augusta would collect her reward, and wouldn't have to suffer the shame of living in Bermondsey.

She remained silent as the carriage turned into Burr Street. The Red Lion Brewhouse loomed on the left, its chimney breathing sour malt into the early evening air. Beyond, the six-storey warehouses rose like brick-built cliffs, not merely blocking the light but choking the last of the day.

The carriage slowed before the last of them.

Mr Irving would be waiting inside with a roll of folded banknotes, perhaps an old chest of jewels, a fitting prize for a scheming devil.

All Daphne had to decide was whether to draw her pistol and waste her only shot on her aunt.

CHAPTER TWENTY

Irving had properties all over London: a townhouse in Mayfair, a counting house in the West End, a percussion cap workshop in Aldgate, a proof house in Bermondsey where they tested munitions.

They had searched six buildings in their hunt for the missing clerk. Four more remained, all near the docks.

Dominic drew his watch from his pocket and checked the time, though his thoughts were in a coffeehouse in Bishopsgate, not outside the Waterman's Arms, where Montfort was certain Irving kept a room.

"Remind me never to fall in love." Stanton rolled his neck as they prepared to enter the dockside tavern. "You can barely string two words together, and that watch hasn't left your hand."

"You forgot the part where he was mumbling to himself and clutching his heart." Montfort tucked the list into his coat pocket. "Frankly, it was embarrassing."

"One more word and I'll remind you why men cross the street to avoid me. Something is wrong." The unease had been building this last hour. "I should have met with her aunt myself, refused to take no for an answer. I don't trust the old crone."

"Isn't your need for dominance the reason Miss Harland left Shadowmere?" Montfort asked.

The memory landed like a blow he hadn't braced for. "I said the wrong thing. But we're not here to discuss my failings. Right now, I need to know you can still take a punch."

Stanton grinned. "I won't need to. And Montfort is so light on his feet they won't hear him coming. Saint-Clair will be sorry he's not here to draw his rapier."

"Enough talking." Dominic strode ahead, pushing open the tavern door as if he meant to take it off its hinges.

Three bearded sailors looked up from the bench, their faces tough as old leather. The lords might know him as a dangerous bastard; to these men, he was just another toff.

The thick-necked man behind the counter went on wiping a tankard with a cloth that had seen better days. "What will it be, gentlemen?"

Dominic glanced around the cramped room, the stink of sweat and stale ale catching in his throat. The dockworkers didn't raise their fists; they only raised their tankards.

"Your friend's mighty generous," the landlord said with a toothy grin. "He paid for everyone's drinks. Told me to serve you brandy, though Jim's downed the lot."

Dominic approached the counter. "Friend?"

The landlord leaned forward. "The one running from the law. He wanted to speak to the *fellow* upstairs." He gave a sly wink. "First door on the right. There ain't no room for all of you, mind. And remember to duck your head."

"Wait here," he said, turning for the stairs.

The wood groaned beneath his boots, each step announcing his arrival. He paused outside the door, fingers closing around the handle, and listened. The clink of metal. The murmur of voices.

When he entered, neither occupant looked surprised to see him. One sat on the shabby bed, a length of chain fixed at the ankle, the iron ring bolted to the frame. Not the clerk. A woman.

Dominic's gaze settled on the man in the chair. "You shouldn't be here."

Saint-Clair wore an amused grin. "I was bored. I thought I might be of some use. Don't begrudge a man a little excitement."

"Did you steal that coat from a vagabond?"

"A drunken sailor, resting beneath tarpaulin. But we've more important matters to discuss now." He gestured to the woman. "The missing clerk. Not Edward but Edwina. She has quite a story to tell."

Dominic looked at her. Men's clothes, hair cropped short, but skin too smooth, no sign of stubble. He knew what it cost a woman to survive on her wits. It explained why her maid was anxious.

"It wasn't my fault." Edwina fought back tears. "Mr Irving sent a note to the house, insisting I meet him on Black-friars Bridge. I had no choice. He threatened to tell my clients they'd hired a woman as a scrivener."

Dominic suspected half her clients already knew. "You told the magistrate you witnessed the murder but couldn't identify the killer."

"She helped toss the body into the Thames," Saint-Clair said dryly. "But Irving abducted her after the magistrate took her statement."

Dominic sighed. "At Bow Street, a missing clerk is as good as a confession."

"Irving made her draft the fake contract, stating Miss Harland had received a three-thousand-pound advance."

Edwina dabbed her eyes with a handkerchief. "I have a terrible feeling he's going to pack me in a crate destined for Bengal. He's had me chained to this bed for more than a week."

Saint-Clair stretched his legs. "Irving told the landlord she was his runaway sister, planning to elope with a wastrel. Paid handsomely for his silence."

"Then Irving is the killer." The motive still eluded him.

Edwina shrugged. "The poor man was dead when I helped lift him from the curricle." She clasped a hand to her chest. "Please. You can't tell anyone. I'll hang for aiding and abetting."

A chill crept up the back of his neck. "What made you specify Bengal? Did Irving mention sailing there?"

Doubtless he wished to escape the Moseley brothers.

A convicted man would forfeit everything. Irving couldn't flee until someone else had answered for Harland's death. His brother would inherit the company the moment he stepped into a courtroom.

"He told the landlord he's sailing on the morning tide to meet his ship in Portsmouth." Edwina blinked back more tears. "He called not three hours ago. Said he's taking his sister abroad for a better life. That he'd be back later but had to collect precious cargo first."

Precious cargo?

The words took the air from his lungs.

A cold certainty settled in his gut.

Daphne had gone to meet her aunt. An aunt who cared more for her own comfort than her niece's safety. The need to race to the coffeehouse had him checking the time again. Half past six.

He wanted to put his fist through the wall.

He'd been a fool to let her go.

Saint-Clair must have read his mind. "Where is Miss Harland?"

"Meeting her aunt at Pickins in Bishopsgate." Less than two miles from the docks. An odd choice of location, now he thought of it.

"Irving has a warehouse near the Red Lion Brewhouse. The landlord heard him mention it to his coachman."

"Yes, Burr Street. It's on our list."

The pieces locked into place he tried not to panic.

"Go. I'll wait with Edwina."

He was already at the door.

"You're certain this is Irving's warehouse?" Dominic watched the shuttered doors from behind a row of wooden barrels. The air was sharp with the scent of scorched malt and the briny exhale of the Thames tide.

"His is the one marked W on the brickwork." Montfort nodded towards the building. "But even at this hour, I'd expect some activity."

All was quiet but for the slap of water against the quay and the ghostly groan of mooring chains. Mist rose from the river, creeping across the stones like an omen.

"We should move." Stanton straightened and pulled his hat down over his brow. "The watchmen do their rounds. I'd rather not explain why we're loitering by the brewhouse."

Dominic agreed. He crossed the yard, his friends at his heels. The main doors were barred from within, but a smaller door to the side yielded to Montfort's knife in under a minute.

"I'll never ask how you learned that," Stanton murmured.

"It's useful if his mistress locks him out," Dominic said.

Inside, iron columns rose into the dark, swallowed by shadows overhead. The warehouse had been cleared. No barrels. No crates.

Montfort stepped forward. "The cargo's on the water. The lighters will have taken it downriver already. If Irving sails on the morning tide, he'll load through the night."

One word turned his blood cold.

Was Daphne the cargo?

Was she being loaded onto a vessel miles from here?

"Irving's been planning to flee from Moseley for days." He should have had eyes on the warehouse sooner. "He'd rather take his chances in India than end up in St Martin's Burial Ground."

"His manager runs the English operations and did an interview for the paper last month, lobbying for the London to Birmingham railway. He has a warehouse there already, and plans—"

The door behind them creaked on its hinges. Dominic's hand went to his coat before he saw it was Jones.

"Thank the Lord it's you, sir," his coachman whispered, scanning the gloom. "I've been hiding outside for an hour. They took Miss Harland through the yard of the coffeehouse and brought her here. But the lady tipped off the waiter and I tracked them to the docks."

Pride hit first. She'd seen the trap before it sprang. Cold fear came next, beneath it the relief that she was still breathing and within reach.

"Here?" Dominic kept his voice low. "Where?"

"The counting house or office, perhaps," Montfort said.

Irving wasn't expecting company. His burly companion was the only obstacle, and large men always fell hardest.

"I would have followed them if they'd moved her, sir." Jones shuffled his feet. "I didn't know what to do. I sent a penny boy to Lady Soanes with a message. He could have reached her by now."

"It's all right, Jones. Where's my carriage?"

"Nightingale Lane, sir. I paid an urchin a copper to watch the horses."

"Go to Bow Street and ask for Sergeant Carter. Tell him everything."

Dominic turned back to the warehouse. Somewhere inside, Daphne was waiting, drugged, wrists bound, silenced by whatever means necessary.

The thought made his jaw ache.

"The counting house first," he said. "Stay close."

He moved with a predator's tread, Stanton and Montfort falling in behind him. Irving wouldn't have gone far. Not with the tide still hours away. He'd be here somewhere, certain no one would come looking tonight.

Irving was about to learn how wrong he was.

They found the internal staircase on the street side, tucked against the brickwork. The air smelled of tallow and old paper. Of the three rooms at the top, light bled beneath the middle door.

Dominic looked through the partially glazed panel of the nearest room. The heavy desk and the dull gleam of weighing scales confirmed it was the counting house. Letters filled the pigeonholes. Books and files littered the table.

He was about to move on when he caught a faint shift in the corner—a bundle stirring. Not a bundle. Daphne, bound and gagged on the boards.

He turned to Stanton and Montfort. "Stay on the landing. Close enough to hear." His eyes moved to the door with light beneath it. "And watch that one."

Dominic's hand closed around the handle.

The door was locked.

Montfort tripped the mechanism without making a sound.

Dominic touched his arm, then eased the door open.

She was on the floor, wrists bound behind her, ankles tied, a strip of cloth pulled tight across her mouth. Her eyes found him and softened in an instant.

He knelt beside her, his fingers already at the gag. "I'm here. You're safe. I'll wring Irving's neck when I see him."

She swallowed hard and drew a breath. "Thank heavens. I feared you'd already checked the warehouses in your hunt for the clerk."

"We planned to search them after dark." He should have been working the knots in the rope, but he clasped her nape and kissed her like a man starved of air. "Tell me your aunt and Irving are here."

She nodded. "Augusta put laudanum in my tea. I let her think it worked because we needed answers. Mr Irving has refused to pay her until I'm aboard the ship. She's up here waiting."

It took a second for the words to sink in. "You came here by choice? You could have been killed."

"No. Mr Irving needs me in India," she whispered, glancing at the door. "He has no plans to marry me himself. It's all a charade. He told Aunt Augusta I'm a gift for some commissioner at the East India Company. Something to sweeten the deal abroad."

A gift. He'd burn the East India Company to the ground before he allowed it.

"Irving won't get far. We have the clerk." He clasped her arm, pressing a kiss to her forehead. "It's likely Irving killed your father. He was the man who threw Harland into the Thames. The clerk had no choice but to assist him."

He watched her, waiting for a small sign of grief.

Nothing.

"Dominic, I was able to prise information from my aunt." She paused, her chin dipping slightly before she found his eyes. "The man who hurt your mother and fathered her child … I believe it was my uncle. I'm sorry. You'll not have your vengeance, not in this life."

His world went still.

Then the memories came like flashes of lightning: his mother's silences, her watchfulness, the strain she had carried like penance. He prayed there was a place in hell where they tortured weak men.

"What about your mother?"

"I don't believe she had an affair with my uncle, more an arrangement to clear my father's debt. It explains why she hated them both. I only wish she'd confided in me."

"She was protecting you."

"But I failed her by not noticing."

He cupped her face. "You didn't fail her. Trust me."

"I know, but the horrible thoughts won't leave me."

One rose inside him, one that had stalked him for years, ugly enough that he had never given it a voice. He asked anyway. "Might your mother have deliberately taken poison?"

She stared at him, the question hanging between them.

Stanton appeared in the doorway. "There's movement next door. What do you want us to do?"

"It will be my aunt," Daphne said. "Mr Irving told her to make me supper. Hide. All of you. But remain within earshot. I'll not leave here without knowing the truth."

"Daphne—"

"Replace the gag. Hurry. My aunt won't hurt me. She

needs me on that ship as much as Mr Irving does." When he hesitated, she mouthed, "Have faith in me."

He kissed her once before raising the gag, then ushered his friends onto the landing. "I'll take the corner by the tall cabinet. The room's dark enough."

Stanton nodded and closed the door behind him. Dominic moved without a sound and folded himself into the shadows, back to the wall.

The clatter of a tea tray signalled the arrival of Aunt Augusta. He could see her silhouette through the glass pane, the high collars of her mourning dress shielding her throat where his hands should be.

She put the tray on the floor and turned the key in the lock, not realising it was already open. She tried it again, muttered something under her breath, then took up the tray and entered, setting it on the table by the door.

"Good. You're awake." Augusta moved closer, bracing her hands on her hips as she studied her prisoner. "Mr Irving insists you eat. The journey will be taxing. He needs you alive when he reaches port."

Daphne made a muffled sound in response.

Dominic gritted his teeth.

If Augusta were a man, he'd wring her scrawny neck.

The woman knelt and tugged the gag free. "It's for the best. We can't have you gallivanting about London, ruining the family name."

Daphne laughed. "Between Father and Uncle Samuel, they did a fine job of that. Wickedness is a trait they shared."

"You mean weakness," Augusta said, standing.

"No. Weak is a term I'd use for you, Aunt."

Augusta recoiled, the movement sharp in the gloom. "Insolent mare. I only wish I were going to Bengal with you, to see that smirk wiped off your face."

"I only wish I were staying here to watch the ton tear you apart when they discover Uncle Samuel used money to buy favours."

"They won't. I've spent my life hiding Samuel's indiscretions. Besides, half the ton are addicted to dipping the wick." Augusta's cackle vibrated with triumph. "You'll be abroad. I'll keep the house in Mayfair. And everyone will presume the missing clerk killed your father."

Daphne said nothing.

Her aunt took that as a sign she'd won and went to pour the tea and lay sliced ham and cheese on a plate.

"Mr Hawke knows Uncle Samuel fathered his—"

"Be quiet!" Augusta spun, her gaze snapping like a whip. "He loaned money to a woman down on her luck. There's no trace of it. No proof he did anything but act as mediator."

Dominic had combed the city and come up empty. Evidence remained as elusive as the villain himself. Now he had a name.

Daphne's sigh was more a weary rasp. "Mother warned me to trust a man's actions, not his words. The secret family in Norfolk who inherited Uncle Samuel's estate tells you everything about his intentions."

Augusta stood, statue still.

"Mother said you wanted children." Daphne spoke calmly. "It must have hurt deeply to learn he'd fathered them everywhere."

Augusta's snort dripped with bitterness. "Yes, like a knife to the gut, twisting when you thought the wound had healed."

"After all these years, it still pains you."

"It won't when you're gone."

"Because you mean to punish me for the terrible way he treated my mother? A woman so desperate to free herself she turned to Mr Moseley."

"Your mother knew what she was doing. They all did. A weak man doesn't take much tempting. Unless it's to bed his own wife."

It took all his strength not to lunge at the woman. He'd dare her to stand at his mother's grave and call her the perpetrator.

"You blamed them for—" The words died in Daphne's throat. "Good Lord. My mother didn't die of dysentery. You poisoned her." Her shallow gasp cut through him. "You killed her because you couldn't stand to see—"

"What did you expect me to do? Eat supper with a woman who bore my husband's child?"

Daphne's breath stuttered, but she pressed on. "And Mrs Hawke? You poisoned her too."

The thud of a door below snapped Augusta's attention to the landing. "Mr Irving has returned. He'll be cross if you've not eaten. You've a long voyage ahead."

Daphne shifted her legs, fighting against her bindings. "We won't see each other again after tonight. You may as well admit to killing her. Though now I think on it, perhaps you didn't. How would you have entered Shadowmere?"

The stairs groaned under a heavy tread, accompanied by humming so tuneless it set Dominic's teeth on edge.

Augusta crowed with delight at Irving's arrival. "You're right. I didn't kill Mrs Hawke. Your uncle did. He just didn't know I'd poisoned the sleeping draught he gave her."

Behind the cabinet, his hands balled into fists. For the first time in his life, he understood what it meant to want a woman dead.

"It may have served you better to kill Uncle Samuel."

Augusta tutted. "One always hopes they'll change."

Irving appeared in the doorway. He removed his hat and

brushed wisps of hair across his pate. "Good. Good. You've brought supper. I don't suppose there's any spare?"

Dominic heard the faint cluck of Augusta's tongue.

"I've bread and cheese in the manager's office, but where's the clerk? You said you'd return with her. You said I'd be paid once they were safely aboard."

"I sent my man to collect her from the Waterman's Arms. He should be here within the hour."

Dominic smiled to himself. Saint-Clair would welcome the chance to bloody someone.

"The clerk is a woman?" Daphne said.

"One attempting to make her way in a man's world." Irving put his hat on the table and stole a slice of ham from the plate. "Life won't be so … complicated for her in India."

Daphne gave a light chuckle. "Don't you just hate it when a plan goes awry?"

"Pay her no mind," Augusta said. "She's a little cuckoo from the laudanum."

Daphne scoffed. "Fine, but expect to leave without her."

Irving stepped closer, bringing the smell of stewed vegetables with him. "If this is a ploy to delay our departure, it won't work. We sail with the tide, regardless."

"Not if Mr Hawke has taken the clerk to Bow Street. He gathered men and visited the tavern late this afternoon. I can almost hear the clack of the watchmen's rattles closing in."

Dominic couldn't see Irving's face from behind the cabinet. He could only hear the hitch in his breath as he whirled to face Augusta.

"You! You and your damned meddling. If you'd left matters alone, I'd be rounding the coast of Spain by now."

"I came to tell you my niece was missing. I wouldn't have needed to hit him with the fire iron had you simply agreed to his terms."

Daphne gasped. "You killed Father?"

"It was an accident. He fell back and landed on the grate. It's your fault for dancing with Mr Hawke."

Irving raised his hands. "If you think I'll explain it away, think again. You hit him when he threatened to tell his daughter the truth."

"No one knows that but us. There are no witnesses. Nothing can be proved in court. We'll invent a story and blame the clerk. If we both keep to the same tale, there'll be no problem."

"And yet there are witnesses to all your misdeeds." Daphne cleared her throat. "You may show yourselves."

Dominic slid out from the shadows first. "I'd like to say welcome to hell, Augusta, but I'm told the journey there is the most harrowing."

Stanton appeared in the doorway, Montfort behind him. "I was looking for something gripping for tomorrow's front page. I presume *The Sentinel* will have exclusive rights."

"If I beat Irving, will you say he fell?" Dominic asked.

Stanton grinned. "*The Sentinel* reports facts, but I can make an exception."

The warehouse door clanged like it had been blown open by a sudden gust. Boots drummed on the wooden treads.

"That could be Bow Street now." Dominic knew it wasn't. They came with lanterns and noise enough to wake the street. The men who appeared on the landing needed no such theatre.

Stanton and Montfort stepped aside to allow one man to enter. He was broad, not tall, solidly built, the kind who would walk through a brick wall without breaking stride.

Dominic assumed it was Irving's man, but Irving looked like he was about to soil his trousers.

"Mr Moseley would like a private word, sir. He's outside

in the carriage. He's heard you're sailing to Portsmouth on the morning tide."

"What? No. He m-must be mistaken," Irving stuttered.

"Then you'll need to put his mind at ease, sir, what with you owing his brother a hefty debt. He's seized your lighter at the dock gates, taken the cargo for the trouble caused."

Irving gulped. "No. Tell him I'll visit the office in the morning. There's been a mistake."

He kept talking. No one listened. At a nod from Moseley's man, the lackeys snared Irving by the collar and hauled his scuffing boots into the dark.

Augusta clutched her throat and shrank back.

"Mr Moseley hopes his intervention was timely," his man said. "He has a proposition, Mr Hawke. One that satisfies all parties concerned, if you're willing to hear it."

Dominic glanced at Stanton and Montfort. "We've enough secrets between us. I'll not ask you to keep another. You can wait downstairs."

Stanton glanced at Montfort and they both shrugged.

"We'll stay," Montfort said. "Justice has always weighed more than the truth."

Dominic turned to Moseley's man. "Give me a moment to free Miss Harland. Any decision will be made jointly."

He crossed to Daphne, drew the blade from his coat and sliced through the rope at her wrists, then crouched and cut her ankles free. He drew her to her feet, his thumb moving in slow circles over her wrists where the bindings had bitten.

"Later," he whispered, his mouth close to her ear, "I'll attend to every ache. Now, would you like to hear Mr Moseley's proposition?"

"After tonight, I'll consider almost anything."

He faced Moseley's messenger. "We're listening."

The fellow reached into his coat pocket and handed

Dominic a letter. A quick scan showed the fifteen thousand had been returned to his account at Coutts.

"Mr Moseley can't accept your payment, sir. It's not how he does business. The debt falls to Harland's beneficiary." He glanced at Augusta when she whimpered. "He feels it only right that Lady Sanders settles the debt in her own way."

"I can raise the money. Give me a week. A month at most. I have jewels—Samuel's mother's pearls—stored at the house in Mayfair."

"Pearls wouldn't cover the first instalment, ma'am."

Daphne snorted. "It's a lie anyway. She hasn't a penny. Samuel left the pearls to his mistress in Norfolk."

"There's a boat waiting at Fobbing Marshes. Mr Moseley wishes to assure you that you'll have no cause to see Lady Sanders again."

Daphne turned to him, her hand coming to rest on his chest. "What shall we do? There's no evidence to convict her other than our testimonies, and Augusta would paint us both as her enemies. Our mothers' names would be dragged through every court in London."

They had all suffered enough. The scandal would taint their children's prospects, though he wasn't about to voice that aloud.

"The clerk's testimony implicates Irving, not your aunt," he said. "Augusta must answer for what she's done. Our mothers deserve justice. But I'd rather London not read every sordid detail."

Moseley's man spoke up. "Bow Street will receive her signed confession, and that of Mr Irving, confirming they both played a part in Lord Harland's death. It will state they've left England." He inclined his head. "Mr Moseley hopes that proves satisfying for all concerned."

Augusta stepped forward. "For heaven's sake, you can't just spirit me away. I'll not sign anything."

"I think you will, ma'am, given the options."

Dominic met Stanton's gaze. A discreet nod passed between them. He turned and reached for Daphne's hand.

"Take her. Moseley will see she pays for her crimes."

"You can be sure of it, sir."

Augusta's protests echoed through the warehouse as she was led out. He barely heard them. Daphne's hand was in his. He did not intend to let it go again.

CHAPTER TWENTY-ONE

The water in the bathtub had gone cold, but neither of them moved. She lay back against his chest, nestled between his thighs, protected, not his prisoner. She understood the distinction perfectly now.

"The only part of me that's not wrinkled is the hand you're holding." She watched as he measured her fingers against his as if the difference were some marvel of nature.

He laced their fingers, locking them together.

She'd defy a heathen army to break them.

They were no longer chasing a villain. Only their future remained, and what lay beyond this hotel room. Perhaps he sensed it too, the need to speak weighed against the risk of saying the wrong thing. Amid the crackle of the fire and the rumble of carriage wheels outside, she could almost hear his questions gathering.

"A penny for them," she said, prompting him to pick one from the long list. "I'm happy to spend my only shilling."

He kissed her hair, choosing the one problem she didn't want to face. "We need to arrange your father's funeral."

We. Not you. One small word that steadied her world.

"It's a kindness he doesn't deserve."

"Perhaps we could fasten a weight to his ankle and toss him back into the Thames. Or pack him into a crate bound for India."

"Yes, a gift for the commissioner Mr Irving mentioned."

"He'd best stay in India. He'll face a dawn appointment if he dares set foot on English soil." The threat lacked its usual spark. His quest for vengeance had not ended as he'd hoped, with a grave he could visit just to curse.

"And Aunt Augusta alongside him." She trusted Mr Moseley to keep his word, though she wasn't entirely sure why. "Hopefully the magistrate will receive her confession, and we can finally lay the past to rest."

In the brief silence, she waited for a pang of guilt.

None came. Her aunt deserved no one's mercy.

She looked at the flames, recalling how many times Mr Beattie had made her build the fire that first morning at Shadowmere. The bitter chill of that room a reflection of her heart.

She wasn't cold anymore. She wasn't afraid.

"I'm not sure Carter believed our version of events." Dominic's hand came to rest on her thigh, the soft stroke a welcome distraction. "Though them fleeing after realising they'd been overheard was a plausible explanation."

"It's fortunate Charlotte came when she did. At least she saw my aunt leave in an unmarked carriage."

He fell silent at the mention of her aunt.

She knew why.

He'd spent years hunting a monster. He hadn't expected her to wear a mourning dress and pour tea.

"We made the right decision." She pressed a lingering kiss to his knuckles. "You can't imagine the horrid things a barrister would have said about our mothers. They don't deserve that."

"No. And I'd have wanted to bury your aunt."

They lay watching the flames in the grate.

His lips brushed her damp hair before drifting to her temple. She tilted her head and met his mouth, the kiss slow and deep. Her hand rose to his jaw, her fingers slipping into his hair as she drew him closer.

"Come home with me?" he whispered, nipping the corner of her mouth, then kissing her softly. "That's a question, but it would be a command if I thought you'd obey."

Her heart missed a beat. There was nowhere in the world she would rather be. But how did he envisage their future? She had to know.

"Will you visit me in the cottage when the stars are out? Will you woo me with hot chocolate and white roses?"

He took her chin between his fingers. "I'd kneel at your feet, pump the water while you washed. I'd dry every inch of you, carry you to our bed. The cottage could be our own personal observatory when we need an escape from the children."

She swallowed. "The children?"

"There'll be many. I can't keep my hands off you."

The heat between her legs took the chill from the water, but practical things filled her mind. "At Shadowmere?"

He paused, as though catching himself. "They're hopes, not presumptions. There'll be no more guests, no more wild parties. It will be a place to raise a family. The home my mother always envisioned."

Oh, he knew how to steal her breath.

How to paint the perfect picture.

She would embrace almost all of it.

"I don't want you to change, Dominic." All the time, she'd thought she would be the one to bend. "I love the man who takes command of every situation. The man who makes me feel safe."

"Don't think I'll be soft, angel."

She shifted in the tub. "There's no danger of that."

"When I lift you out of the water, I'll drive the point home. But let's not fool ourselves into thinking I'm the one in control."

She smiled. "You think I hold the cards."

"The one that matters."

"And what's that?"

His eyes held hers. "The answer to the question I've been keeping close to my heart since the day you left me. Will you marry me?"

Tears filled her eyes.

She'd once told him he could never give her what she wanted. Love. A home. A family. She'd been wrong. She looked at the ring on her finger, his mother's peridot catching the firelight.

"I love you, Dominic. I'd be proud to be your wife."

"Is that a yes, angel?"

"You know damn well it is."

One month later

"You're here as a guest, Beattie, not to direct the hired staff," Dominic said when he found his housekeeper fussing with the champagne.

"Sir, I've managed Shadowmere for a decade. Such things are second nature. At least let me make sure the kitchen is running smoothly."

He placed a hand on his man's shoulder. "You know I don't tolerate disobedience. For you, I'll make an exception."

Beattie smiled as though he'd been given a knighthood.

Ramsey approached as Beattie departed. "You know he's barely slept this week. The list ran to ten pages. I doubt there's a white rose left in London."

Dominic glanced at the vases of flowers in the drawing room, white roses taking pride of place amid the myrtle.

He thought of his mother and smiled.

"Things will be less chaotic here in future. I'll have to give him a project. The man lives for a list." Given the time Dominic spent in bed with his wife, Beattie could organise a nursery.

His gaze moved to her. Her silk gown was simple, and she wore it like a woman who knew her own power. He was not in the habit of counting his blessings, but he knew a rare fortune when he saw it.

She was laughing at something Charlotte said when she turned her head and saw him. Her eyes softened. Her lips parted. And everything they meant to each other was there in that single beat.

He turned to find Stanton staring at him as though making notes for the morning edition. "I can see the next headline in *The Sentinel*. The formidable Dominic Hawke tamed by a woman. We'd sell out within the hour."

Ramsey laughed. "He's been this way for over a month."

"I wasn't tamed. I handed myself over willingly," he said, his gaze moving between them. "A man obsessed with facts should choose his words carefully. I look forward to the day you both meet the same fate."

Ramsey took that as a cue to check on Beattie.

Stanton merely found the idea amusing. "God help the woman who thinks she has a hold on me."

"I recall saying something similar once, when Shadowmere was the netherworld for the depraved."

He was not ashamed. It had been a means of survival. Life was different now.

"One of your disappointed guests has turned her attention to *The Sentinel*." Stanton checked that people were occupied with their champagne. "Though she had the grace not to name you while debasing my good name."

"What the devil are you talking about?" Dominic gripped Stanton's arm and drew him aside. "Who is it? What did she say?"

He should have walked away.

The last thing he needed was another damn quest.

"Like a true coward, she remains anonymous. Apparently, being friends with you must make me a bare-faced liar."

He pursed his lips, trying not to grin. "A low blow. The lady has done her research."

"Not well enough."

"What does she want?"

"My head on a spike."

"Not everyone agrees with what you print. It's never bothered you before." Stanton had survived religious fanatics, rotten tomatoes, and a brick through his office window.

He drew a letter from his pocket and thrust it under Dominic's nose. "Smell that and tell me this isn't a wicked form of intimidation."

He inhaled once. "And you have the gall to accuse me of losing my mind. I can't smell a thing."

Stanton drew back and frowned. "It's potent. I hate the woman but love her perfume. It's a bloody conspiracy."

"We'll discuss this tomorrow. Not on my wedding day."

Stanton drew his hand through his hair. "Forgive me. It's

nothing. I was wrong to mention it. She'll tire of writing eventually. They always do."

Thankfully, Beattie appeared in the doorway, gave one ring of his handbell and invited everyone to take their seats in the dining room.

The wedding breakfast passed in a blur of toasts and laughter. Montfort rose first, glass in hand, and said something about love that made Charlotte snort and Stanton reach for more wine.

Dominic kept Daphne at his side, his chair drawn close enough that their shoulders brushed when he turned to speak. Beneath the table, his hand found hers. Their fingers laced, hidden by linen, the quiet pressure of his grip a silent promise.

When the guests rose to return to the drawing room, he leaned in, his mouth close to her ear. "We could slip away to the cottage for half an hour."

"Won't our guests wonder why we keep disappearing?"

"Let them wonder. I need to know if you're wearing the garters I saw in that silk-lined box."

She smiled. "Always so impatient, Mr Hawke."

"Only with you, angel."

Her breath caught. "Call me that and I'll follow you anywhere."

They were about to sneak through the terrace doors when Ramsey found them. "There's a delivery. A wedding gift. The fellow wants you to check for damages before he leaves. Beattie told him to take it to the cottage."

"Can it not wait?" The sigh was for Ramsey's benefit. He turned to Daphne. "As it's a wedding gift, we should both inspect it."

"Yes, we should study it closely."

He held her hand as they walked to the cottage. The last

time he'd made this journey, he'd been half out of his mind with panic. Today, he was the luckiest man in England.

Propped against a chair and wrapped in hessian was a gilt-framed painting of Shadowmere. Not the dark, fortress-like structure he knew. Not the house where the past clung like cobwebs in every hallway. The sun shone. White roses filled the Grecian urns on the steps. The doors stood open.

It was the home he'd imagined as a boy.

He recognised Saint-Clair's hand in every brushstroke. A dream made real. His mother would have hung it above the fireplace.

Daphne stepped back. "It's beautiful. But there's no card. Where's the man who delivered it? He may know."

"We don't need a card. I know who painted this, and who delivered it. That's his greatcoat on the chair." He looked to the door leading to the kitchen. "You can come out. I know how you hate hiding in dark corners."

Dominic laughed when Saint-Clair appeared. He'd grown a goatee, wore an eye patch, and a dusty tricorn hat. "Been grave robbing again?"

"I got the hat for a shilling from an ostler at the Pig and Whistle." He crossed to Daphne, took her hand, and bowed. "I trust you know who I am, Mrs Hawke."

"I haven't the faintest idea, sir," she teased.

Saint-Clair knew Dominic kept no secrets from her.

"Good. Then I come merely to pay my respects and meet the woman who ruined my poor friend before the ton." Saint-Clair looked at him when he said, "You've made an honest man of a rotten scoundrel. There's hope for us all yet."

Yes, even for a man destined for the gallows.

"Don't let it unsettle you," Dominic said, though the threat of the noose had never unnerved Saint-Clair. "It won't happen overnight."

"Never in my case. Women want roots. I was born for the open road."

Daphne touched Saint-Clair's arm. "Well, you paint like a master, sir. That involves considerable time standing in one place."

Saint-Clair grinned, knowing she could see through his bravado. "Master is somewhat of a stretch, but I'm a fool for a compliment."

"It's deserved." Dominic met his friend's gaze. "We couldn't have asked for a more poignant gift."

Saint-Clair brushed it off like road dust on his sleeve. "Take a turn about the kitchen with me, Mrs Hawke. Tell me what Hawke's really like when no one is watching."

He heard whispering and Daphne's laugh. Saint-Clair could charm the birds from the trees or freeze a man where he stood, depending on his mood.

A minute or two passed before they returned.

Saint-Clair kissed Daphne's hand and gave Dominic a sly wink. "Well, I've left Armand in charge of the carriage, and the man is a self-professed drunk." He retrieved his greatcoat from the chair and was gone in the blink of an eye.

Dominic slid his arm around her waist. "You'll get used to him, though he has a habit of appearing like a ghost in the night." He didn't wait for her reply, but kissed her like he couldn't breathe without her.

"Dance with me," she whispered against his mouth.

"There's no music."

She smiled as she wound her arms around his neck. "We're so in tune we always find the right rhythm."

"You're wearing your mother's locket." Only the chain was visible. He knew she wore it against her heart.

She glanced down. "And your mother's ring."

"I have a gift for you in the house."

"What is it?"

"Something Mrs Foster helped me find in return for paying off Ainsley." The lord was lucky he'd not knocked out his teeth.

She stopped, her throat bobbing. "Pearl earrings and a cameo brooch? Were they still at the pawnbroker's?"

"Not quite, but I paid enough to see them returned to you."

She collapsed into his arms, weeping and laughing at the same time. "I knew the night we met that my life would change for the better."

He brushed her hair behind her ear. "I was set on ruin until a woman with sad eyes waltzed me to salvation." He'd never forget it. The instant recognition he fought to dismiss. The rightness in that first touch. "Still, I could have missed the signs and been poorer for it."

"Not when I'm skilled in entrapment." Her mouth brushed his. "All I had to do was stand there and kiss you. And suddenly, I belonged to no one but you."

I hope you enjoyed reading *The Sins of Shadowmere.*

Will Hugh Stanton unmask the mystery letter writer? Is her perfume as potent as her pen? When truth puts them both in danger, will desire prove their greatest threat?

Find out in:

The Devil of Fleet Street
Rotten Scoundrels - Book 2

More titles by Adele Clee

Lost Ladies of London

The Mysterious Miss Flint

The Deceptive Lady Darby

The Scandalous Lady Sandford

The Daring Miss Darcy

Avenging Lords

At Last the Rogue Returns

A Wicked Wager

Valentine's Vow

A Gentleman's Curse

Scandalous Sons

And the Widow Wore Scarlet

The Mark of a Rogue

When Scandal Came to Town

The Mystery of Mr Daventry

Gentlemen of the Order

Dauntless

Raven

Valiant

Dark Angel

More titles by Adele Clee

Ladies of the Order

The Devereaux Affair

More than a Masquerade

Mine at Midnight

Your Scarred Heart

No Life for a Lady

Scandal Sheet Survivors

More than Tempted

Not so Wicked

Never a Duchess

No One's Bride

Rogues of Fortune's Den

A Little Bit Dangerous

Temptress in Disguise

Lady Gambit

My Kind of Scoundrel

The Last Chance

Tales from The Burnished Jade

A Lesson in Scandal

One Wicked Secret

A Devil in Silk

A Marquess Scorned